The SUMMER OF IMPOSSIBILITIES

The SUMMER OF IMPOSSIBILITIES

RACHAEL ALLEN

AMULET BOOKS • NEW YORK

Cataloging-in-Publication Data has been applied for and may be obtained from the Library of Congress.

ISBN 978-1-4197-4112-8

Text copyright © 2020 Rachael Allen
Book design by Hana Anouk Nakamura

Printed and bound in U.S.A.
10 9 8 7 6 5 4 3 2 1

Amulet Books are available at special discounts when purchased in quantity for premiums and promotions as well as fundraising or educational use. Special editions can also be created to specification. For details, contact specialsales@abramsbooks.com or the address below.

Amulet Books® is a registered trademark of Harry N. Abrams, Inc.

ABRAMS The Art of Books
195 Broadway, New York, NY 10007
abramsbooks.com

To mothers and daughters,
especially Kim Laver,
who taught me to chase big dreams
and helped me realize that writing books
made me feel like me

MAY

CHAPTER 1

Skyler

I NEED THIS TO BE THE LAST PITCH I THROW FOR THE rest of the scrimmage. On a regular day, I'd strike Carter out no problem. She always swings a half second too late. But today, my fingers and wrists have turned against me. My best friend, Paige, our catcher, signals to throw a change-up—my least painful pitch. I cringe. *She knows.* But I'll worry about that later.

I wind up, attempt to lock the pain away where I can't feel it, and send the change-up flying.

Carter gets a piece of it, and it pops up up up. It's gonna be a foul, I can tell, but she's already tearing toward first, because you don't wait around to see. And then the ball is coming down, and Paige is rushing to get underneath it. I close my eyes. If she catches it, the inning is over. I hear the thump of the ball in her glove. Thank. Goodness. I run over to her, screaming some unintelligible softball raving. Our first rec league scrimmage is finally over. She claps me on the back on the way to the dugout.

"You okay?" she asks as we slump onto the grass with our water bottles.

I nod. I'm always okay.

The doctor says it's senseless to fight my pain. That I have to listen to it.

Which kind of goes against everything I know about softball. Daddy taught me and my sister, Scarlett, how to play when we were five. I remember Scarlett throwing the ball down after about two minutes and saying, "This is boring." But I threw it back, hard as I could, and you should have seen the way my dad looked at me. He grinned and said, "You've got an arm, kiddo."

I was used to my sister getting all the attention, usually by any means necessary. I threw the ball back to my dad even harder.

Today, my hands couldn't hurt more if someone ran them over with a truck and lit them on fire. But none of the girls seem to notice (well, except Paige, who is totally looking at me with question-mark eyes). I want to keep it that way, so I paste on a grin and skip over to Emmeline.

"You killed it today, girl!" I bump my hip against hers.

"Thanks." She blushes. The freshmen, they are big on blushing.

"Just, like, keep waiting for your pitches, and you're going to crush it this summer."

"Awesome. I will! Hey, you're pitching next game, right?"

"Uh . . ." My smile falters. "Well, my hands have been bothering me a bit, so I don't know . . ."

All the girls—all my favorite girls from years and years and years of playing rec softball together—start pressing in on me and talking all at once.

"Sky, you have to!"

"We can't win without you!"

"You said that last practice too, but you always push through, don't worry!"

"Yeah, and even if you have to sit out a few games, you can be like our mascot!"

Is that what I am now? I don't want the girls to see how that makes me feel, so I plaster on an even bigger smile and say, "Totally. Her-ricanes for life."

And then they're cheering and dancing and yelling around me, and it feels wonderful. But also like it's going to be the thing that breaks me.

I remember a game a couple months ago, midway through the varsity season. The pain was so bad I had been planning to ask Coach if he could sub me out and put in a closer. But then my dad came down to the dugout, and he was all, "How are your hands feeling? How's the new medicine working?" He couldn't keep the eagerness out of his voice. The thought of telling him the truth made me queasy.

So, I went back in and finished the game.

Because that's what athletes do. Because you always give 110 percent and pain is weakness leaving the body and winning isn't everything—it's the only thing.

And we did win.

Three outs and sixteen broken-glass-in-my-knuckles pitches later.

I iced my hands and thought everything would be okay.

Until the pain knocked me out of bed in the middle of the night.

I remember my dad kneeling on the floor next to me, saying, "What's the matter?"

And my mom standing over him. "What in the damn hell do you think is the matter? You pushed her too hard, and now she's paying for it. She needs to quit the team."

It turned into one of the worst fights they'd ever had. I remember being surprised that it was over me and not my sister. While they yelled at each other about what to do with me and everything else under the sun, Scarlett got me into a warm bath. She tried to distract me, but I couldn't block it out. The pain or the fighting. Even when they went in their room and shut the door.

I was hopeful at the start of rec season. Dr. Levy said that since my rec softball team is less intense than varsity, it would give me a chance to see how my arthritis does in a lower stress environment. It felt like my last shot at making softball work.

But it's too much, trying to play softball and sorting through this arthritis stuff at the same time. Too much for all of us.

I walk up to Coach after practice. I wait until no one is close enough to hear. And I open my mouth.

"See you tomorrow!" is what comes out.

"See you, Skyler," he calls back.

I hesitate, shifting my weight from foot to foot, hoping for something—the truth? A miracle? But I can't seem to make myself tell him.

I'll do it tomorrow.

Paige drives me home, but since Emmeline and Carter are in the car, I still have to pretend like everything is OMGOMG-AMAZING. It's really not that hard. Beyoncé comes on, and I turn it up, and we sing at the top of our lungs as we fly through downtown Winston-Salem in Paige's convertible.

Mama's car is at the house when we pull into the driveway, but not Daddy's. He'll be home from his work trip later tonight though.

"Hey, call me if you change your mind about the sleepover, okay?" says Paige. "I don't mind driving back over here to get you."

She's making the Paige face—the one that means she can see right through me. "Thanks. You are such a sweetheart. My mom's forcing us to do family time since my dad's getting back, but next time?"

"Next time!" they yell.

Then Paige turns the car around in my driveway while they squeal/giggle/fight over music.

I smile and walk up the cobblestone path to the front porch. I smile and climb the steps. I smile so dang hard I think it might break my teeth, and I open the door and I close it.

It is such a relief to finally be able to stop smiling.

I sag against the front door. I have to come up with an alternate plan for this summer. Because going to practices is killing me by degrees, but quitting the team feels just as impossible as playing through the pain. Why does everything have to hurt so much?

I really don't think the pills I'm on are working. I've been thinking it for a while, first a creeping suspicion and then a bell clanging over my head. I picked the pills over a biologic, because needles scare the bejesus out of me, and they expect you to do the injections yourself. But even needles would be better than this. I'll tell my parents today. When Daddy gets home. I'll ask them to take me back to the doctor. Maybe I'll even talk to them about how I don't think I can play softball anymore. If I'm calm, if I say it right, everything will be fine, and no one will get upset.

I'll have to sew my smile back on. But first, a break. I imagine closing the door to my bedroom and sliding down to the floor, ready to let the sobs flow through me.

Then I hear the noises coming from upstairs, and I realize I've got bigger problems.

"Scarlett?" I call. No response. She's probably still out with her boyfriend.

I pull out my phone and text her, even though my fingers hiss at me with every letter.

Something bad is happening at home. Can you get here soon?

CHAPTER 2

Scarlett

"I CAN'T BELIEVE WE GET TO SPEND THE WHOLE summer like this," I say.

"I know."

Reese kisses me to oblivion in the backseat of his car while his fingertips make circles along the outside of my leg. Circles that move farther up my thigh with each passing second. I shiver. My hand twitches, ready to block him, but he stops on his own when he reaches the hem of my skirt. He pulls away, and I realize his face is way too serious for oblivion-kissing.

"Do you want to, you know—? Have you thought any more about sex?"

Well, yes, actually. I think about it all the time. The bulk of these thoughts are devoted to how to keep myself from having it. With you. Before I'm ready. In the heat of the moment (because holy hell, are you good at creating heated moments). "I always thought I would wait," I say. "Maybe not until I'm married, but at least until I know for sure I'm in love."

"Thought?"

"Think." Stupid oblivion-kissing. "Still think. I just. I really want to make sure my first time is with the right person."

Reese scoots close to me and holds my face in his hands and looks into my eyes like he's trying to see my soul. "I love you. I want to spend the rest of my life with you."

I objectively know that if I heard anyone else say something like that to another person, I would think snarky thoughts about how cheesy they sounded. Instead, the words make me feel a little dizzy (though maybe that is a residual effect of the kissing).

"Me too."

He smiles. "Cool. I just want to make sure you know how I feel. I don't want that to be the reason you're not ready to have sex with me."

"Okay." We've only been dating five months. How are we already here, at this conversation?

He runs his hands down my shoulders, my arms, gently touching the scars that lead like ladder rungs from the crooks of my elbows to my wrists. They're white now—faded. It's been months since I've cut. When we started dating, they were still an angry purple-red. I had almost no friends. Reese plucked me from the fringes, and I became someone people wanted to be around. He kisses my scars here and there like he's making me all better.

"You're perfect," he pronounces.

It bugs me and makes me feel beautiful at the same time, but I don't say anything. He's so steady and calm and *good*. I'm lucky he sees something in someone like me.

"I still don't think I'm ready," I say.

His face falls.

"For sex," I add quickly. "But maybe I'm ready for other things."

He grins. "Other things would be cool too."

Other things. My brain is sizzling. Holy hell, I actually told Reese I'm ready to do other things. And I am. But I don't know, I've never done these other things, and what if I'm bad at them or what if I like them so much I totally lose control of myself or—

His fingers run along the hem of my skirt, and this time they don't stop.

Oh. So apparently Other Things are starting right now. Cool.

My phone makes a pinging noise from where it's sitting on the floorboard, effectively interrupting my summer of oblivion kissing. I see a text from Skyler.

Something bad is happening at home. Can you get here soon?

"Hang on." I push away Reese's chest and sit up straight. He stifles a groan. "It's from Sky. I think it's important."

I text back: What's going on? Is Grandma okay?

My brain starts running through a list of possibilities to be anxious over; I can't help it. My sister is kind of sensitive, but she's very low drama.

Everyone is fine. Just try to come home now, okay? And maybe have Reese drop you off at the bottom of the driveway.

wtf sky

Just do it. I twin promise.

Oh, shit.

"We need to get home now," I tell Reese.

His hand is on my arm, his face concerned. "What's going on? Is everything okay?"

"No. I don't know. Skyler said I need to come home right now. It sounds bad."

"Of course. I'll get you there as fast as I can."

For the moment, Other Things are completely forgotten.

When we get to my house, I ask him to stop at the mailbox, per Sky's instructions.

"Are you sure you can handle it on your own?" he asks. "I'm happy to go in with you."

"I'll be fine."

Reese doesn't look convinced. "Well, call me when you find out what's going on."

"I will." I kiss him on the cheek and wait for him to drive away.

Then I jog up our driveway—it's long and kind of winding, with huge oak and beech trees that block most of the house from the street. When I get halfway up, I see why Sky told me to have Reese drop me off at the road.

There are clothes all over the front yard. Button-down shirts scattered across the grass. Gym socks in the hydrangeas. A pair of plaid boxers hangs forlornly from a dogwood tree. What the ever-loving hell.

I look at our house, trying to locate the source of the mass laundry exodus, and I find it in a second-story window. My parents' bedroom. The window is open, the screen is gone. My mother has her head poked out, and she's waving a red flag. Nope, those are my dad's swim trunks. Mama flails her arm, and the trunks end up flattening some hostas.

"Asshole!" she yells.

And then she spots me.

"Oh. Not you, dear. Your father's not going to be with us much longer."

Really loud, angry '90s music pours out the window all around her silhouette. Something about reminding someone of the mess they left when they went away.

I open the front door, and Sky flings herself at me, wrapping her arms around my neck.

"Oh, thank goodness," she says into my shoulder.

"What the fuck is going on?"

Her mouth pinches the way it always does when I swear, but she knows we've got bigger problems than F-bombs right now. "Daddy cheated on her," she says, her face white.

"Wait. WHAT?" I can't even put those words together in any kind of way that makes sense. My dad would never—I mean, he couldn't. My parents are happy. Like, for parents. I look at my sister as if I'll find the answers in the scrunch of her delicate eyebrows, in the 80,000 pounds pressing down on her shoulders. The words finally fall into place. "That fucking bastard."

"Scarlett."

"Don't tell me he's not, Sky. I swear, I'll—" I don't know what I'll do. Join Mama throwing clothes out the window? Maybe.

"I tried to ask her if she was okay, and it just made her throw the clothes harder," Sky whispers. "I'm not going up there again without you."

We climb the stairs, hand in hand, like when we were little, and the jagged voice over the speakers gets louder. Every now and then I pick up a piece of what she's singing, and—ugh, why would you want to do that with someone in a movie theater?

We get to the door of the bedroom. All of Daddy's drawers are empty, and Mama has moved on to his shoes.

"Oh, good." She smiles brightly when she sees us. "Pack your bags, girls. We're going to the lake."

She looks like she's wearing a mask of someone else's face—that's how little I recognize her right now. I have about a million questions, but the only thing that comes out is "The lake house? For how long?" Are they separating? Leaving means they're probably separating, right?

"I don't know. A few weeks? The whole summer? Your daddy's a lying son of a bitch, and we are not gonna be here when he gets back."

Sky frowns. "Doesn't he get back from Chicago in a few hours?"

Mama's head practically explodes. Her curly brown hair looks like tentacles. "From Ber. Mu. Da." She says the syllables like shotgun bursts. Like the entire island of Bermuda has personally wounded her. "He went to Bermuda with that ho from HR with all the cat photos on her desk, and I found the receipts on his laptop."

Usually I would correct someone for calling someone else a ho, but sometimes you make exceptions, like when a person's eighteen-year marriage is unraveling. "Are you sure—" I begin.

"Yes. Yes I am sure because I found texts and pictures starting two months ago, and he's been coming home from work at lunch and sleeping with her in our own damn bed, and apparently that's why he was 'sick' the night of Skyler's awards banquet."

I look at my sister in horror. She and my dad have shared this weird softball connection since practically forever.

Sky's blue eyes fill with tears and she whispers, "That fucking bastard."

Amelia Grace

MY ANGEL COSTUME IS GIVING ME A RASH. EITHER that, or I stepped in some poison ivy when I was hiking yesterday. I tug at the costume where it scratches against my rib cage. Not sure how the poison ivy would have gotten that high though.

Under layers of itchy white fabric, I am wearing jean shorts. Because I am pathetic. Because jean shorts mean pockets, and pockets mean a place to put my phone, and two weeks ago I emailed the girl I've been in love with for four freaking years, and no, she hasn't emailed me back on any of the past fourteen days, but what if today is the day and I don't have my phone? So, like I was saying, pathetic.

I tap, tap, tap my foot against the wooden black stage they built right over where the preacher preaches on Sunday. I'm not usually so impatient, but something about waiting in both literal and metaphorical darkness gets to me.

Mrs. Bellcamp turns around and whispers, "Who's tapping?" Only, her eyes narrow in a way that makes it sound like she's really saying, *Stop fucking tapping*. Not that Mrs. Bellcamp would ever say *fucking*. She's too "nice" for that.

I stop and take a step backward, pressing myself against the back wall of the stage. I can hear people acting on the other side of the curtain, but the angels don't make their appearance until the grand finale. Also part of the finale: the children's choir I helped teach this year. I'm so excited for them. They're pretty much the only reason I'm willing to wear this costume. And then my phone buzzes in my pocket.

HOLY CRAP, MY PHONE IS BUZZING IN MY POCKET.

I pull it out, and my heart does a backflip when I see the Gmail icon. I unlock it with shaking fingers. Mrs. Bellcamp gives me a dirty look when she notices the light, but she can deal with it. I'm already spinning fantasies of what might be waiting for me in my inbox when I see the message from Change.org. Do I want to sign a petition because Windex is doing some kind of evil thing? Um, no. And I'm grateful for the work that gets done there, really, but just because you sign one petition against oil pipelines on native lands does not mean you want to sign EVERY OTHER PETITION EVER. Especially on days when you're expecting an email from the most wonderful girl in the entire world.

I hike up my angel skirt and slip my phone back in my pocket. Then I think about clawing off all the skin around my midsection, because holy crap, these angel costumes. If real angels had to wear these, they'd decide to become fallen within a day, I'm certain of it.

Carrie Sullivan leans against the wall, next to me. "They're pretty awful, huh?" She smiles sympathetically.

I smile back. "The worst."

Carrie and I do all the church stuff together—Sunday mornings and Wednesday nights, lock-ins on the weekend, camps over the summer, workdays to assemble nonperishable items whenever there's a natural disaster somewhere. She gets this smile on her face whenever she's helping someone, and I think it's really cool. Other than that, we couldn't be more different. Carrie has long blond hair and looks a lot like Princess Aurora from *Sleeping Beauty*, minus the resting bitch face. She's tiny and perky and a cheerleader, and she wears these adorable little owl pendant necklaces. And I'm . . . well, the opposite of that.

Maybe that's why there aren't any emails for me.

Carrie inches closer. "Amelia Grace?"

Mrs. Bellcamp turns and attempts to shoot lasers at us out of her pupils. Then an iPhone flashes from the other side of the stage, and she hurries off to heckle a different pair of angels.

Carrie rolls her eyes and lowers her voice to a whisper. "Are you okay?"

"Oh. Sure." I nod like that'll make it true.

"You look sad."

Her sympathetic smile is back. It makes me feel seen though, not pitied.

"I—" Am I really going to tell her this? "I have this friend that I really like."

"Like-like?" Carrie asks, her voice singsong.

My face flushes. "Yeah. Something like that. Only, we've been friends forever, and we used to be really close, and, like, email each other every day and stuff. But I just emailed two weeks ago, and I haven't heard anything, and I'm scared that we've grown apart. I don't know. Maybe she doesn't like me back." My heart stops. "I mean, he."

My cheeks are so red, I just know it, and I hope like anything that Carrie can't see them in the darkness, and the seconds stretch out like hours, and then she gets this tiny smile on her face.

"It would be okay if it was a she," she says.

I gulp like a cartoon character. "It would?"

"Uh-huh." And then she steps closer, so close that her breath is tickling my ear, and she whispers, "And I think she's stupid for not liking you back."

And then Carrie Sullivan is kissing me.

Gently, like she's trying to send me a message without words: *I think you're pretty great.*

So I hold her hand in mine and kiss her back. *I think you're pretty great too.*

Her lips taste like strawberries and self-discovery. Maybe that's what all first kisses taste like, I don't know. I feel this overwhelming sense of rightness, and the very air seems to shift around us. No, wait. The air is *actually* shifting around us. All of a sudden, my skin feels hotter, and the insides of my eyelids change from black to orange. I realize what has happened even as I open them.

The curtain has gone up.

And all hell has broken loose.

The stage lights make my eyes burn, and I'm pretty sure I can hear the collective gasp of the congregation from all the way up here. Carrie and I jump apart, but it's too late. Everyone has seen. Well, everyone except the guy playing the prodigal son at the front of the stage and the man playing his father. They soldier on through the last scene, while Carrie and I scurry to our places and try to act angelic.

Is Carrie out? Because I had no idea. Heck, I'm not even out, not really. My stepdad, our small town, and our church were the three biggest reasons why I figured I wouldn't come out until college. I've just told a few people: our youth minister, my best friend, Abby, and this guy Grayson, who, to my knowledge, is the only other gay person at Ranburne High.

I know my mom and stepdad are in the crowd, but I can't see them through the lights, which is probably a blessing. And then it's over. The curtains go down, and we make our way off the risers and through the set pieces of past plays backstage, into the hallway. Which is, thankfully, empty. All the angels go straight to the girls' dressing room, which is usually the room where Carrie and I have Sunday school.

I wonder if any of them saw us. They would have been facing the crowd.

"Is Amelia Grace your girlfriend?" asks Jamie Marlowe, a fifth grader who pretty much follows Carrie everywhere like a puppy.

Uh-oh.

Carrie blushes, but before she can say anything, Mrs. Bellcamp pulls off her halo with a particularly shrewish frown. "When my girls are older, I'm going to make sure they know to set a proper example for the younger girls."

It feels like a slap.

"There's nothing wrong with—" Carrie begins.

"There is, and you know it. You need to get your life right with God before you come back here."

Carrie's lips disappear inside her mouth. I'm fixing to say something terrible to Mrs. Bellcamp—I don't even know what, but I can feel it bubbling inside me. Carrie must be able to see

17

it too, because she touches my shoulder and shakes her head. Then she runs out of the room.

Mrs. Bellcamp stares right at me in a way that makes me feel like I need a shield. She opens her mouth, but I am not about to listen to a lecture from this woman who just made Carrie leave in tears. The terrible thing bubbles to the surface again, but all that comes out is "I don't think God is who you think He is."

She blinks at me. I tear off my angel costume and throw it on a chair before she can say anything back. Then I run out into the hallway and hope I'll be able to find Carrie.

A few people are milling around, including my mom, but her back is turned so she hasn't seen me yet. Each step in her direction feels like a step toward fate. This isn't what I imagined coming out to her would be like. I always figured I'd wait till college, once I found someone I was really in love with (well, someone who loved me back). Then I'd sit her down and tell her, and maybe it would be a little awkward, and she wouldn't know what to say, but she would definitely hug me, and that's how I'd know everything would be okay.

"Mom?" My voice doesn't crack but only just.

She turns. Her face isn't at all how I pictured. Her eyes look a little weepy, but her lips are a hard line. She holds her arms tight around herself like it's the only way she can keep it together.

She does not hug me.

"We should go," she says, her voice anxious. "Jay's pulling the car around."

Is that all she's going to say? I wait, but no, that's really it. Nothing else is coming.

"Okay," I say softly. For the first time, I want to cry. This isn't who my mom is. She's supposed to tell me she loves me or maybe that she had a feeling all along. That's what people do on TV, right? I know she's really religious. *I'm* really religious. But I thought we felt the same way about God's love. I want to grab her arm and say, *Why aren't you hugging me right now?* But I don't. Maybe because I'm scared of what the answer would be.

My stepdad is waiting for us at the curb, as promised. He doesn't say anything to me when I get in the car. It's when he's quiet that you have to be really scared. I buckle my seat belt, and he pulls out of the church parking lot. We cruise past Jake's ice cream shop and an antique store. The silence hangs, heavy and uncomfortable. Jay keeps a stranglehold on the steering wheel. Mom picks at her cuticles until they bleed.

I try to distract myself by checking my phone for emails (nothing), and for the first time tonight I feel a little guilty. I always imagined my first real kiss would be with someone else.

We're farther away from the church now. Jay sighs, and the stranglehold relaxes an eensy bit. Mom must decide this means it's safe to talk, because she clears her throat delicately. "I was thinking of making pot roast for dinner tomorrow night."

His favorite.

He grunts in reply.

Mom looks down at her hands.

A few minutes later, she tries again. We're passing the multiplex, and she says, "Oh, look, the new Avengers movie is playing. We really liked that last one, didn't we?"

He says yes, and she beams at him like he invented toilet paper.

"I thought we did. What's the name of that actor that plays Captain America?" Her voice takes a particular tone when she asks it, but I feel like I'm the only one who hears it.

"Oh, that was that guy. Chris, um, Everett."

Mom winces.

"No, Evans. Chris Evans."

She beams again and touches his arm. "I knew you'd know it."

He smiles, and it's smug.

I want to throw up.

But at the same time, I don't know. If he's smiling this soon after what happened, does it maybe mean I have a chance? I start to feel cautiously/haltingly/marginally hopeful. Then some kid pulls out in front of us from the Walmart parking lot.

"What the fuck!" My stepdad slams on the brakes so hard my head whacks Mom's seat in front of me. "WATCH WHERE YOU'RE FUCKING GOING, ASSHOLE."

He doesn't just say it. He screams it.

"Fucking teenagers. Think they can do any goddamn thing they want."

He hits the gas and zooms around the kid, flipping him off as we pass. Mom has to grab the door handle to keep from slamming into the window.

Things are not going to be okay.

Jay goes at least twenty over the rest of the way home. Mom no longer tries to make conversation.

As we pull into the driveway, her phone rings, a chipper Bon Jovi ringtone that feels out of place.

"It's your aunt Adeline," she says. "I'll call her back later."

Aunt Adeline isn't really my aunt. She's one of Mom's best

friends from college, and she hasn't called us in forever, but I kind of have bigger things to think about right now. I keep my head high as I walk inside.

I will not apologize. I will *not* apologize. No matter what happens.

My stepdad heads straight to the fridge and cracks open a Coors Light. "They have camps," he says. "For people like you. I'll ask Pastor Mike. They sent one of the deacons' sons there a couple years back, and it straightened him out."

I know I'm supposed to have God's love in my heart for everyone, but sometimes I think I hate him.

"There's nothing wrong with me to fix." I meet his eyes and don't look away. I wonder how I will pay for this later.

A muscle in his jaw twitches, but when he speaks, his voice is even. "It's not up for discussion." He disappears into the bedroom.

"We care about you so much," my mom says. "We just want what's best for you."

I stare at her across the kitchen, and my anger turns into something else.

"Please don't send me away." My voice quivers.

Mom crumples. "Did you have to do it in front of everyone?"

"Is that what bothers you, Mom? That I'm gay, or that I was gay in front of everyone?"

She kind of wrings her hands, glancing back and forth between me and the bedroom.

"Mom, *please.*"

My tears spill over. Mom cries too—sobs and tears and snot and blubbering—and she finally gives me the hug I've been waiting for. I let myself slump against her soft body, feel her arms around me, holding me to her. Maybe everything will be okay.

"I love you so much," she whispers into my hair. "I'm going to do everything I can."

I can't sleep, so instead I press my ear against the air vent in my room and listen to them fight. It's an endless loop of him saying they've got to get me out of this town. It's the only way to fix me. And then Mom tries to stand up for me, but she's so out of practice, it's easy for him to knock her over. Not physically, only with his words. Words can be enough though.

This is your fault. You've always been too easy on her.

We can't let her stay here, not after that.

Hate the sin, love the sinner.

I curl into a ball on the floor and tell myself that I don't need to be fixed. I'm a good person. God loves me. It would be a whole lot easier if there was someone else to tell me.

Ellie

....

I DON'T USUALLY LEAVE THE HOUSE WITH IT. BETTER
to keep it in the box under my bed. Safe. Hidden. Today felt
like the kind of day that needed the extra magic. Today, I
have plans.

I wait until Momma's car is all the way out of the parking
lot. I don't think Momma would be angry exactly that I have
it, but she might not be pleased that I went through her stuff
and read her journal. I pull the friendship bracelet from my
duffel bag. Its threads are every shade of ocean and sky. I make
sure no one is watching before I put it on. Attempt to put it on.
Several times. Turns out bracelets are really hard to put on by
yourself. See, Ellie? This is why you need friends.

I finally get it to clasp. Then I walk into tennis practice and
spot Riley tying her shoes.

"Hey, girl," I say, sitting next to her.

"Hey."

My shorts go tight around my legs as I stretch. They don't
fit because I've gained weight. No, I correct myself. They
don't fit because I have more muscles now, and muscles take
up space. I ignore my shorts and turn to Riley.

"Can you believe how humid it is today? My hair hates me."

She laughs. "I know, right? Like, why do I even bother blow-drying it in the morning."

This talking thing is going really well. Thankfully, Emily Rae isn't around. She's the ringleader, and she scares me a little. Maybe I should just go for it. I touch the bracelet on my wrist for courage.

"Hey, so, my mom has a bunch of errands to run today. Think you could give me a ride home after practice?"

Riley pulls her legs into a butterfly stretch. "Sure."

"Cool, well, I'm gonna go fill up my water bottle, but I'll catch you after practice."

NAILED IT.

I knew the bracelet would work. I found it in our attic when I was eleven years old in a box of my mom's college stuff. That box taught me everything I needed to know about friendship. Namely, that I needed to find three best friends as quickly as possible so we could forge a lifelong sisterhood and make pacts that change the world.

That part has proved trickier than I'd thought.

But today? Things are happening. Me, Riley, Autumn, and Emily Rae. It's gonna be perfect. The three of them are already really close, and they wear the cutest tennis gear, and they're always doing Instagram-worthy stuff after practice. And, okay, sometimes they make fun of people more than I'd like, and I've seen other girls try to be part of their group and fail, but the challenge only makes them that much more interesting.

I smile at Emily Rae as I square up across from her on the court during two-minute drills. I've been killing myself trying to make first court since I started at the academy a few months ago. I slice the ball at her, and she slams it back. She's ahead and then me and then she's saying one of my shots was out even though I kind of thought it was in. There can't be much time left. I make a spectacular serve. And then another. Holy wow, I just might—

The whistle blows.

Yes! I am made of electricity and muscle, and my racket is an extension of my body. And I am screaming "YESSSS" at the top of my lungs. And I am running around in circles and pumping my hands in the air. And I am yelling, "First court! Hell yeah!" And I am remembering that there are a lot of other people here and now some of them are watching me.

Oops.

Sometimes the winner's high hits me a little hard, and I can't be held responsible for my actions. Oh well. If anyone will understand, these girls will.

I've finally found my people. I've never really had girl-friends before. Partly because being homeschooled so you can spend most of your day playing tennis and taking lessons doesn't exactly allow for a lot of social interaction. And partly because I'm so competitive, like more competitive than people think a girl should be.

But not these girls. These are fellow tennis freaks, and I know I've only been with the tennis academy a little while, but I swear, I can already see us being best friends. That thing with me and Riley today? BFFs in the making!! Sadia waves at me from where she's sitting on the bleachers next to Heather. Feeling the movement beside her, Heather looks up from her book and smiles. Sadia's the only other Muslim girl at the academy, and yesterday she told me about how she wanted to be the first woman to play in the US Open while wearing a hijab. I wave back at them both, but I'm really looking for Riley right now.

I spot her talking to a few other girls by her car, so I weave through the parking lot. I'm just squeezing past one of those huge mom vans, when I hear someone say, "Do you want to go get Snow Pops?"

"Hell yes, I do," says Riley.

I'm about to jump in and be like, *OMG I LOVE artisanal popsicles* when Emily Rae says, "Aren't you giving Ellie a ride home?"

Something about the way she says my name makes me duck behind the van.

"Um, yeah," says Riley. "I mean, she asked me or whatever."

Autumn snorts. "She's kind of weird. You know she's never been to a real school?"

"She's a total psycho," says Emily Rae.

It hurts, but I shake it off. A lot of people get really pissed when they lose and just need to vent. It doesn't necessarily mean she hates me. I'm sure they'll still invite me to Snow Pops. Well, maybe not Emily Rae of the ableist insults, but I'm sure Riley will. This isn't going to be like that time in seventh grade. These are tennis girls.

I wait a minute, to be safe, before I walk over to them.

"Hey!" I say.

"Hey," says Riley. "You ready?"

"Yep!"

Emily Rae takes shotgun, and I get in the back with Autumn. I think of how cool it would feel to put Snow Pop pics on Instagram. The irony of having tons of friends on the internet but none in real life is not lost on me. OMG, stop being such a baby. These girls could still be my friends. Maybe.

My phone buzzes with a text from Momma.

Will you be home soon? We're going on a trip tomorrow, and I need you to pack.

Huh. Well, that's not mysterious.

Emily Rae pulls out a bag of gummy bears and pops a few in her mouth before jiggling them at the backseat. "Want some?"

Autumn giggles and grabs a handful.

"Ellie?"

OMG, did you see how she just offered them to me?

"Sure, thanks." I take a few, making sure to get a clear one because those are the best. There was a time a couple years ago when I wouldn't have taken any because my brain had basically equated sugar with poison, but I'm different now. I pop them into my mouth all at once and bite down. A bear squishes between my teeth and liquid comes out. What the—?

Autumn and Riley bust out laughing.

"Vodka," smirks Emily Rae.

"Oh, ha-ha." I don't really drink.

It's technically against my religion, but I don't say that. I really want these girls to like me. But I also really don't want to drink vodka, so I just sort of sit there, holding the gummy bears in my mouth awkwardly so I don't bite down and release more alcohol. I feel like it's going to happen anyway if I don't get home soon. Also, hi, don't vodka-injected gummy bears count as an open container? Maybe only if you decapitate them.

"Ellie, you want some more?"

"Mmm, no thanks." I barely get the words out. Okay,

this is definitely not going to work. My mouth is making too much spit.

I glance around to make sure no one is looking. Try to be as inconspicuous as possible. I spit the whole gummies and the half-chewed gummy into my hand and hold them in my lap. Please don't let anyone notice. Please don't let the juice drip all over me.

"I need more gummies!" yells Autumn, and the other girls laugh.

Emily Rae tosses the bag at her, but it flies in between us, and Autumn's shoulder knocks against mine, and my hand opens for just a second. A bead of green liquid hits my leg.

Autumn narrows her eyes. "Are you *holding* your chewed up gummy bears in your *hand*? Ewww, she is. It's dripping down her legs."

Record scratch. Everyone stops laughing. More than that, they are un-laughing.

"I, um, don't really drink. Religious thing." I fish the bag out from between Autumn and me. "Here, you can eat them for both of us." I pass the gummy bears to Autumn, who doesn't quite meet my eyes.

"Okay, but just a couple more," says Autumn. "I don't want to eat too many on the way to—home."

Emily Rae turns around and gives her a Look. Pretty sure my popsicle dreams are dead.

Riley stops at a big wooden sign that says LAUREL CREEK.

"This is your neighborhood, right?"

"Yeah, you can just drop me at my house. Or . . ."

I wait. And wait. Long enough for it to be awkward and plenty long enough to extend a Snow Pops invitation.

"Um, yeah, my house is fine."

I feel my cheeks get hot. I somehow manage to direct Riley to my house. The other girls are quiet. Conspicuously quiet. Until I get out of the car and shut the door.

They burst into giggles as I walk up my driveway.

"Do you think she knows?" I hear Emily Rae say just before they drive off.

And I know I could get really mad and call them bitches and stuff, but the thing is, it's not like they're bullying me or something. They just don't seem interested in being my friend or inviting me to things. Which is fine, not everybody has to like everybody. But why doesn't anybody ever like *me*?

CHAPTER 5

Scarlett

MAMA IS BASICALLY KIDNAPPING US. SKY AND I
loaded up all our crap (seriously, Mama only gave us thirty
minutes, so there's a 200 percent chance one of us forgot socks
or tampons or something), and we sat in the backseat of the
SUV until Mama got in and slammed the door (looking completely unhinged, I might add) and peeled out of the driveway.
I think about my dad coming home to an empty house and an
apocalyptic display of what used to be his wardrobe decorat-
ing the front yard. Bastard deserves it.

Skyler

I'm a little scared. Mama doesn't usually drive this fast, and
her mascara is smeared all down her cheeks. It's not like my
parents have never gotten into fights before. I mean, of course
they fight. Sometimes. Everyone does. But I can't remember

either of them ever using the D word. I can't stop worrying about it—them getting divorced I mean. And because I'm a really selfish person, I also worry about softball and joint pain and how I'm ever going to be able to tell them now.

I can't believe Daddy would do something like this. And that we've left him. Because it doesn't feel like *she's* leaving him—it definitely feels like a we.

Scarlett

After about half an hour of driving like a trucker on methamphetamines, Mama turns down the angry '90s music and clears her throat.

"I'm sorry," she begins.

"Why are *you* sorry? You have nothing to be sorry about." He cheats, and she's sorry? I could Hulk-smash something right now. Ideally, his face.

But my mama's voice comes out calm and even. "I could have told you what happened without giving you all those details. And I should have. There are things that parents should shield their children from knowing." She sweeps a hand over her hair, smoothing flyaways all around, pulling herself back together.

"I'm glad we know the truth." Even if it does set my teeth on edge.

Sky nods. "I am too." She leans forward and squeezes Mama's shoulder. "We love you so much. Everything will be okay."

Mama starts sobbing again. Oh, for Pete's sake, Sky. Just when we were making some headway.

Skyler

....

I try to put myself in Mama's shoes. What must it be like to build your entire life with someone, and then have it all just ripped out from underneath you? Last fall, I thought I was in love with this guy who plays saxophone in the band—Jonah. We even had sex, but I don't know. Sometimes I feel like people's stories are only meant to overlap for a little bit. That's what I told Jonah, and he took it pretty well. He's still my friend, and we still get Kernol's Donuts together sometimes.

I don't think Mama and Daddy are the type that could stay friends. Maybe if your story gets too wrapped up in someone else's, the only way out is to tear everything to pieces.

Scarlett

....

Mama has finally stopped crying again. As long as Sky doesn't unleash any more of her capital-F Feelings, we should be okay. I decide it's safe to voice some reservations about our current trajectory.

"How long are we going to stay at the lake house?" I ask. A week? Two weeks? I have a job. And a boyfriend.

"Definitely for the summer. I'm not teaching any classes," Mama says. "I'll have to figure out something more permanent for the fall, but don't worry. Everything will be fine."

Everything will be fine? "What about my job?" And Reese? Mama sighs like that will be the one little thing that pushes her over the brink. "I'll call Mr. Thornton on Monday and explain things to him. I'm sure he'll let you pick back up in the fall."

"No, I'll do it." Rule of professionalism no. 1: Your mom does not call your boss for you. I guess there's also the possibility that I could live at home with my dad, but just, nope. Not happening. "Ugh." I throw my empty water bottle against the floorboard. Sky cuts her eyes at me.

I hate when she gives me that look. The you-are-not-meeting-my-impossibly-high-standards-of-how-to-be-a-good-person look.

"Wait. What about Sky's softball?" I shouldn't be the only one acting like a spoiled brat right now.

"I'll just take a break from playing rec this summer," says my sister serenely. "This is more important."

Mama almost starts crying again over that one. This time I'm the one giving the look. The why-do-you-always-have-to-be-such-a-martyr look.

"I called my sisters," says Mama. "They're all going to be here tomorrow."

An important distinction: My mother has no biological sisters. She bought her friends in college. Seriously, what's more pathetic than joining a club for women with more internalized misogyny than you can shake a stick at? *Paying* to join that club. We are about to be the victims of an Alpha Kappa Nu invasion.

33

"Aunt Neely is driving down from Tennessee with Amelia Grace, and Aunt Seema is schlepping all the way from DC with Ellie, but they should all be here by the afternoon. Aunt Val and Heidi are already at their house."

No joke: Aunt Val bought a house on the lake RIGHT NEXT DOOR to ours because she and my mom are that kind of friends. She and Heidi live at the lake full-time.

"We thought it would be fun if the four of you girls stayed in the carriage house together."

"Fun" is not generally a word I'd use to describe a summer with no job, no boyfriend, and no friends. That goes double when your family is falling apart.

Skyler

At least 30 percent of the tension I'm feeling releases when I realize I don't have to make a decision about softball. It's already been made for me. I have time to figure out how to tell someone about the pain and my meds. And I'm so glad I get to see Aunt Val. I can't think of a life without her in it. She's come to almost every birthday party Scarlett and I have ever had, and last year we did Thanksgiving with her and her wife, Heidi.

And Aunt Seema and Aunt Neely, I haven't seen them or Amelia Grace or Ellie since we were little, but all my life, I've heard stories about these women. And about the lake. Whenever my mom talks about it, it sounds like one of those beach novels stacked in bookstore windows: friendships forged in sunscreen and secrets, in Jet Ski races and dancing around bonfires at midnight. Four women who are strong and beautiful and brilliant and most important, always there for each other. I can't wait to be in a sorority someday. Sometimes when Mama talks about them I get a little jealous.

But now, I'm just feeling so relieved.

This might be the thing that gets Mama through this.

This might be the thing that gets all of us through it.

Scarlett

I would rather gnaw off my own arm than go to this effing lake house right now.

Skyler

I hope the girls like me. They'll probably like me. Have they grown up their whole lives hearing about me like I've been hearing about them? That's weird to think about.

Scarlett

But seriously, who in their right mind thought this was a good idea? I don't want to spend an entire summer at a house with a bunch of strangers just so our moms can sit on the dock and drink wine until belting out Journey at two o'clock in the morning suddenly seems like a really good idea.

I guess it will be kind of cool to see Ames though.

Skyler

"I'm really glad everyone is coming," I tell Mama.

Scarlett rolls her eyes where she thinks I can't see, because she thinks I'm brown-nosing again.

Mama smiles at me in the rearview mirror. "Me too."

The roads are getting smaller now. We're only a few miles away from the lake house.

And then Mama's phone rings.

My eyes flick to the clock on the dashboard. 8:45 p.m.

Mama doesn't answer, but we all know who it is.

Scarlett's phone is next, and I don't know why, but that hurts a little.

"Don't," says Mama.

Scarlett looks at her screen and winces. "You don't think he'll see the yard and think we got murdered or something, do you?"

"He'll be fine," I say.

Scarlett gives me this raised-eyebrows appraising look, like she's impressed by my hard-hearted resolve.

"I left a Post-it on the fridge," I mumble.

And . . . the moment of admiration is gone.

"SKYLER, YOU TRAITOR."

"Well, I just wanted him to know we're okay. What if he was worried?"

"He should be worried. He should be spending a hell of a lot more time worrying about his own daughters than banging people at work."

"Scarlett!" I jerk my head in Mama's direction.

It is only then that I realize we've come to a complete stop.

"We're here," Mama announces.

Something about the way she says it feels very meta.

Scarlett

"Oy vey, there's no way I'm tackling all the lake check-in stuff tonight," says Mama. "That means we won't have water, but we can brush our teeth with bottled water, okay?"

"Sure," Skyler and I say together.

Daddy would never have saved the water till morning.

We unload the car and do a quick check inside the house. Sky and I are putting the last of the things in the fridge when Mama comes downstairs in her pajamas.

"I'm gonna go to bed early, but I just wanted you to know that everything is going to be okay. We'll figure this out."

She looks like she's going to cry again.

"Okay," I say. Skyler says it too.

"We'll get you an appointment with Dr. Dabkowski next week, okay?" Mama says to me, turning on her Concerned Mom Eyes. "It would be good for you to talk to someone."

Just me. Not my sister. Just in case I was thinking about forgetting that I'm the broken one.

Mama gives us both one of those awkwardly long mom hugs and goes upstairs to bed. It is 9:15 p.m. Is it a good sign or a bad one that she's going to bed so early?

"Scarlett?" my sister whispers.

"What?" I whisper back and then feel tricked into whispering.

"Will you sleep in my room with me?" she asks.

"Sure," I say in my normal voice. I'm really glad she asked. I didn't want to sleep by myself either.

We put on our pajamas, but it's so early that we snuggle under the covers of Sky's canopy bed and watch old episodes of *Pretty Little Liars*. Aria's dad is cheating with a student, and Aria's mom doesn't know yet. Maybe this was a bad idea.

We turn off the TV and try to go to sleep. I toss and turn under the covers, trying to get comfortable, but it isn't the bed or the covers or the itchy place on the back of my leg or the sliver of light coming in under the door. I feel like I'm walking through one of those funhouse tunnels, and the floors won't stop moving, and the pieces of my life are spiraling overhead and all around, and I have no idea how they're going to settle. Will they get a divorce? Who will we live with? Do we have to sell the house? I'm not the kind of person who can just roll with changes like this. I'm not my sister.

"Sky?" I whisper.

She rolls over so she's facing me. "Yeah?"

I don't know how to say it so I just do: "I'm scared."

"It's gonna be okay." She rushes to say it the way you do when you want to make someone feel better, but I want it to be true, so I try to believe it.

"Okay."

"Okay."

She puts her hand on my shoulder under the covers. I roll over and try to go to sleep again.

It's going to be okay. It's going to be okay. It's going to be okay.

But what if it's not?

CHAPTER 6

Amelia Grace

I LET THE WATER RUN OVER ME FOR WHAT FEELS LIKE forever. Normally, I'd have to worry about my stepdad pounding on the door and telling me time's up, but I guess I get a reprieve, seeing as how I'm about to get shipped off. If I can stay under long enough, maybe I'll forget about the car ride home last night. When I come out, Mom is sitting on my bed waiting for me, and Jay is—mercifully—gone.

"I know you're angry, but I really think this is what's best for all of us," she says.

"All of us?" I don't try to keep the bitterness out of my voice.

"Your stepdad could use some time to cool down."

That might be true, but it doesn't make it right.

"I just— I wish you could try to understand me," I say.

"Maybe this trip will do that. Give us time to understand where the other one is coming from."

I bite my lip to keep from crying. I will never understand being able to treat your child this way.

Mom gets out my suitcase and helps me get my clothes together.

"Where is it we're going?" The only thing I know for sure is that we can't afford one of those camps.

"Your aunt Adeline has a house on Lake Hartwell. She said we could stay there." Mom shrugs. "And it'll be free."

"Oh. That's really nice of her, I guess." It's not enough to put me at ease. I feel like there's still some piece of this I'm missing. "Why are you packing so many clothes? That's, like, every pair of underwear I own."

Mom winces. "Well, we'll be leaving later this morning." Yes. This is something I already know. "And we'll come back at the end of July. The week before school starts."

July. "But—I'm leading Vacation Bible School. It'll be my first time as a junior youth minister. All my kids from choir are so excited."

This isn't just for a week or two. This is an entire summer of banishment. The funny thing? Even if I stayed, I don't know that there would be anything with Carrie. It was just the one kiss, and it came out of nowhere. But honestly, if I stayed, I probably would want to see where it goes with her. Gosh, I hope she's doing okay.

Mom doesn't meet my eyes. "The church doesn't want you working with kids after what happened last night. People have been complaining that you're not spiritually fit."

"Oh." Tears prick my eyes, but I'm not going to cry. "How many people?"

"Well, Mrs. Bellcamp—"

"*Mrs. Bellcamp?*" *You need to get your life right with God before you come back here.* "Mom, she's terrible. She once made Peyton Reed cry for 'dancing sinfully' at a lock-in. Please tell me you didn't let her get away with whatever bigotry she was—"

41

"Everyone agreed that a summer away might be the best thing for you."

"What about you? Mom, you know I'm a good person."

She puts her arm around me. "Of course I do. And the church said if you go away for the summer, we can revisit the idea of you being a junior youth minister when you come back."

"But only if I come back the way they want, right?" I whisper.

"Amelia Grace—"

"I can't talk about this anymore."

I turn my back on her. Hope she leaves. I've been volunteering at church since I could walk, dreaming of being a junior youth minister since one of the older girls taught me how to use a power drill at a Habitat for Humanity build. But now? I don't think I'll ever be able to be the person they want me to be.

I knew there were people like Mrs. Bellcamp and my stepdad at church. Even our pastor has had some sermons that made me curl my hands into fists. But when I came out to Pastor Chris, our youth minister, he was so kind, and I really thought he was on my side. I thought things were changing, and I wanted to be at the front of that change.

I can feel my mom there, hovering, when the doorbell rings.

"It's for you," she says. "I told Abby we were going, and she wanted to come over and see you before you left."

I almost want to hug her for that. Almost.

"Thanks," I whisper.

I go answer the door. And I fall into Abby's arms.

"It's going to be okay," she says. "Everything is going to be okay."

I wish my mom had said it. I somehow get out the story of everything that happened last night and this morning. Abby was at church last night, so she seems to know most of it already. We sit on the front porch of my trailer and talk for a while before I work up the courage to break it to her about our summer plans.

"They're not going to let me be a youth minister this summer."

Abby squeezes my shoulder. "I heard about that. I'm so sorry."

I wonder if her mom was one of the people who called about me and that's how she knows, but I can't bring myself to ask.

Abby fidgets with the hem of her shorts. "Do you think—? I mean, what if you just promised you wouldn't kiss any more girls or go on dates or anything?"

"I shouldn't have to change who I am." I finally get to live this piece of me. I don't want to give it up.

"I'm not saying change. I'm just saying . . . make things easier on yourself. You could just try."

She wants us to be junior youth ministers together, I know that's the only reason she's saying it, but it still doesn't feel good to hear. "I don't know," I say.

Abby nods. "I better go."

"Me too. I gotta go finish packing."

She gives me one last hug. "I'm going to pray for you."

"Thank you. And thanks for coming over. I'll pray for you too."

She frowns. "No, I mean. I need to pray for you. I think you— I think it's important."

It finally clicks. I'm embarrassed it took so long. Sometimes "I'm going to pray for you" is a blessing, and sometimes it's a judgment. And now I understand that this is the second kind. A brittle, awkward silence rises up between us. I thought she was cool with it. When I told her I thought I might have a crush on this girl I'm pen pals with, she was like, "Oh, wow," and then she gave me a hug. But now it's hitting me—it's not just people like Mrs. Bellcamp. And my stepdad. It's Abby. It's my mom. It's everyone.

And when she was trying to get me to hide—

I stand up, fast. "Um, I need to go put some clothes in the dryer."

Abby gets in her car, and I go back inside and finish packing on autopilot.

I'm still feeling numb two hours later when Mom and I are on the road. I stare out the window at the wildflowers growing in the median. Purple blur. Pink blur. Yellow blur. At one point, I pull out my phone and dash off a quick Are you okay? to Carrie. She doesn't text back though. I wonder if she still has her phone. Mom's eyes keep flicking to the passenger seat like she wants to say something. Or maybe she's just checking on me.

"Amelia Grace?" she says on the two hundred and sixty-seventh check.

I grunt noncommittally in response.

"There's . . . something else I need to tell you. About Aunt Adeline's."

The needle on my BS-ometer slides to Seriously Effing Fishy. "Yes?"

"Aunt Adeline just found out her husband is cheating on her."

"Oh, gosh, I'm so sorry. Is it okay that we're going up there?" Because we could turn back around. I am totally that selfless.

"That's actually a big part of why we're going up there. She called all the girls last night." She smiles, but it's the sad kind. "I think she really needs us."

"I understand. That's really terrible." I wish she would have framed it for me like that at breakfast. I would have felt a whole lot better about—

"Your stepdad doesn't know."

And that would be why.

"I think it might be best if he thinks it's just us at the house."

Because Aunt Adeline thinks my stepdad, and I quote, "isn't worth the pot he pisses in." And the feeling is definitely mutual. Sometimes I wonder if that's why she and my mom haven't talked so much these past few years. They used to be so close.

"I won't tell him," I say, my voice as unforgiving as the hot stretch of asphalt in front of us.

"Thanks." The relief radiates off of her. "And, um, there's one other thing."

I don't know if I can handle another thing. What's next? Does the lake contain mermaids? Actually, that'd be pretty freaking sweet.

"We thought it would be fun if we all brought our daughters this time," Mom says. "I don't even know how many years it's been since you've seen Skyler or Scarlett or Ellie."

Mom said *her* name. She'll be there. I whip my head back to the wildflowers because if I don't, I'm certain Mom will be able to see everything running through my brain right now—

namely, one long glittery streamer with the words I'M IN LOVE WITH HER. I'M IN LOVE WITH HER. I'M IN LOVE WITH HER.

It's pathetic, but I can't help it. I check my phone to see if maybe she emailed me back, in light of the fact that we'll be seeing each other in, oh, a few hours.

Nothing.

And then, even more pathetic, I search for this one particular email thread. It's from three years ago, and I've read it at least a hundred times since. Our moms had set us up as pen pals (well, more like email pals) in middle school because "they thought we'd have a lot in common and get to be good friends," which was actually code for "we were both really lonely and hardly had any friends and people were picking on us at school." We emailed and texted almost every day. She had kind of a tortured loner thing going. And I, well, I came to school every day in soccer shorts and big giant T-shirts, and the girls at my school . . . didn't.

So, she emailed me all upset one day because some stupid cow uninvited her from a sleepover. And I wrote back and said, A) she's a stupid cow. Because B) you're amazing. And C) you can't change how other people act, but you can change how you act. I told her about this article I read about friendship notebooks and how you can take a hurtful thing that someone has done to you and use it to teach yourself about the kind of friend you want to be. You take the hurtful thing (getting disinvited) and turn it into a pledge: I will never disinvite a friend from an event. And you write it down in a notebook, so you'll never forget the person you're hoping to be.

She emailed me back a couple hours later saying she'd tried it, and it'd made her feel so much better. And then she said the thing that has been haunting me ever since. I scroll down until I find the line I'm looking for.

You are like the most perfect person, do you know that? If you were a boy, I would totally marry you!

I read it again. And then again. And, okay, fine, maybe half a dozen times after that.

I realize Mom is watching me. Oops.

But she smiles. "You seem happy."

I shrug. "I guess I am. Kind of. It's been a long time since I've seen any of them."

Her. Since I've seen her.

Ellie

MOMMA EYES ME FROM THE DRIVER'S SEAT. "IF YOU want, you can stay for a long weekend and fly back Monday or Tuesday. You'd only miss a couple practices."

"It's fine," I say. I try not to look too happy about leaving. "How long are we going for anyway? A week or two?"

"I'm not completely sure, but at least a few weeks. I brought my laptop, so I can work remotely."

"Oh."

"I know how disruptive that would be for your tennis, beta. Are you sure you don't want to stay home with Dad?"

I try to maintain my composure even though I'm freaking out on the inside. The lake is where it all started. Momma's journals and photos make that pretty clear. I am on a friendship pilgrimage, and there will be three other girls dying to be friends with me, and maybe, if I'm lucky, I can find the remnants of the SBDC. I don't actually know what that stands for because Momma's journals didn't say, but I gather it's some kind of Ya-Ya Sisterhood club for female empowerment/ shenanigans.

I hope the other girls will be up for re-creating it with me. I haven't actually seen any of them since I was five, but I'm sure we'll be best friends. How could we not? First, though, I have to make sure I get to stay at that lake house.

"Well, maybe I can find a coach in South Carolina," I say slowly, like I'm just now thinking of it. "We'd be driving all over the southeast for my tourneys anyway. We can do that from the lake house. That way I could stay with you and pick back up at the academy later."

Momma brakes hard at a stop sign and turns to face me. "You have been begging to go to a tennis academy for years."

"I know." I try to keep my face neutral. Why does she have to be so good at seeing me? Don't most kids have parents who don't see them at all? I'm pretty sure that's a thing.

She squints. "Did something happen?" (Told you.)

"What? No. I just really want to meet your friends and their daughters. You've talked about them for so long."

And if all of you are such good friends, then all of us will be good friends too because it's like hardwired into our DNA, right? It won't be like tennis academy. I won't be such a dork this time. I will make this summer of friendship happen if it's the last thing I do.

"We'll see," says Momma.

I imagine her saying no. Spending the rest of the summer at the academy. I start to go into one of those spirals where you think about all the ways everyone hates you. Focus, Ellie. That's not helping. I pull out my Things to Pack for the Lake House list. Lists always help. I know it's technically too late to add anything, but just looking over it soothes me. I wonder if I really needed to bring a curling iron AND a straightener or if I could have gotten by with one or the other. Maybe a curling iron plus hair dryer? This may seem like a lot of contingency planning dedicated to hair, but it's kind of my signature thing about my look on Instagram. I have long brown hair with golden highlights that goes most of the way down my back. I get it from my dad—he's white, and he still has super-light-blond hair even as a grown-up. Did I remember to tell Momma to pack the cooler? I think she put it in the trunk somewhere. My brother, Zakir, and I are like his and hers kids. When I was little, like if it was just the two of us at the park or something, people used to ask Momma if she was the nanny. I remember it would always make her eyes go sad. Now I understand why. I wonder if I have enough conditioner for two weeks of swimming in lake water. I also wonder how hard it is to be a travel writer. Like, as a career.

As I'm in the middle of pondering these important life decisions, my brother FaceTimes me.

"Hey, what's up?"

"Just got to camp," says Zakir. He's working at a camp for kids with juvenile diabetes over the summer. "What are you doing?"

"Double-checking my pack list, *obviously.*"

"I can't believe you make those."

"And I can't believe how many times you're going to wish you took me up on my offer to make you one. Bet you forgot shampoo AND deodorant. Those poor children."

"Hey, Ellie, wanna be stressed out? I woke up fifteen minutes before we left. *And* I threw all my stuff in a duffel bag. *And* I didn't even put my shower stuff in one of those plastic bag things you and Momma use. It's probably oozing all over my—"

"Okay, stop!" I cannot believe he shares 50 percent of my DNA. "Oh! We're crossing the South Carolina border!"

I pick my feet up off the floor of the car like I do every time we cross a state line. Zakir makes a redneck joke, and I make one back, and then we go into a full-on joke battle. Momma even lets us go for a while before she gives me a whack and says something about classism. I feel like the fact that she didn't stop us sooner means something. See, Momma and Daddy met at college in Atlanta, and that was all cool, but then they got married and moved to some dinky Deep South college town where Daddy got a job and Momma could go to law school. And they almost never talk about what it was like, living there, but it's what they don't say that gets me.

You guys are so lucky we live where we live in DC.

The people here are so wonderful.

Things got so much better after we moved here.

There's always an unspoken comparison that makes me wonder exactly what "there" was like and exactly how bad it was.

Momma ruffles my hair. "You want to stop for a snack soon?"

Zakir snorts. "Dare you to Instagram your hair like that."

I roll my eyes, but it doesn't stop me from fixing my hair in the mirror. Or Zakir from teasing me about said fixing.

"BYE, Zakir."

My brother has been teasing me for as long as I can remember. He's also the reason people call me Ellie. He had a really hard time saying Jameelah as a kid, so he called me Ellie, and then everyone else started calling me Ellie too, and it just stuck. Sometimes I feel a little guilty about it—like it's one more way for me to pass and him to not. But mostly it just feels like me.

I lean against the window in a way I hope looks both bored and cute at the same time and snap a selfie. *At least I got in a run before this car ride. I hate sitting still for so long,* I type before posting.

The worst part of road trips: having to sit still for hours on end (no joke, sitting is the new smoking) and not being able to drink adequate water. I mean, I guess I *could* drink as much water as I usually do, but then I'd have to pee every twenty minutes, and I don't think that'd go over very well with Momma.

She pulls off at the next exit. I'm not used to seeing so much land with so few buildings and people. Barns with rusted tin roofs and fields full of cows and stuff. The gas station's paint is peeling, and the bunny on the sign has seen better days, but they appear to have gas and food. A car pulls up next to us, a convertible bug, and four girls pile out, looking for all the world like they're starring in their own teen movie. I stare at them wistfully.

And then we get out of the car.

Everyone else at the gas station is white. And it's not like I've never been in a situation like that before, but sometimes you feel it more than others, and this, this is a lot. The way people are looking at us makes me wonder if they've ever seen a brown person before. Their eyes stick like flypaper as Momma pumps gas, her black hair rippling in the wind.

I go inside and go to the bathroom and pick a snack— Vitamin Water and pistachios (with shells, because a study showed you eat fewer nuts that way but still feel just as full). Momma comes in to pay, and I meet her at the register. The woman behind the counter smiles stiffly, but her eyes are kind. Then we turn and this older man (sixties, maybe?) scoffs like we almost ran him over, even though we totally didn't, and he makes a big radius around us on his way to the bathroom.

"Let's go, Ellie," my mother says quietly.

The man glares at us as he pushes the bathroom door open. I don't *think* we were in his way. No, you know what, I know we weren't.

If I was by myself, that man wouldn't have looked twice. People always think I'm white because of my hair and my green eyes, unless I happen to be rocking a really good tan, but even then, I usually just get The Squint and some rude question about what I am. Nothing like what Zakir and Momma have to deal with.

By the time we get back outside, the people at the pumps have downgraded from outright staring to the occasional meant-to-be-covert-but-not glance. It's not that our family never gets looks in DC, what with me looking like Daddy and Zakir looking like Momma. Sometimes when the four of us are together, people will watch us, and you can see it breaking their brains trying to figure out how we fit together.

I just wish it wasn't so hard.

CHAPTER 8

Scarlett

WE ARE SO COMPLETELY BADASS. IF WONDER Woman and Beyoncé had a baby together and then that baby got coached in badassery by Ruth Bader Ginsburg, she would still only be *almost* as badass as us right now. See, my dad has this cabin-opening checklist. And usually it's his job to do all these little things to open the cabin and Mama's job to open a bottle of wine, so I was kinda nervous as to how today would play out, but nope.

Check the deck, check the house, check the dock. We got this. Make sure the roof is okay and the window screens are intact? All in a day's work for three badass ladies like us. It's like Skyler has Dad's entire check-in list memorized. She even directed us on how to do all kinds of fancy boat stuff to the boat. (She's about as obsessed with boats as those guys who talk about sailing all the time and wear shorts with whales on them.)

I'm thinking it's all going to go off without a hitch when I hear a shriek from the living room. I take the deck stairs two at a time and find Skyler jumping up and down on the couch and pointing at a bookshelf.

"Mouse! There's a mouse! I saw it go under there!"

I peek under the bookshelf.

"BE CAREFUL! IT ALMOST BIT ME."

I go to the kitchen and grab a broom.

"OHMYGOSH, DON'T KILL IT."

I give her some extreme side-eye. "Do you want me to leave it there?"

"NO! Just, like, sweep it out of there gently."

"I'll see what I can do."

I wedge the broom under the bookshelf (gently, before Skyler has an empathy-induced heart attack), but I still make sure to give the mouse a good nudge, because vermin. The mouse is more than happy to run out the open front door, and Skyler is more than happy to screech at it until the tip of its pink tail disappears.

She steps down from the couch cushions and throws her arms around me dramatically. "You saved my life."

"I mean, I don't want to brag, but you would pretty much have rabies right now if it weren't for me."

"Truth." She lets me go.

"But if we see any spiders, those are on you," I say.

"I'll take spiders over mice any day."

"Are you kidding? That mouse was adorable. It was all fluffy, and it gave me this look, like, 'Hey, Scarlett, what if you just carry me around in your pocket and feed me cheese on occasion?'"

"It gave no such look."

"Like you would know. You were too busy screaming."

"Okay, but speaking of cheese—"

"What are you—"

"*Speaking of cheese*, I think we should go eat some and, like, celebrate how awesome we are."

I shrug and follow her to the kitchen. I'm an easy sell where cheese is concerned. My sister grabs some kind of hard white cheese with a purple wine-flavored rind. She picked it this morning when the two of us decided we'd better go to the grocery store seeing as how A) neither of us had seen Mama eat anything since before the clothes-pocalypse, and B) there was nothing at the lake house but coffee (Mama took every last bit of it with us and said she hoped like hell Daddy woke up jet-lagged). Skyler plucks a knife from the knife block. She keeps tugging at the plastic packaging on the cheese and biting her lip, but her fingers can't seem to grasp the edges. I've never seen her struggle so hard to open something before.

"Sky, do you—?"

She jerks her hands away and lets the cheese fall to the counter. "Here. I just put on lotion, and it's super slippery. Do you mind?" She laughs weakly. I pick up the cheese package, but I don't feel any lotion.

I want to say something to her. She's silent behind me as I tear open the plastic on the first try.

I pick up the knife. Put it back down. "Sky, are you okay?"

That weak laugh again. "I'm fine. It was the lotion."

I try to make my voice as sweet and un-Scarlett-like as possible. "Are you sure?"

"Scar, just cut the cheese."

Cut. The cheese. We both happen onto the double entendre at the same time. We have the combined humor IQ of a twelve-year-old boy, I'm not even kidding. I crack first, and then Skyler starts snickering, and then I snort, and it's all over.

We laugh until my stomach aches and I slap the counter. It takes a good two minutes for us to recover, and then I can cut the cheese (the block of cheese on my counter—get your mind out of the toilet). We each grab a slice and clink them together like they're wineglasses.

"L'chaim," says Skyler.

"Cheers to having giant lady balls and knocking out the entire list by ourselves."

We both stuff our faces with cheese. After a few moments, Skyler tilts her head to the side, listening.

"Is that . . . Mama?"

I freeze and tilt my head too. From somewhere outside, I hear: "Dadgum-fercockt-POS-water-pump-bastard!"

I withhold a snicker (mostly). "Yeah, we should probably go check on that."

Skyler and I hop up and run outside. Well, first, I put the cheese back in the fridge (priorities). We rush to the shed where the water pump is.

Mama's hair is a mess, and her clothes are splattered in water and dirt. She sweeps her curly brown hair back into a ponytail, smudging her cheek with her dirty hand in the process.

"Is everything okay?" asks my sister. She makes her patented Skyler-question-asking face. All big blue eyes and blinking lashes, and you feel like you have to say something comforting because she might cry if you don't. She is really freaking exhausting sometimes. It seems to work on Mama though.

"I'm fine, baby." She scratches her temple. Another smudge. "I just had to get the water pump going, and it doesn't work worth a damn." Da-yum. Mama's accent stretches all the four-letter words from one syllable to two. "Can you go in the house and turn on the faucet to see if it worked?"

"Sure," we both say at the same time (twin jinx!) and run back inside.

"I totally forgot about the water pump," says Skyler.

"Me too, and it's the worst part."

I go to the kitchen sink and turn on the faucet. *C'mon, we've got this.* Instead of water, a hissing noise comes out. Okay, maybe we don't got this.

"Sky, run and tell Mama it didn't work."

She nods and runs back outside. After a few seconds, I hear her yell, "Okay, turn it o—"

Did she say on? I think she did. The sink is still hissing in front of me. "It *is* on!" I yell back.

Or maybe she said off.

The hissing is getting louder. And I think I just heard a clunk. And maybe a rushing sound, like—

Water explodes out of the sink and hits me in the face and soaks me all down my front. I scream some things. And by things, I mean swear words. Footsteps coming my way, Mama and Sky, but I manage to get my act together and turn off the sink. Unfortunately, not before they get splattered with water too. I sweep my wet hair out of my face. Why is there still the sound of water running?

"The fridge!" yells Mama.

The water dispenser on the fridge is shooting out water even though no one is pushing the button. Mama runs over and tries to catch it with her hands and fling it into the sink, but she mostly just gets herself wetter and more frantic.

I leap over and hit the lock button on the water dispenser, so it stops coming out.

"I think we were supposed to turn off the water before we opened the faucets," I say. Understatement of the year. Then I notice Mama's face. "But, hey, we did it, right?"

She doesn't say anything. Tightens her lips until they practically disappear.

"Why does everything have to be so hard?" she whispers. And then her posture goes all to hell.

"Mama?" I do my best to say it in a Skyler voice. It's the first time I've seen her shoulders slump. Maybe ever. I grip the counter.

Her eyes lock on my white knuckles, and she forces a calm smile onto her face. "It's going to be fine, sweetie. I didn't mean to get so upset."

She's lying. She is not okay, and she's only saying she is because she thinks I can't handle it. And maybe I can't if my own mother doesn't trust me with the truth.

She turns away from me and walks out of the room.

Skyler chases Mama up the stairs. I cannot go live with Dad. I need her to be okay.

I think of a night last September, right at the beginning of sophomore year. Earlier that day, I had accidentally spilled to my English teacher that I was cutting myself, and she said she'd have to tell my parents, since I was hurting myself. I walked into my house knowing it would be bad. I made Sky go upstairs because she's a terrible liar, and I didn't want them to know that she already knew and didn't tell them.

Mama was reactive and dramatic, as always. She couldn't sit down, I remember that. Almost like her frantic pacing would take her steps closer to solving what was wrong with me. Daddy was calm. He took my hand and said, "We'll get you help. We'll find someone you can talk to."

But later that night, I heard them talking. Daddy was crying, and I remember thinking it was the scariest thing I had ever heard. "I don't know if I can do this," he said.

And Mama was all, "I don't give a damn what you think you can or can't do. She's our daughter. You don't get to pick when you are and aren't her parent. It's the hardest thing you'll ever do, and we have to be better people than we are. For her."

"I just— I need for something to go right. I need a break."

I could picture him through the wall, sitting on the bed with his head in his hands. I grit my teeth thinking of it now. I wonder if that's when he started seeing that lady at work.

Mama's voice was strident in reply. "Well, that's too fucking bad because parents don't get breaks. Our little girl needs us right now, and we're gonna get up tomorrow morning and we're gonna help her. And we're gonna do it the next day, and the next day, and every day until she's okay because that's what you do."

Her rage warmed me like a cup of hot cocoa. I had always thought that Daddy and I were kindred spirits. That was the night I knew I was wrong.

And I realized, much as she vexed me, that when they fashioned my mama's soul out of carpenter nails and lipstick and fireworks and glasses half empty, they saved the blueprint for mine.

I can survive without my dad. But I don't know what I'll do if losing him makes me lose her.

The doubt makes an empty space inside me, and all my darkest thoughts rush in to fill it.

We're not going to make it. I've been trying so hard to be strong for her, but I don't know if I can do this.

I'm fixated, a dog with a bone. Breathing is starting to seem really hard, and there are all these terrible things trying to reach their bony fingers into my brain and pull at my nerve endings until they snap. And the cheese knife is sitting so still on the counter where I left it, and a part of me is very tempted. More tempted than I've been in a long time.

Everything is your fault. Mama has to spend so much time worrying about you, and they're always fighting because of you and your problems, and if they can't be happy just having you in their lives, then you're never going to be able to be happy with Reese. You're never going to be able to be happy with anyone, and you're never going to be able to figure your life out, and you're probably going to cut again, and then Reese will break up with you or at least be really disappointed. He'd be so much better off with someone else. Stupid. Ugly. Hopeless. Worthless.

Every bad thing I've ever thought about myself, amplified and looping.

Too many and too much and now now now now now.

Do it now.

Make it stop.

I trace my fingertips along the scars that mark my forearms in straight lines, one by one by one. I could make another.

I won't.

It would end the way I'm feeling right now.

Seven months and six days. Seven months and six days.

I cross to the freezer and grab a couple ice cubes and

squeeze down on them as hard as I can, a coping strategy from my therapist that usually works. Usually. I walk over to the knife and pick it up. And put it down. And pick it up.

That's when I realize there's a girl standing in the doorway, watching me have this freak-out. I smile and try to pretend that I wasn't doing what she definitely just saw me doing.

"Hey, Ames."

CHAPTER 9

Amelia Grace

I WAS HOPING SHE WOULD BE THE FIRST PERSON I saw. Only, now that I'm here, I have no idea what to do. I know what she was thinking about doing with that knife—it's why I stopped dead in the doorway, so she'd have a chance to put it down and paste a smile on her face before my mom could see around my body. But maybe I would have stopped dead no matter what. There's something about seeing her in person after so many emails that makes me forget how to breathe.

"Scarlett, hi." Mom gives her a hug. "You've gotten so tall."

She's definitely taller than I imagined she would be, but I'm only five foot four, so everyone is tall. And she's even more beautiful than in her pictures, all long red hair and curves and freckles. But somehow different. Edgier or sexier.

I stay on the other side of the room. If I get too close to her, will she know? I feel like my mom would know.

"Is Adeline around?" Mom asks, brows furrowed with concern.

"She's upstairs." Scarlett bites her lip, and I have to look out the window. "I think she's not doing so well. Can you check on her?"

"Of course." Mom squeezes her shoulder and leaves immediately. There's something about the way she walks out of the room—her steps are so purposeful. I almost don't recognize her for a second.

Skyler bounds in just as Mom is leaving. She grins at me, but her eyes are red.

"Amelia Grace!" she squeals, giving me a big, bouncy hug. "I haven't seen you in forever! You look just like your pictures on Insta!"

And then it feels like it would be weird for Scarlett and me not to hug after I've just hugged her sister, and she must be feeling the same way because she takes a couple steps toward me. Her shirt is wet in patches, and so is her hair.

"Are you okay?" I ask. It's a general *Are you okay*, but buried underneath is a very specific *Are you okay*? Because back when things were really bad, with the girls at school and the cutting, she used to email me every day. But that was three years ago, before our emails trickled to every few weeks and then every few months. A part of me wants to pick back up right where we left off, but—

"I'm fine," she says.

She hugs me, and it isn't a big or bouncy one like Skyler's, and it's over too quickly, and it doesn't answer any of my questions. I guess I thought we meant more to each other than that.

There's the sound of another car pulling up outside, and Skyler runs out of the room to meet them, her chestnut ponytail swinging behind her. Scarlett takes exactly one step closer. She lowers her voice and says in a whisper that's just for me, "I'm really glad you're here."

My heart squeezes in my chest, and I almost choke on my own spit. "Me too."

The kitchen gets really quiet. I can hear Skyler outside, greeting the new arrivals with some unintelligible bubbliness. A trickle of water from the faucet goes drip-drip-dripping down the sink.

"I should, um, go upstairs and change." She gestures to her shirt.

"Right. See you." *See you?* Of course I'll see her. We are living in the same dang house for the summer.

Her footsteps echo up the stairs, and I feel like I'm on the cusp of realizing some great truth. Then my phone dings in my pocket. Carrie? I type in my password. Nah, just a bunch of social media updates. Including one from Carrie. It's a photo of a book she's reading—she posts those a lot—with a tiny caption.

weekend plans

So she does have her phone. Well, maybe she doesn't know what to say or maybe she's feeling really bad about things or maybe she wishes it never happened and she never wants to see me again but she's too sweet to tell me.

What if you just promised you wouldn't kiss any more girls or go on dates or anything?

Maybe it wouldn't be such a big deal to promise that after all. If Carrie doesn't want to talk to me, I mean, I don't know anyone else in Ranburne who might be interested. And Scarlett, well. She's in a relationship. I know this. She has emailed me about this. I have pretended to be happy for her on multiple occasions.

I could email Pastor Chris—he's our youth minister, the one I was going to be serving with. See about being a junior youth minister when I come back in the fall, maybe sooner. I could promise him, like Abby said. I only have one more year of high school anyway. And it wouldn't be changing who I am so much as it would just be . . . waiting.

Sometimes I imagine what life will be like on the other side and all the shapes my life could take, but mostly I'm scared to even think about it. Because if I do, all the possible futures start to shift like a kaleidoscope, each one falling into place, forming a single dream. I want to marry a sweet girl who I'm in love with. And I want us to have kids; I don't even know how many. Two? Three? Seven plus a menagerie of pets? I don't even know how the baby-having part would work exactly, but who cares as long as they're ours? And she and I will walk down the street holding hands and we'll sit together in church on Sundays, each holding up one-half of the same hymnal.

That's about where the future starts to fall apart. Because I already know I'll never be able to have all those things at the same time.

I realize I'm still staring at the stairs, so I go outside, because I don't want to seem like I'm creeping around Scarlett's kitchen waiting for her. Skyler is dancing circles around a woman I recognize as my aunt Seema, and her daughter, Ellie. I remember playing with her brother, Zakir, when I was little. I haven't seen them since Mom married Jay and moved to Tennessee. We stopped seeing all the aunts after that.

I walk up to the group of them, everyone talking at once. I say hi to Ellie, who is impossibly gorgeous and who gives me a hesitant side-hug like she isn't sure what else to do.

Seema beams at me. "Amelia Grace, love, you look beautiful."

I smile and allow myself to be scrunched into a hug. I remember that about her from when I was little—she gives the best hugs.

A tan SUV pulls up next to us. There's not exactly a driveway, more just a dirt road that makes a circle in front of the house. A tall, Latinx woman with golden brown skin and glossy hair gets out. She has a piercing through one eyebrow and a flower tucked behind one ear. Definitely Val.

"I'm here, and I have everything we need!" she hollers. She pulls out a cardboard box from the passenger seat. "My 'fasten seat belt' alarm has been going off since the liquor store. You know it's a good day when you have enough alcohol in your seat that your car thinks it's a person."

She sets down the box so she can give Seema a hug. It's like watching family members get reunited at the airport.

"How are you, Seema?"

"Good." Seema smiles slyly. "I'm good. Because I have everything we need."

"Wh—? Excuse me? I have wine, whiskey, bourbon, *and* tequila. I'm not sure there's anything else a person could need."

Seema swings a wrinkled brown paper bag. If she has weed in there, just, I don't know, shoot me dead. I am so not prepared for this.

"Every kind of Cadbury you can imagine from when I visited my mother in Canada."

Val clutches her heart. "You brought Cadbury? Did you bring—"

"Coconut cashew? Yes, five bars of it, one of which I instructed Ellie to write your name on in Sharpie."

"God bless you."

I used to think Cadbury was just those eggs you get at Easter, but it turns out Canada has a whole new level of chocolate going on. I remember I would totally freak out every time a care package from Aunt Seema came in the mail.

"Is that whole bag really filled with chocolate?" I ask.

Seema smiles. "About three kilograms."

"I love it when you talk metric to me," says Val, and Seema cackles.

And then it's like they both remember why they're here at exactly the same time.

"I am going to kill Jimmy Gable," says Aunt Val.

"You'll have to arm wrestle me for it, jaan, because I'm going to kill him first."

I stare up at the blue house with the white wraparound porch, where my mom is no doubt holding my aunt Adeline like she's trying to put her back together. Scarlett stands in the second window from the left, looking down at the lawn. The way the light hits her makes her look like a ghost. She's never even talked about liking a girl, so I know she'll probably never feel the same way, but the things I'm feeling, they're so big, it doesn't even matter. I look at her, and I feel lucky just to feel this way.

The great truth finally takes shape inside my head: If I was ever thinking about doing what they want, of going back to the way I was before and locking away the part of me that likes girls and hiding the key until college—seeing her makes me realize that is no longer an option.

CHAPTER 10

Ellie

....

THIS IS IT. THE MOMENT WHEN REAL LIFE FINALLY gets to be like Instagram. Skyler seems sweet as can be with her huge blue eyes and her bubbliness. Amelia Grace hangs back, quieter, so I tell her I adore her pixie cut and ask her how long she's had it. And then there's Scarlett. She stalks out of the house wearing combat boots and black tights under jean shorts, looking so freaking cool. I bounce over and give her a hug.

"Hi!" I say.

She stiffens, and I pull away.

"Hi," she says back. Her "hi" feels like a wall I have to get over. It only makes me more determined to be her best friend. All of their friends. Because they're all even more perfect than I could have hoped for. And watching our moms together—I want that. I want friendship that feels as easy as breathing and stretches over years and miles.

Two hours later, and I have made approximately zero progress. For someone who just Instagrammed an unbelievably picturesque #nofilter photo of the sun setting over the lake, I am not feeling so good about things right now. Maybe it's the way Scarlett alternates between looking at me judgmentally and not looking at me at all. Or maybe I'm imagining that.

I've mostly been helping out (read: hiding) in the kitchen. Preparing the mountain of food required to feed nine people. Making sure there are at least a few healthy things on the menu. I'm making my nani's gosht biryani, except with butternut squash and chickpeas instead of mutton because I'm feeling vegetable deprived. Also, this recipe takes kind of a while, and frying up the onions and simmering the veggies with the yogurt and spices relaxes me (plus, there's the hiding).

My brother wouldn't be able to make biryani if his life depended on it. And it's not a sexist thing—my parents are big on that. More like: I've always felt the need to be at Nani's elbow when she is in the kitchen, soaking up everything she is saying and showing her that I can make everything just so. Sometimes there's this little voice telling me that I'm not as Muslim or as Indian as the rest my family. Food makes me feel like I belong.

I pour saffron milk over the rice/veggies/gravy mixture and cover the pan. "Done!"

Val's wife, Heidi, is cooking some kind of ginger chicken that smells ungodly good, and Momma is making world peace cookies, which are so ridiculously delicious but so full of sugar and butter. There was a time when I would have passed them up. A part of me still wants to, and I have to remind myself there are reasons to eat food other than macros. My stomach growls, and Aunt Val hears it.

"Here." She hands me a serving plate of hummus, carrots, and pita chips. "Why don't you see if the girls want some of these?"

"Um, sure."

I take the plate. Her smile is too big. She is definitely trying to give me an excuse to go out there and talk to the other girls. I think I'd be insulted if I weren't so grateful. Plus, I'm about to devour this hummus.

When I get to the door, I close my eyes and take a deep breath. I have to try harder to be the kind of person they'll like. To be cool. Confident. Confident Ellie skips out to the deck and places the plate on the table. "I come bearing snacks!"

I wince at the perkiness in my voice. So does Scarlett. I freaking knew it! She hates me.

I sit down anyway, but I don't reach for a carrot. I don't feel so hungry anymore.

Scarlett

Ellie of the anemic side-hugs plops down next to me like being at this lake house is the absolute worst thing that has ever happened to her. (Spoiler alert: It probably is.)

She's pretty. Too pretty. *Mean* pretty. It's like a law of physics: People who are that beautiful cannot also be nice. I cross my arms so that my scars don't show. I used to wear long-sleeved shirts all the time, even in summer, to hide them, and I may be a lot more confident now, but something about this girl puts me in protection mode.

"Do you want some?"

"What?" I realize Amelia Grace is pushing the snack plate in my direction. "Oh, um, sure."

I take some pita and rake it through the hummus. Mmm, somebody got the roasted red pepper kind.

I check my phone. Dad called me again. Twice. So now the constant loop of what's-happening-to-us, how-am-I-going-to-survive-this gets some extra stress stirred in: What is Dad doing right now? Is he gonna drive out here since we're not answering? Is Mama gonna freak out on him? I can't handle this.

Skyler

Maybe I'll write a book this summer.

Ellie

I cross my legs. Then uncross them. Then cross them again.

Nope. This isn't awkward at all.

Skyler

Or start a podcast.

Amelia Grace

Holy crap, my hand just touched Scarlett's when we both went for a carrot just now. Not that she noticed. Or cared. Or even looked up from her phone.

Scarlett

WHY IS REESE HANGING OUT WITH CARTER RIGHT NOW? She just posted a selfie of them at the bowling alley with the caption Careful. This guy's a shark. I bite down hard on the insides of my cheeks, but I manage to stop before I break the skin. Calm down. I breathe in through my nose and out through my mouth. When I do, I notice that Sky's friend, Paige, is eating nachos behind them.

Paige is a notorious over-poster. And I have never been more grateful. I go to her account. There they are. Not just Reese and Carter, but at least seven people from school. They've got two whole lanes to themselves.

So, okay. It's not like he's on a date, and he's allowed to have friends. I pop back to the photo of him with Carter. But do they have to be sitting so close together?

Skyler

I'd need a topic for the podcast. How to Cope with Your Parents' Divorce? Meh. I don't know if that's something I'm ready to talk about on the interwebs yet. I just— I'm tired of feeling crappy about losing softball, and I want to use all that extra time to do something big, you know?

Ellie

I can't take it anymore.

"So, do you guys come here a lot?"

Skyler is staring blankly at the sunset, but Scarlett looks up from her phone. Holy resting bitch face, her eyebrows are intense.

"I mean, yeah. It's our lake house."

Right. Guess I deserved that one. I laugh and try to make my voice even brighter. "Yeah, I guess I just meant, like, do you guys have friends that you hang out with around here? Like, lake friends?"

OMG, every time I say the word "like," I swear her eye twitches.

"*Yes.*" She says it almost indignantly.

"Oh! Are any of them boys?"

Is it possible to roll your eyes at someone telepathically? Because that is totally what she does.

"I have a boyfriend at home." Again with the indignance. She goes back to her phone.

I dial up my smile until it hurts. "Cool! So, more boys for me!"

She tilts her head back up. Gives me the deadliest of side-eyes. "There's a lot of other stuff to do here."

Skyler

Maybe a memoir *would* be better than a podcast. Or a novel. Wait, crap, when did things go DEFCON 5?

I do a quick rewind of the conversation in my head. Boys. Stuff to do. I don't get why Scarlett is being so dang salty. But then, why is my sister ever being salty?

"There are so many cool things to do here!" I rush to say. I need to give this tension a good roundhouse kick to the face or this is going to be one awkward summer. "We can go wakeboarding and tubing." Both of which require fully functional finger joints. "And ride Jet Skis!" Which would totally wreck my body right now. "And we can take the boat on moonlit cruises and go swimming. Scarlett does a mean cannonball."

I nudge my sister. This is your chance to not be an a-hole.

"Sounds awesome!" says Ellie, just as Scarlett says, "Yeah. When I was twelve."

"Scarlett!" I hiss.

She smashes her phone down on the table. "What, Sky?" She sighs, the angry kind. "I'm sorry I'm not bulletproof like you, but I can't do this right now. I don't know why Mama thought this was a good idea. Our parents—" Her hazel eyes go glassy, and she can't finish her sentence. Then she tightens her jaw, and her fists, and her everything, and rolls her head around on her neck. "They fucked everything up," she finally says.

She marches off, leaving fires in her wake that I'll be forced to put out.

Yes, Scarlett, I'm aware. They are my parents too. Oh, and in addition to that, I've lost my favorite thing to do in the whole world, and I hurt all the time.

But, you know, my feelings could never be as deep or important or painful as your Scarlett Feelings, so by all means, let's make this all about you just like we do EVERY-THING ELSE.

I'm breathing heavier, and there are flashes in my head of Mama and Daddy fighting after my softball game, but I shove it all down until I can pretend it doesn't hurt me anymore. It's funny how even the people who know you best can get it so wrong. I'm not bulletproof. Not at all. I've just learned to hide the impact. Because when I don't, I'm not the one who ends up bleeding.

I put on a candy-coated smile. "I'm really sorry about that. How 'bout I show y'all where we'll be staying this summer? You're going to love the carriage house."

Amelia Grace

I only look around for Scarlett a little bit as we walk with Skyler to the cars to get our stuff.

There was this time in seventh grade. Mom used to nag me about not dressing up for church. And one day I saw this picture of Emma Watson on someone's Tumblr. It wasn't even new or anything, but she had this short pixie cut, all tousled up, and a white sleeveless tuxedo shirt and suspenders. She looked so dang cool. I remember thinking, maybe dressing up could be all right after all. I made an appointment at Charmaine's the same day. I usually wore my straight brown hair in a ponytail, but I showed the stylist the photo, and said, "Please, can you make me look like this?" And she grinned and said, "This is going to be fantastic." And she snipped and she moussed and when she was all done, she turned me around to face the mirror, and I whispered, "This is amazing."

I already had a white button-up, so I cut off the sleeves just above the elbow and rolled them up (not as cool as E.W.'s tuxedo shirt, but we do what we can). I found a pair of black suspenders at Walmart. The next morning, I put the whole outfit together. I even wore eyeliner.

And I went to school.

I emailed Scarlett crying as soon as I got home.

A lot of people were whispering and snickering. I noticed people talking to me less, even my friends, and this guy Casey called me something awful at lunch. But the thing that hurt the most was when I was playing basketball during gym with my friend Jacob. I made a jump shot with a perfect swish, and he said, "Can't you just dress like a girl? I'm not saying you have to be like Melanie Jane Montgomery, but it would make things so much easier for you."

I asked Scarlett if she thought I should stop wearing so many boy clothes. And I'll never forget her email back.

I pull it up on my phone while I wait for Ellie to unload a truly impressive amount of matching purple luggage from her mom's car.

Dear Ames (I loved that she always started the emails with "dear." It made me feel like the heroine of some old-timey love story.)

I'm sorry people are so terrible. If it makes you feel any better, they're terrible here too. Sometimes I get so upset, I bite my lip or, like, my mouth on the inside. Today, I bit down so hard, my lower lip got stuck on my teeth and I had to pull it off. It was gross. You're the only person I've ever told, so please don't tell anyone, okay?

Anyway, sorry, I wasn't trying to make this email about me. I guess I was just trying to say that you're not alone. And also, I like the way you dress. You look cool as hell, and I don't think you should change it for anyone. Not even one little thing. Because you're amazing.

xoxo,
Scarlett

We used to know exactly what to say to each other and exactly how to be there. Half of me feels like I should have run after her just now, and the other half of me feels like a stranger and my best friend are living inside the same person. Have you ever built up a moment in your head until it's this huge unwieldy thing, and when you finally get to it, all you can do is choke? And the worst part is how you can feel yourself going down in flames and you're powerless to stop it and you wish you could get a redo and make it like any one of the billion possibilities you'd imagined because it wasn't supposed to be like this.

That's what being with Scarlett is like right now.

Ellie

Skyler doesn't offer to help me carry my stuff, but that's okay because I'm a travel badass, and I can wheel two roller suitcases while holding a purse and a beach bag. It would be a whole lot easier if I wasn't wheeling them on gravel though. One of the wheels gets stuck for the fifth (fiftieth?) time, and Amelia Grace offers to carry one of the suitcases for me, since she only has a duffel bag.

"Thanks," I say, flashing her a grateful smile.

Skyler bites her lip. "Yeah, thanks, Ames. Sorry, I, um— Anyway, here's the carriage house."

I've only ever read the words "carriage house" in Momma's journals, but it appears to be an apartment stacked on top of a really big garage. Something about the shape of the windows or the cross-hatching of the wood seems vaguely magical, though that could just be my brain going to town over the word "carriage." Skyler opens the door to the garage, which has room for two cars and a boat, and leads us up the stairs to the apartment above. It's really charming—one long skinny room with a sloped ceiling and lots of exposed wood in a sun-bleached gray. On one side, there's a kitchen and breakfast bar, on the other, a living room with a sectional couch with cheery yellow throw pillows. Next to that room is a bedroom with two sets of bunk beds. It's cute, everything done up in red, white, and blue like a Taylor Swift Fourth of July party. I look for the other bedroom. Door number one is a bathroom. Door number two is a storage closet. I reach for the handle of door number three. It is a linen closet/laundry room combo with a tiny stackable washer/dryer. It is not a bedroom. HOLY CRAP THERE IS ONLY ONE BEDROOM AND THE FOUR OF US ARE SHARING IT. From a BFF perspective, this is fabulous news, but oh gosh, the bathroom. There is only one of those too, and I have a lot of hair, and I do not wake up looking like this, people!

Ahem. I mean, it's going to be okay. There was that time we went on a family trip to Nepal to see Everest Base Camp, and you can't exactly take a shower there, and I still looked pretty damn fierce even after a wet-wipe bath.

I sit down on one of the beds for a second. Is this the one Momma slept in? I know they used to stay in the carriage house when they came up here. It said so in Momma's journals. And there's this one photo of the four of them lying on their bellies with their chins in their hands and their legs crossed behind them. I think they're in the clubhouse Momma's journal mentioned. They're definitely lying on a wooden floor, and—if you scan the photo and digitally enhance it (not that I did that)— you can just make out a stack of notebooks next to a candelabra. I wonder where that clubhouse is. Or if there's anything left of the club. I know it's a long shot, but even a burn mark from a candle would be exciting. The air in here smells like sunscreen and old wood, but there's something else. A feeling I can't shake. It feels like possibilities.

Amelia Grace

HOLY CRAP I AM SHARING A BEDROOM WITH SCARLETT.

Skyler

Watching Ellie unpack is like watching the folks at NASA prep for a space mission. Only, with fewer tampons. (Did you know they thought that packing a hundred for Sally Ride would be a good idea because they weren't sure how many she'd need for seven days? And also that they tied them together by the strings? I will never look at space travel the same way again.) It only takes Ellie, like, seven minutes, and then there are dresses in the closet and clothes in the drawers and suitcases stuffed under the bunk bed.

"I feel like efficiency is key to sharing a small space," she says when she notices Amelia Grace and me watching. "This room is super cute, by the way. Are you guys as obsessed as I am with T. Swift's Fourth of July extravaganzas?"

We shake our heads blankly. Ellie shrugs. "Okay, you need

to get on that. Don't worry. I'll totally help. We're going to have so much fun rooming together! Do you care if I take a top bunk?"

More headshaking from me and Ames.

"Oh! I'll take the bottom one," I say, bouncing over and setting my sunglasses on the pillow. I don't know how well a top bunk would work out for me right now.

Ellie positively beams at me and bumps her hip against mine. "Sounds good, roomie."

I smile back and sit on my bed and take a couple slow yoga breaths. The pain in my fingers and wrists is worse than it was this morning, worse than it's been all week, but I try not to let it show on my face. It hits me that this is what my entire summer is going to be like. At home, I can keep it in until I get to my bedroom, and once I close the door, I know I can lie on the floor and cry if I need to, and knowing that helps me get through. There won't be anywhere to hide here.

Amelia Grace is still standing in the doorway looking lost. I feel you, girl.

Amelia Grace

But seriously, they just picked the beds, and we are sharing one, and THIS IS NOT A DRILL. I am sharing a bed with the girl I love. Okay, yes, it's a bunk bed, and we'll be separated by three feet of space, so it's not like we're going to accidentally spoon each other, but still.

I have zero chill left. ZERO. There is a zombie apocalypse taking over my body and heart and brain (braaaains), and the part of me that's in love with Scarlett keeps multiplying/intensifying/electrifying. It's a piece of me that feels too big to hide. But we live in a world that's either/or. Be in love with this girl or be a junior youth minister. Pick a piece of yourself to give up.

But how do I do that? And which one do I choose? And how do I take care of what's left of my heart after?

Ellie

Okay, so I think Skyler might finally be warming up to me. She's going to be the key—Amelia Grace and Scarlett will be a lot harder to crack. There's something about Scarlett that really draws me. I know, I know, she's kind of being a jerk to me, but I like how confident she is. That she's not afraid to let the ugly things out in the open.

I slip Momma's friendship bracelet under my pillow and grab my purse. "I'm gonna go touch up my makeup before dinner," I say.

Amelia Grace nods. Skyler says, "Cool," and goes back to staring out the window like she's about to solve world peace if she can focus on the horizon hard enough.

I shut the door to the teeny-tiny bathroom behind me (holy wow, are all four of us really sharing this thing?!) and let out a breath I didn't know I was holding. In addition to being tiny, the bathroom is painted a pretty washed-out blue, and over the back of the toilet is one of those stencil-painted wooden signs that Southern people always have in their houses. This one reads HEAVEN IS A LITTLE CLOSER IN A HOME BY THE WATER. I ponder the validity of that statement. I also ponder the fact that someone hung it over the toilet. I try to imagine for a minute someone painting a dua on a piece of wood and hanging it in a bathroom. Yeah . . . no.

I check to see if there's anything SBDC-related in the bathroom cabinets. I'll need to check the other two rooms thoroughly later. I fling open the last little white door with a flourish. Toilet paper. Not exactly what I was hoping for. I know I've got all summer to search, but with the way things are going, I feel like I need to find something sooner.

I dab under my eyes with a tissue—my mascara got all smeared in the heat. I redo my eye shadow and add a touch of bronzer, because really, what else do I have to do right now? I'm just deciding between bee sting lip balm and sugar gloss when I hear voices in the bedroom.

"You okay?" says Skyler.

"Yeah." It's all Scarlett has to say. Her tone says not to ask her anything else. "Where's Ellie?"

"In the bathroom putting on makeup."

"She's pretty enough already."

I can hear her eye roll through the door.

For the first time, I think about giving up. I close my eyes and try really hard not to cry as I screw the cap on my lip gloss. This was supposed to be easier than tennis team. But maybe it's not the tennis team girls or the seventh-grade girls or any of the girls. Maybe it's me.

I could leave. Book a flight home and spend the rest of the summer knocking around the house and playing tennis while Dad's at work. The only thing that keeps me from picking up the phone is the feeling of failure that would come with it.

So, okay. Failure is not an option. Leaving is not an option. I'll just do what I do best, i.e. Make a plan for how to make this summer not suck, which will obviously include a bulleted list. I stuff my makeup bag back in my purse and root around for a pen and my daisy-print notebook.

Step 1: Make friends
Step 2: Locate the nearest tennis court and also a trainer
Step 3: Study for the PSAT (goal: 1500+)
Step 4: Have my first kiss
Step 5: Write one letter a week to a Muslim woman who is changing the world
Step 6: Try a ton of new healthy recipes and post the results
Step 7: Go to some Instagram-worthy parties
Step 8: Find the remains of the SBDC. Tonight.

Skyler

Everything is fine.

Scarlett and Ellie totally hate each other, but I'll fix that when Ellie gets out of the bathroom.

Mama keeps doing weird things like stopping me in the hallway so she can hug me and cry into my hair, but the aunts will fix that. I hope. Ever since they descended on Mama in a cloud of hugs and chocolate and booze, she seems a little better.

Daddy keeps calling me, and I don't know how to talk to him yet, but it's okay. I'll fix that too.

And my fingers and wrists won't stop screaming at each other, and that's not really something I can fix, but I'm sure it'll be better when I wake up tomorrow. I don't really have the energy to worry about it today.

"Are you okay, Skyler?" asks Amelia Grace.

I realize I'm cradling my right hand in my left.

"Everything is fine," I say.

Scarlett

The door to the carriage house opens.

"Dinner!" calls Aunt Val.

We file down the stairs. She tucks a flower behind each of our ears. Ellie looks entirely too excited about it. Ten bucks says she takes a selfie and Instagrams it.

None of us says much on the way to the house. We are a stark contrast to the kitchen, where our moms are listening to the Backstreet Boys while simultaneously doing a weird dance/drinking wine/operating dangerous things like stoves. It is possible we will be visiting Urgent Care tonight.

I pull out my phone to see if Carter posted any new pictures. She hasn't. Probably because you can't use Instagram if you're busy making out with someone.

"Scarlett, baby, can you put this on the table?"

I hide my screen. "What?"

Mama shoves a serving bowl of rice at me. I must be making an awful face because Sky jumps on it like a grenade.

"I've got it!" she says with a smile so wide it almost feels violent. She gives Mama a quick hug and a kiss on the cheek. "Smells delicious."

It is plain white rice.

Skyler carries it out of the kitchen and sets it on the table, where plates and glasses and even name cards are already arranged. I follow her. She glances at the table and then switches Ellie's name card so that she's sitting by Sky instead of me.

"What are you doing?"

She jumps. "Nothing."

"Sky—"

"I just want us to have a nice dinner."

Skyler

Mama gives me my forty-seventh hug of the day. "Thank you for being so strong. I don't know if I could get through this if I had to worry about both of you."

"Of course." It feels good and bad at the same time. And

it tells me everything I need to know. That I have to keep on keeping things calm at all costs. That she needs me.

Mama carries the decorative bowl of ginger chicken to the dining room. I hover around the kitchen, trying to figure out if there's anything left to do. Her phone starts vibrating on the counter. My daddy's face appears on the screen. If she could just stay in the dining room. Please, please, please don't—

Mama pops back into the kitchen. "We need a new bottle of wine." She grabs one out of the wine rack, but then she stops. "You okay, babe?"

I slide a dish towel over a few inches so that it covers her phone. Paste on my biggest smile.

"I'm wonderful."

CHAPTER 11

Skyler

....

THE PAIN IS EATING AT ME SO BADLY IT'S HARD TO eat my dinner. Playing peacemaker and trying to make sure everything's perfect takes its toll. I don't want Mama to see how gnarled my hand is as I attempt to spoon ginger chicken into my mouth. I don't want her to notice how the pain seeps into my eyes and around my lips until my smile is so brittle it could shatter. So when Aunt Seema brings out dessert, I make an excuse about how I'm not hungry (which, if you've ever had my aunt Seema's world peace cookies—chocolate, sea salt, more chocolate—you'll know is a lie). I say I'm just going for a quick walk, and I'll be right back. Thankfully, no one tries to follow me because there are cookies.

I make my way down the hill to the dock, each step away from the house bringing relief. And then I lie on the wooden slats and stare at the sky and wait for the stars to come out.

This is a bad flare-up. Definitely my worst one yet. They say stress can make juvenile arthritis worse, but I don't know what could possibly be stressing me right now—oh, wait, my dad cheating on my mom and totally exploding our happy family. Lying on the dock helps though. I don't have to worry about taking care of people or making sure everyone gets along. I get a break from the full-time job that is trying to hide your pain from other people.

I must lie there for a while because people start to move out to the porch. The moms crack open another bottle of wine, and even though Aunt Val is hi-larious when she's tipsy, I really don't want anyone to see me. Or ask me if I'm okay. Mostly that last one. The old canoe that Scarlett and I used to love playing in when we were younger bumps against the dock. I wish I could crawl inside and just float away.

And then it occurs to me. Maybe I can.

I'm reminded of that scene in *Anne of Green Gables*, the Lady of Shalott. I could totally Lady of Shalott this canoe right now. I slip over the side of the dock as quietly as I can. A note about this canoe: It was not designed for stealth. And then the hard part—I have to untie it. Working the knot free with my fingers is so painful, I nearly give up, but luckily it wasn't tied very tightly. I'm shaking by the time I push away from the dock, but it's done. The worst part is over, and now I can just lie back and pretend to be a cursed dead lady from Camelot or wherever.

And that is exactly what I do. Lie my body out stiff as a board the way Anne did. Shut my eyes. I even take the flower Aunt Val tucked behind my ear and use it as my final bouquet. It's really too bad I'm not covered in that awesome blanket thing Anne had in the movie, but we do what we can with what we have.

As I drift across the lake, I recite as much as I can remember from Lord Tennyson's poem. Then I just lie there. The movement of the boat on the water is so delightfully peaceful. I feel as if I'm being rocked to sleep. I take a few deep breaths in and out like Dr. Levy taught me. This is the most relaxed I've felt all day. I wonder what Anne would do right now. Think up new ways to kick boys' butts at spelling bees? Probably. Although, now that I think about it, didn't this whole boat thing end kind of badly for Anne? Like with the boat springing a leak, and her clinging to the side of a bridge, and getting rescued by— Oh! Gilbert! Does this mean I get a Gilbert?!

My boat knocks against something hard, and I can't help but let out a yelp.

When I open my eyes, the most beautiful boy is standing over me. "Gilbert?"

"What?" I realize that the beautiful boy is standing on the bow of a boat, and also that I have bumped into said boat, and also that he looks angry.

"Nothing."

He narrows his eyes at me. "Are you drunk?"

"No. I'm Skyler."

"What are you doing out here?"

I don't think I like his tone. "Reenacting iconic scenes from classic Canadian literature. What are you doing?"

His face grows, if possible, even more skeptical. "Are you sure you're not drunk?"

I sit up, possibly too fast, definitely making my canoe wobble (this is probably not helping my case). "No. I. Am. Not. Drunk. Why do you keep asking me that?"

"Because it's really dangerous to be out on the water at night without a light. And I can't imagine anyone would be stupid enough to do that. *Unless* they were drunk. You could get run over, you know that?"

"I don't need a lecture on boat safety. I've been coming to

the lake my whole life." Seriously, who is this guy and why does he think someone died and made him king of the lake?

He sighs like I am the most annoying person ever and I'm doing it on purpose just to hurt him. "Then you really should know better. Whatever. Look. I'll tow you back to shore."

"I don't need your help," I say.

I pick up a paddle and attempt to use it. There are barbs inside of my knuckles where I grip the handle. I sweep the paddle through the water. The barbs light themselves on fire.

"Maybe I do need a little help," I say through gritted teeth. "One second."

He walks off into the dark of his boat, and I can't see his face, but I'm sure his smug butt is smirking. The boat surges forward, gently—he's probably got it on idle—and inches up alongside mine until I'm at the very back. He grabs the end of my canoe. Steers it around ninety degrees so it's flush against the back of the boat.

"Do you think you can get out?" he asks.

"*Yes.*"

And I do a pretty dang good job of it (despite my joint pain, thank you very much).

"Huh." He scrutinizes me as the waves rock the boat and I shift my weight from leg to leg like a surfer. (What I lack in grace, I make up for in softball quads.)

"What?" I ask, not even bothering to hide my irritation.

He sniffs at the air. "You really aren't drunk."

"I flipping told you I wasn't!"

I stomp my foot, which apparently is absolutely hilarious, because he can't stop laughing as he tethers my canoe to the back of his boat. As you might imagine, this does not exactly endear him to me. "Why are you out here anyway? Other than the obvious."

"The obvious?"

"Making fun of girls and accusing people of binge drinking. Your hobbies." Oh, snap. I can't believe I just said that. Usually sassy flirting is Scarlett's thing. Mine is being run-of-the-mill adorable and bubbly.

He gives me that long-suffering look again. "I don't *have* to rescue you."

"You're not going to throw me back." I fling the words like a gauntlet.

He runs his entire hand down his face. "No. I'm not."

I point across the lake. "I live over that way."

I don't say anything for a little while. Neither does he. I wouldn't say there's silence though, what with the mosquitoes and cicadas and frogs and owls and water lapping against things. Picturesque lakes are a lot louder than people think.

I look at him while trying to pretend like I'm not actually looking. He's tall, much taller than me, with reddish-brown hair and eyes the color of celery.

"I needed to get away for a while," he finally says. His voice is different, softer.

"That's why I'm out here too."

I feel like there are entire life stories packed into those two sentences. A novel in fourteen words. I realize I want to know everything that happened to make him say it.

I take a deep breath. "Do you ever get so tired of pretending, that you feel like if you have to keep it up, even for one more minute, you might just explode?"

"Yes. Absolutely, yes. My dad's always riding me about

stuff." He winces and stares out across the lake. "Just having something to look forward to helps me get through countless hours of lectures. The boat. At night. That's my thing."

I smile. "I get that."

But do I? What do I actually have to look forward to?

I feel like I'm on the cusp of something huge. I also realize we're approaching the part of the lake where I live.

"This is me," I say, pointing to the dock.

He maneuvers in. Ties up the canoe. I'm so relieved I don't have to handle the knots again that I almost hug him. Almost. Then he helps me hop from the boat to the dock, holding my hand like the good guy in a black-and-white movie.

"Thank you." I smile at him. The bubbly, charming kind.

"You're welcome," he says. He's leaning over the railing of the boat, and then he shakes his head like he remembers where he is. "If you ever want to get away—you know, together—give me a call." He slips back into the driver's seat, and his mouth spreads into a smirk. "You know. When you're not drunk."

I'm pretty sure I'd rather punch myself in the face than call Sergeant Mansplainer.

And besides, he didn't even give me his number.

He drives away, but I'm not ready to go inside yet. I pull out my phone and look at the pictures my friends are posting. Eight of them crammed into a row of seats at the bowling alley, Emmeline laughing, Carter trying to make a duck face, and Paige—her grin is so big.

It's the caption that gets me though: Victory bowling is the best bowling.

It's not that I don't want them to win. I totally do! It's just that it stings a little.

Just having something to look forward to gets me through countless hours of lectures.

This is what I have to look forward to. Watching other people live my dreams. If anyone had ever asked, I'd have told them I'd be playing this game until I was a creaky old lady. And now I am one. At sixteen. And there is nothing I can do about it.

I need something for me.

CHAPTER 12

Scarlett

....

"WHERE HAVE YOU BEEN?" I FLING THE WORDS AT Sky as soon as she walks up the stairs from the garage and into the carriage house. I guess I use a little too much force because Ames and Ellie jump. Oops. Well, Sky shouldn't have left me like that.

Her face turns as red as my name. "I don't know. I went down to the dock."

"Really? Because I went down there, and you weren't there. I had to say you were tired, so you came over here to take a nap." I also had to "show Amelia Grace and Ellie around the carriage house" and "help them get settled" all by myself. Translation: Get out of our hair so we can drink more wine and talk about grown-up things. Which would have been fine, except I'm not great at small talk, and I really needed Sky to keep this awkward ship from sinking. My sister's always been the one who's good at making friends, the popular twin.

Amelia Grace stops texting whoever on her phone, and Ellie stops painting her nails. They both stare at us like this is the most interesting thing that has happened all day. Or like they're scared. One of those. They probably think I'm a total freak show after my meltdown before.

Sky just kind of shrugs and blushes even harder.

"Dude, DID YOU MEET A BOY?"

"What? *No*." She shoots pointed glances at Ellie and Ames.

I shrug, the grandmother of all sarcastic shrugs. "They don't care." I realize I technically don't know if this is true. "Do you?"

Ames says no, and Ellie caps her nail polish in a way that is positively gleeful. "Tell us all about him. Or her." She sits cross-legged on the floor like a kindergartner ready for story time.

"Nothing happened," says Sky. Bullshit. "I'm gonna go sit on the deck."

She crosses the tiny room and weaves around the coffee table, and then she's out the door. Ellie sighs audibly. Tell me about it. I almost wish I hadn't covered for Sky, but the thing is, we made this pact when we were seven years old after coming to the realization that our constant tattling to Mama and Daddy was only getting us in more trouble. And that if we stopped it, if we banded together, it would save us untold hours in lectures and time-outs. So we made a pinky promise, our tiny faces set. The very next day, Sky accidentally knocked my dad's electric razor into the toilet, and I told him I was pretty sure the dog had done it. When I said that, when I protected her, her chin shot up and our eyes met and I knew. From that day forward, it would be us against them. It would be us against the world.

Just, like, not today, apparently. Ames goes back to her phone, and Ellie gets out hers too. I'm so desperate, I'm thinking about reaching for Sky's copy of *Goblet of Fire*. This carriage house is way too small for this much awkwardness. I always thought it was so cool when I was little, the way there are all these little nooks and crannies for storage and the walls slope smaller on the sides. Now I feel claustrophobic. Ames is biting her nails. Ellie starts smacking her gum. And then the balcony door opens again. OH THANK GOODNESS.

Sky shuts the door behind her.

"Back already?" I ask.

She quirks an eyebrow at me. Opens the door again. I can hear their voices all the way from the dock.

Stree-eet-light. Pee-eo-ple. Whoa-ooo-ooo.

"Oh." I snicker. "So I guess going down to the dock is out."

"Wait, is that our moms?" Amelia Grace is out of her chair in a hot second, and she does not look nearly as mortified as she should.

Sky winces. "Yes."

"All of them?"

There's something in her voice when she says it. It almost sounds like hope, but that can't be right. And then she's out the door, and she's standing on the balcony, and the silhouette of her there, pressed against the slats so desperately, short brown hair blowing around in the wind—she makes me think of the stories of the women who would pace the widow's walks waiting for their husbands to return from sea.

Before I can help myself, I'm standing next to her, trying to see what she's seeing. All I see are four grown-ass women singing at the top of their lungs. One of them is holding a bottle of wine that she sometimes passes to the others. They're jumping up and down like they're at a concert but they're the only ones who can see the band. Also, like they are operating under different rules of rhythm and gravity than the rest of the universe. I look at Amelia Grace's face. I think she might be about to cry. It is possible we are not seeing the world the same way right now.

"You okay?" I ask.

Amelia Grace can't tear her eyes from the scene in front of us. "I've never seen her this way before."

I giggle. "Drunk?"

She shakes her head. "Happy."

My mouth opens, but my brain is entirely blank. I wish I could say something profound right now. I wish I could do pretty much anything besides stare. Amelia Grace's brown eyes go big and she blushes.

"I mean, um, anyway." She looks around like she's hoping a push-in-case-of-awkward button will appear. "Hey, what's that window up there?"

Really? That's what we're going with?

She's pointing at a spot above my head. "It looks like a miniature set of French doors. I don't remember seeing anything like that from the inside."

I decide to humor her because crying in front of people is no joke.

"There's a little loft inside. Not even tall enough to stand in. You didn't see it because Mama packed it with decades' worth of crap and ran a curtain across it."

Ellie bounds outside. "What are we talking about?"

Amelia Grace points again.

"Secret window!" squeals Ellie.

"It's not really a secret," I say.

Ellie puts her hands on her hips. "It totally looks like the doorway to another world AND it's hidden, but sure, okay." She's bouncing around like it physically hurts to hold still. "So, what are we doing tonight?"

"Not going down to the dock," I offer.

She looks at our moms and wrinkles her nose, and my opinion of her goes up a smidge. "Yeah, nope."

"Sometimes we take the boat and drive around till we find a party or something."

Ellie's eyes light up.

"But that would require us being able to get to the boat without our moms seeing us. Mama doesn't really let us take the boat out at night anymore."

And . . . the light dies. I decide not to mention any of the factors that led to this new boating policy being instituted last summer. Namely: me, Jim Beam, some college kids, a not-so-minor boat crash.

"Well, we *have* to do *something*."

A) If she is one of those people who emphasizes random words, I am never going to survive the summer. And B) I am so over popular girls and how they expect you to constantly entertain them.

"Can we *walk* to these parties?"

I grip the banister. Hard.

"It'd be through woods and briars and stuff, and it might be muddy," calls Sky from inside. "And, um, I don't really feel like walking tonight, if that's okay with you guys, but I'm totally cool staying here if y'all want to go."

Have I mentioned how much I love my sister? It is impossible to disagree with someone that sweet without looking like a Grade A bitch.

"Well, sure, we don't have to do that," says Ellie. "Hmm . . ." She taps her fingers against her chin dramatically.

Sky is scrolling one finger down the screen of her phone and whatever she sees makes her mouth go tight. She lets the phone flop on the couch and closes her eyes.

"Sky?"

She opens them. "Aunt Val brought a metric ass-load of wine," she says.

Wait. WHAT? My sister does not say "ass." And she definitely doesn't steal our parents' wine.

"I could go for a glass of wine," says Ellie. "Maybe a nice Shiraz."

I have no idea what a Shiraz is, but I feel this weird desire to know more about wine than Ellie right now. "I bet we could take a bottle, and they wouldn't even notice." I cock my head in the direction of the dock like it's whatever.

Ellie's green eyes flicker mischievously. "Are you brave enough?"

"*Yes.*"

She grins. "Cool. We'll keep watch."

She struts out onto the deck. Wait, how did that just happen? I don't even like this girl, and now I'm fetching wine for her? I glance from Skyler to Amelia Grace. If I say no now, I look like a coward. If I say no, Ellie wins. But if I get her the wine, she also wins.

I stomp off to get the wine.

This girl is turning out to be a real pain in my ass.

CHAPTER 13

Ellie

SCARLETT COMES BACK VICTORIOUS WITH THE
wine. I shove my hands in the pockets of my shorts so I won't
fidget. Because now that there's wine, there's drinking, and
I don't drink. Which is probably something I should have
thought about before I convinced Scarlett to get us wine. But
also: I've spent two hours reading magazines and feeling like
bottled desperation, and if I don't make something happen,
I'm going to explode.

"Woo! Let's get this party started!" I yell.

The three of them just kind of stare at me.

But that's okay. I can deal. Step 1 of making these girls my
friends: Procure wine. Done. Easy.

Step 2: Open the wine. This one proves to be a little more
difficult. Mostly because the only corkscrew in the carriage
house is rusty and looks like it hasn't been used since 1995.

"Why. Is. This. So. Difficult?" Scarlett's tongue is between
her teeth and she is working the corkscrew for all it's worth.
"Oops," she says.

"What, oops?" says Skyler.

"I broke the top half of the cork off."

We laugh at her misfortune. She narrows her eyes at us. Playfully. I think.

"It's fine. I'll get the bottom half next."

She finally manages to pry it out, and then she pours me a glass in a little mason jar because the wineglasses are in the big house. It's actually really cute. I'd totally take a picture, except that I'm pretty sure their judgment would slip over the scale into unbearable.

"So. We good now?" says Scarlett.

I turn my head so she can't see, just in case the hurt shows on my face. And then my eyes land on something that may just turn this night around.

"We will be." I grin at her and point at the curtain that hides the loft. "When we drink it up there."

Scarlett looks at me like I've suggested going down to the dock and taking shots with our moms. "Why would you want to?"

Because I'm hoping to uncover the secrets of our moms' friendship, and Amelia Grace inadvertently may have located their clubhouse. "Because. We could either drink it down here where it would be super easy for our moms to peek in and catch us, or we could drink it up there in front of the portal to Narnia."

Skyler's head shoots up at the mention of Narnia. We trade smiles, but then she goes back to her phone.

"*C'mon.*" I'm saying it like an obnoxious little kid, and I don't even care.

"I am kind of curious to see what it looks like up there," says Amelia Grace.

"See!" I take a pretend sip of my wine. I've never actually had alcohol before unless you count that accidental gummy bear. I know there are Muslims who drink. My momma drinks. But she still hides all the alcohol in the house whenever Nani visits from Toronto, and I don't know. I'm still figuring out how I feel about drinking.

Scarlett rolls her eyes. "It's just a bunch of junk. I don't even know where the ladder is."

"It's in the closet in the bedroom," says Skyler without looking up from her phone.

I don't miss the look Scarlett shoots her.

"Perfect!" I set down my wine, clap my hands together, and search out the ladder. Amelia Grace helps me set it up.

I wonder if I should play a joke on them when I get to the top. Pretend to find a rabid raccoon or Mr. Tumnus or something. I have to stop a couple of rungs short so I don't hit my head on the ceiling.

"There's nothing up there but junk," calls Scarlett. "Sky and I went up there a couple times as kids, and it was super disappointing."

I sweep back the curtain. A crate of Legos. Another of cords and electronic-looking things. A third entirely filled with CDs. That's just the first three boxes though. Secret sisterhood materials probably wouldn't be at the very front.

"There is some really exciting stuff up here. You guys are totally missing out."

"I can see the Legos from here," says Scarlett.

"Damn it!"

She busts out laughing. I squeeze the Lego bin to the side so I can crawl into the loft.

"Don't blame me if you scratch yourself on a rusty nail and get tetanus or something," yells Scarlett.

I snort. She wishes.

The rest of the loft is really more of the same. Dust and stuffiness and a smell that is kind of like a library only not as good. Lots of old books/clothes/toys. Cans of paint that look older than me. All the CDs and VHS tapes. Most of it is in those plastic bins with the snap lids, because apparently the twins' mom is too fancy for cardboard boxes. There's also a ridiculous amount of old lake toys. I'm just inspecting a box of water guns shaped like sea creatures and feeling as though this could come in handy, when I stand up too fast and crack my head on the ceiling.

"Son of a—"

"Are you okay?" yell three voices.

I duck and take a step backward at the same time. And slip on an ancient roll of wrapping paper. I'm pretty sure I scream, twice—once for the slip and another time when I fall butt-first against the wall and hear a crack. Luckily, it's the wall and not me.

Amelia Grace's head appears over the top of the bins. "Whoa, Ellie, are you okay?"

"I'm fine." I groan and try to stand up, but the wall gives behind me, and I almost fall again. Okay. Let's take it slowly.

"Are you sure you're okay?" one of the twins calls from below. Skyler, I think. The voice is soft.

"Yeah. But I think I broke your wall." I get back into my half-standing, half-crouch position and start dusting myself off.

"It's really no big deal," says Scarlett. "No one ever goes up there. We don't even have to tell my mom about the wall."

"Thanks," I say. I brush my hair out of my eyes. And that's when I realize. It's not a wall. "Holy crap, you guys, it's a door."

"There's a door up there?"

"Yeah. I mean, it looks like it's just a little closet, but—" I take a step closer. I realize now that the cracking noise was me making the door open the wrong way in. It's tiny—too small for me to go inside and stand up all the way—built into the triangle shape of the roof. I shine my phone inside, because I will forever and always be an eight-year-old at heart, and there could be pirate's gold or a secret passage or a unicorn in here. Unfortunately, the closet is unicorn-free (okay, I guess it would've had to have been a very tiny unicorn), but what it does contain is even better. Namely, some creepy-ass candles and a box of very fancy-looking cigars. And tacked to the wall is a list of rules with a name at the top: The Southern Belle Drinking Club. THIS IS IT. THIS IS MORE THAN I COULD HAVE HOPED FOR. "Okay, I really think you guys are gonna want to see this, and I swear I'm not kidding this time."

Skyler crawls into the loft with me (YESSS!!!), and I pass her the paper. It reminds me of those treasure maps Zakir and I used to make when we were little. We'd dye them with tea and rub dirt all over them, then get my mom to burn the edges. When we were done, we were positive they looked like 100 percent authentic pirate artifacts. Except this piece of paper looks *actually* old—it's fragile, and the pink and blue lines of the notebook paper are faded, and it's also kind of yellowed.

The Southern Belle Drinking Club

Rules:
1. You must meet once a week to play poker and smoke cigars.
2. You must drink Southern Comfort and Diet Coke.
3. You must wear pearls.
4. You must be 100%, no-holding-back, salt-in-the-wound honest.
5. You must accomplish something impossible before the end of the summer.

"This looks real," she says.

"Of course it's real!" I say. I can't believe I found it the very first night! It feels like a sign.

"What's real?" Scarlett calls from below.

"If you came up into the loft, you'd know!" I say.

"There's not any room."

"We can totally fix that." I push some boxes around so there's room for all of us, if we don't mind cramming and if we're cool with getting covered in dust. Scarlett does not seem cool with it, particularly the part that involves getting a mean gray streak on her shorts. Amelia Grace climbs up after her. Their knees bump when they both try to sit cross-legged and Amelia Grace jumps like a cat.

"So that's it?" Scarlett asks. "It's just that piece of paper?"

She is not impressed, but I just make this big show of being mortally offended, like I'm in on the joke. "No. No, that is definitely not it. Look inside that little closet thing. It looks like the remains of a secret society." I clasp my hands together. "I hope there were blood oaths."

Scarlett gives me a look like "You are so weird," but even she is smiling a little. "Do you really think someone ran a secret society out of this carriage house? How would that even be possible?"

I shrug nervously.

"It must have been some girls who were staying here," Skyler says. "We have a lot of people who come back every summer. And people who stay for weeks at a time."

"I'm sure that was it," I say. I'm certain Scarlett won't be up for it if she knows it's our moms. Even now, she wrinkles her nose at the paper.

"So, the point was . . . what? Drinking a lot while smoking cigars and being obnoxiously Southern?"

I pop up on my knees. "No, it was so much more than that! The drinking and poker were just the details, but having a place where you can be honest, where you can try to do big things in the world and have other women supporting you? They were each other's lifelines." Scarlett raises her eyebrows. "I mean, that's how I imagine it at least."

Skyler stand up and peers into the closet.

"Sky?" says her sister.

"I just wanna see. Ohhh."

I know how she feels. Eerie, that's the best word to describe it. But there's also something majestic about it. Something that speaks of secrets and history and magic, old magic.

Amelia Grace and Scarlett cram in behind her so they can see too.

"Are you thinking what I'm thinking?" I ask.

"That Pennywise and the little girl from *The Ring* probably have secret tea parties in this closet?" says Scarlett with a smirk.

"Ugh. No. I was thinking that we should totally re-create this drinking club thing this summer."

Amelia Grace shakes her head. "Do you know how much trouble I would be in if my mom caught me doing some of the stuff on this list? More than I can fathom. And I can fathom quite a lot. I'm already on, like, razor-thin ice."

"I don't think we have any cigars," Skyler says.

"Plus, smoking is super bad for you," says Scarlett.

"Smoking would totally jack with my ability to play tennis," I concede. "Cool. So, we're all in agreement on the smoking. Um, but the poker once a week, that could be cool."

I feel like I'm losing my grip on this thing. Like there's no way the other girls are going to do it with me.

"You know what?" Skyler says, looking at the rules again. "We definitely have some playing cards downstairs."

I smile. "Yeah?"

"Sky, we're not even—" begins Scarlett.

"Be right back. I think I know where they are."

She gets the cards quickly, which is good, because it was starting to get awkward up here.

"Awesome!" I say, just as she says, "I think I have pearls. Do you guys have pearls?"

Amelia Grace: No.

Scarlett: No.

Me: Yes.

"Scar, yes you do. Aunt Amy gave us matching earrings and pendants for our bat mitzvah."

"Oh. Well, I don't have them *here*."

"I do!" I say. "Probably even enough for all of us." I hurry down the ladder, trying not to flinch when Scarlett mutters, "Of course she does."

I return with the pearls—earrings for me, bracelets for Scarlett and Amelia Grace, and a necklace for Skyler. Scarlett wrinkles her nose, but she puts on the bracelet. I take it as a sign to plow ahead.

"So, we'll do the poker part but not the cigars part."

"What about the Southern Comfort part?" Scarlett asks.

"Huh?" I ask.

"Rule number two," she says.

I frown. "What even is that? I mean, like, besides alcohol?"

"Whiskey?" Skyler says.

"Bourbon?" says Amelia Grace.

"Definitely something brown," says Skyler.

"I'm *not* going back over to that house and stealing anything else," says Scarlett.

"Um, well, we'll just do wine for tonight. That's just details. I think the important thing is the meeting together and the honesty. And this part here. Would you guys want to do it?"

Skyler reads number five aloud. "You must accomplish something impossible before the end of the summer." It gives me shivers just hearing it.

Everyone goes quiet. But it's not real silence. You can almost hear the thoughts pinging around in people's heads. It makes me want to cup my hands over my ears like earmuffs. Keep all the secrets safely in place.

I laugh nervously. "Heh-heh. No pressure, right?"

"I'll do it," Skyler says.

We all turn to stare at her.

"Me too," says Amelia Grace. "It could be cool." The words flow out of her mouth so calmly, but there's this look on her face, like now there's more light in the world.

Yes! This is totally happening! Mostly. There's an awkward silence while we all wait to hear what Scarlett will say.

She shrugs. Grudgingly.

"Awesome!" I pop up so I'm sitting on my knees. "Now we just have to figure out the impossible."

CHAPTER 14

Amelia Grace

I'VE ALREADY THOUGHT OF MINE.

I want to get reinstated as a junior youth minister by the end of the summer.

But more than that. I want it to be on my own terms. I want it to be okay that I'm queer. I want my mom to go to bat for me. And maybe possibly even see what it would be like to have a girlfriend. No eithers and ors. Just me.

And Scarlett. I wish it could be Scarlett. I can't look anywhere near her right now. My cheeks feel so very hot.

"Look at you, you totally have yours already." Ellie pushes my shoulder. "And it is GOOD."

"What? No. I don't know. Skip me for now."

If I could shrink to the size of a dust bunny and not have everyone staring at me right now, that would be excellent. It's not that I don't want to make a pact about impossible things—I can't tell you how badly I want to do this. But telling them means coming out to Skyler and Ellie tonight. I don't know if I'm ready for that.

Scarlett sits straight up beside me, breaking me from my thoughts. "I'll go."

We all turn to stare at her.

"You will?" asks Ellie.

She laughs. "Sure." She makes a big show of clearing her throat. Lowering her voice like she's about to divulge state secrets. "This summer, I solemnly swear that I will"—she leans forward, and so do we—"get a tan."

"Oh, come on!" squeals Skyler.

"Pretty sure that doesn't count," I say.

"Why not?" Her eyes twinkle. I swear she can make them do that.

"Getting a tan is not impossible," says Ellie, who is apparently the commission on all things possible and not.

Scarlett holds out a freckled arm. "Have you seen me? I have to wear SPF hundred or I go from ghost to tomato."

"Okay, cool. Mine is to eat the El Gigante meal at Los Lobos," says Skyler.

"Also doesn't count," says Ellie.

"But it's *seven* tacos!"

"And I'm going to pet a giraffe," I say.

"You guys!" Ellie looks exactly like a frustrated kindergarten teacher. "We're supposed to be sharing our secrets and stuff!"

Scarlett makes that noise that sounds like half a cough and means *Hell no*. "Hi, we literally just met."

I give her the side-eye. "Um . . . ?"

"You know what I mean." She makes a move like she's going to get up. "I'm just feeling kind of weird about this. Some stuff is too personal. I'm sorry."

"Wait!" says Ellie. "What if we write them on paper? That way no one else can see?"

Scarlett turns, but her frown doesn't go away. "Right. Until someone sneaks up here and reads them all."

Skyler pokes her. "Someone's paranoid."

But Ellie just grins. "I know what to do about that too."

She dances over to the recently discovered storage closet and after some rooting around and a sneeze that sounds like a kitten's, she emerges with several candles and an old wooden crate. She flips the crate to form a makeshift table and arranges the candles. "Now I just need something to light them with."

She crawls down the ladder, and when she comes back, she has one of those long lighters and a large ceramic bowl with squirrels painted around the sides.

"What's the bowl for?" asks Scarlett.

"So we don't burn our fingers." Ellie sets the bowl on the crate. Inside the bowl is a sheet of paper ripped from a notebook and four pens.

She lights the candles and tears the paper into four pieces and passes them around. We all kind of look at each other, waiting for someone else to start writing first.

"Do you think they really accomplished the impossible?" I ask. It feels significant, knowing someone else was able to do this first.

"I really do," says Ellie, giving me a soft smile. "Um, I'll start." She scribbles something down on her paper with her hand covering it and her back all hunched. Guess I'm not the only one with a secret. Then she folds it into quarters with tight creases. Her hand moves toward the flame.

"Wait!" says Skyler.

Ellie freezes. Scarlett and I raise our eyebrows in unison.

"I just want to do something," says Skyler.

She reaches for the curtain and carefully pulls it closed across the loft so that the candles are our only light. I'm relieved, because the loft is completely visible from down-stairs with the curtain open, and I don't want Mom to come in here and catch me drinking. Then Skyler crawls over to the little window and, after struggling with the latch for a second, pushes the two halves of it out and open. A breeze much cooler than you'd expect for late May rolls in off the lake. I shiver. So does Scarlett. The candles flicker, but they don't go out.

"Sky, if Grandma comes to haunt us in the middle of the night, it is one hundred percent your fault."

We all start giggling, partly nervous, partly giddy, partly legitimately creeped out by the idea of impending dead grandmas.

Then the loft goes silent.

Solemn like a cemetery. Bright like a beginning.

Ellie's face glows in the candlelight as she leans forward. She touches her paper to the flame.

It snaps up the paper faster than I expect, and she says, "Oh," dropping it in the bowl where the edges turn black and curl in on themselves.

She scoots back, proud and maybe a little relieved.

Skyler goes next, writing slowly with her lip clenched between her teeth. She lights her paper without folding it and waits for the fire to creep from one side to the other before dropping it in the bowl with a huge grin.

And then Scarlett.

She smirks at her blank piece of paper.

Skyler pokes her. "No cheating!"

"I'm not cheating!"

And the care with which she hides her writing lets me know she's telling the truth. Her eyes dart from side to side, daring anyone to peek. Then she adds her tiny truth torch to the pile of ashes. And everyone looks at me.

"Right," I say.

I write down the words: *I want to get reinstated as a junior youth minister by the end of the summer.*

I've already thought them. I knew this was what I was going to write. But something about putting the words down on paper makes them feel final. More real. Like now there's intent behind them. I've crossed the boundary from wishing to doing.

I realize I'm taking forever, and the girls are waiting, so I fold over the paper real quick and shove it into the flames. *I want to get reinstated as a junior youth minister by the end of the summer*, I think as the paper catches fire. *And I want to do it without losing any of my pieces.* My eyes meet Scarlett's and my breath catches, and I accidentally hold on for a second too long.

"Ow, shit." I drop the paper into the bowl.

I feel . . . different. Braver. I look from Ellie to Skyler to Scarlett.

"I think I want to tell you guys what I wrote."

Oh, wow, I really just said that.

Okay, so I guess I'm doing this. I kind of can't believe it, but you know what? Yeah. It feels right.

"I want to get reinstated as a youth minister by the end of the summer." I do not look at Scarlett. "And, uh, I want it to be okay that I like girls. I know that's stupid because it's not like that's one hundred percent under my control to have other people accept me or whatever, but I just, I don't know, I've always wanted to be a youth minister."

I wait for their reactions, stomach churning.

"That's awesome," says Ellie. "It's not a stupid goal at all."

Skyler agrees, but Scarlett still looks stunned.

"That is really wonderful." She says it like the words feel funny in her mouth. "I didn't know. I mean—"

"That I was out yet? I wasn't two days ago."

"Ohhh." She smiles like it finally makes sense. Touches my shoulder in a way that lets me know she'd be hugging me if we weren't in a cramped attic.

Ellie looks back and forth between us, biting her lip. "So, how come—?" she begins, but Scarlett interrupts her. "What's yours?"

Ellie blinks at her. "Huh?"

"What did you write on your paper?"

Ellie's eyes go big and scared. "Um."

"I'll go next!" Skyler jumps in.

Ellie seems desperately relieved.

"I'm—" Skyler's voice seizes up, and she has to start again. "I'm going to play softball again."

Scarlett frowns. "I thought you were quitting so you could be with Mama this summer."

"It may also have had something to do with my medical stuff."

Scarlett may need to surgically reattach her jaw. "Holy shit, that's really why you did it."

"What happened?" asks Ellie. "Like, to keep you from playing? If you don't mind me asking."

"Oh. I— Well, I had some issues with injury this past season, and I had to quit the team partway through." Skyler doesn't take her eyes off the floor. "I know it'll be hard, rehabbing and getting back into it, but I really want to try."

"I can totally help you!" squeals Ellie. "I've had two elbow

117

surgeries and a sprained knee from tennis, and I've been to like eighty billion hours of physical therapy. Do you—"

"What was yours again?" Scarlett cuts her off.

Ellie's eyes dart around like she's looking for an exit. "I don't know . . ."

"C'mon," says Scarlett. "You swore to tell us the truth. This was your big idea to begin with, and everyone else is womaning up and sharing."

Ellie opens her mouth. And closes it. Opens. Closes. Opens. Closes. Oops, I think we broke her.

"The truth is," she finally says, "mine is kind of stupid. I'm embarrassed to tell you guys after you've all said such big important things. I need to think of something better. Maybe next time? We could still play poker though."

"Huh." Scarlett shrugs her shoulders in a way that is effortlessly cool. "Well, I'm pretty beat," she says. "I think I'm gonna go to bed. But you guys knock yourselves out."

Ellie's face falls and the smile she covers it with makes me feel even sadder for her. "Well, sure. Maybe another night."

Scarlett crawls back down the ladder. I don't realize until she gets to the bedroom that she didn't share hers either.

CHAPTER 15

Scarlett

MY SISTER IS THE FIRST PERSON I THINK OF WHEN I wake up in the morning. It hasn't always been this way. I mean, it probably was when we were little, and we had this thing where whoever woke up first would go pounce on the other person's head. But now there's a different reason.

I sneak down the ladder from the top bunk. It's almost 7:30. I've always been an early riser. The instant the sun comes up, I can't be asleep anymore, especially if the blinds are open like today. I quietly dig around in Sky's suitcase. Good grief, where did she put them? I unzip a pocket. Amelia Grace tosses around under. her blanket. Oops. But the heating pads I'm looking for are in the pocket, so we're good.

I tiptoe out to the tiny kitchen/breakfast bar/miniature living room and pop both of them into the microwave for a minute. While they're going, I start the coffee. Sky doesn't drink it, but my parents do, and so do I. (I may be a morning person, but that doesn't mean my brain is ready to work yet.) The microwave beeps, and I shake the heating pads around and throw them back in for another minute. The whole kitchen smells like lavender now. Well, and sunscreen. One time my cousin Joey squeezed an entire bottle onto the floor because he said it was magic sauce, and the carriage house has never smelled the same.

When the microwave beeps again, I pull out the heating pads and tiptoe back to the bedroom. I wrap one around each of Skyler's hands and then pull up the covers so no one can see. Not that there's anything wrong with her needing heating pads to get out of bed in the morning, but I can tell she's not ready to tell Ellie or Amelia Grace about her arthritis yet, and I want that to be her choice.

I walk through the wet grass to get to the main house but stop dead when I open the patio door. It looks like a tornado picked up a liquor store and discarded the windswept wreckage in our living room. I trace my way through upended cups and empty wine bottles—quietly, like an anthropologist studying the habits and behavior of wine moms. The coffee table is so covered with limes, salt, and shot glasses you can barely see the crisscross lines that form the repurposed window underneath.

The room is a metaphor for our lives. The difference? I could probably have this living room put back together in half an hour.

I make a pot of coffee over here too, because given the amount of tequila not left in the bottle, our moms are sure as shit going to need it. Then I make myself a slice of peanut butter toast and weave around the living room gathering empty wineglasses and shot glasses and martini glasses while I eat. Truth? I am not actually this nice of a person, I'm just looking for a way to keep myself occupied until it's a socially acceptable time to text Reese. 7:58 is just plain desperate, but 9:45? Much cooler. And to be safe, I'll text at 9:46 so it seems more organic. He was definitely the subject of my goal last night, and it's definitely why I wasn't feeling like sharing.

My phone buzzes in my pocket. Reese!

Oh. It's Daddy. And I know we're on radio silence and I judged the eff out of Sky for leaving him that Post-it, but something comes over me, and I answer.

"Hello?"

"Scarlett." There is so much relief in his voice. "I didn't think you'd answer."

"Me neither."

He clears his throat. Ha! That one stopped him in his tracks.

"So, you're at the lake?" he says after a beat.

"Yep."

"Um, well, good. I saw on Valeria's Facebook that your mom's sisters are there. You guys having fun?"

"Yeah. Tons." I try to squeeze as much venom into the words as I possibly can. It does not go unnoticed by my father.

"Scarlett, I'm trying here."

"Are you? Are you really?"

"I'm sorry," he says.

Some things are too big for sorry.

"That you got caught?"

"What? No. You don't understand—"

"Pretty sure I understand a lot of things," I snap, and I hang up the phone.

I'm not ready for apologies. I am ready for scorched earth and destruction and karma in its most sledgehammer-y form.

There's a wedding picture on the table in front of me—my parents wrapped in each other's arms, looking so blissful it's gross. How can something so good go so wrong? They seemed happy. I mean, yeah, I guess they were fighting more the past year or two, but shouldn't there have been signs? Like, big ones? How can something be crumbling around you without you even realizing it?

The smell of coffee hits me from the kitchen, so I take a couple deep breaths and pour a cup and take it upstairs to Mama. She's still in bed, her brown hair tangled around her head, her mascara a study in smudges—one black stripe across her cheek, another across her pillow. I set the coffee on her nightstand, and she jumps.

"Sorry."

"Don't ever be sorry for bringing coffee, baby."

She sits up in bed so she can take a sip. Even with her hair and mascara and stuff, she's pretty. "Are you doing okay?" She squeezes my arm and asks it with Concerned Mom Eyes, so what she really means is "Are you cutting?"

"I'm fine." My voice has spines in it. "So, Daddy called me this morning with some crappy apology."

I brace myself, but her eyes soften. "At least he's trying."

Wait. *What?*

"He's been calling me too."

"And you answered?"

"Well, no. But it's nice to see the effort."

Hitting a button on his phone is effort? "Right. I have to get back downstairs."

"Scarlett—"

"Sorry, I just realized I forgot to heat up Skyler's heating pads," I say before rushing out the door.

I can't do this with her, or I'll say something mean. How is she not more angry? I'm furious. Like a firework going off inside a glass jar and everything exploding because there's nowhere for all that pressure to go. I pass by the table with my parents' wedding picture again, those blissful smiles digging into me. I don't want to let a picture affect me so much. I want to keep my cool. To be the kind of person who's strong enough and calm enough to deal with things. I slam the picture frame against the table so I don't have to look at their stupid faces anymore.

And then I realize Ellie is standing in the doorway watching this entire meltdown play out. I also realize the frame may have made a cracking noise when it hit the table. I turn it over. Yep. There's a spiderweb of cracks where my parents used to be. Oops.

"Do you need some help with that?"

Ellie and Sky could have a competition for best judgy face, not even kidding.

"I've got it," I say tightly.

She shrugs in a way that makes me think of a wounded animal and goes to the kitchen, digging around in the fridge for eggs and spinach. Okay, but seriously, who eats spinach at eight thirty in the morning voluntarily?

"Omelet?" she asks.

"No, thanks. I already ate."

While I clean up the picture frame, she makes one for herself, cracking the eggs one-handed and folding the yellow circle of cooked egg over the spinach just so. Because of course she even makes omelets perfectly. She slips the omelet onto a plate and turns to face me.

"My, um, cousin's parents got divorced last year."

"Oh, yeah?" I try to look appropriately sympathetic, but

I'm already squirming from worrying where this conversation is going.

"Yeah," says Ellie. Amelia Grace walks in stretching, and Ellie's eyes go kind of frantic, but she plows ahead. "So, if you ever need to, like, talk to someone or anything, I know what it's like."

My jaw actually drops. She knows what it's like? I start to say something, but Amelia Grace puts her hand on my shoulder.

"You wanna go canoeing? I really wanna go canoeing."

Which is probably the best thing that could've happened, because I'm pretty sure yelling "You know nothing, Jon Snow!" in your guest's face is not in Emily Post's guide to etiquette.

"Yes," I say quickly and follow her out the door.

I know a life preserver when I see one.

Ellie

....

I position my plate on the table outside, and it takes a couple (read: twelve) tries, but I manage to get a shot of the lake and the cotton ball clouds in the background between the porch slats. Perfect. I take a bite. My omelet got cold while I was taking all those pictures. I shrug and post the photo with the caption Eating the most glorious omelet with the most glorious view. #lakelife #summer

I take another bite. Eggs really do taste like rubber when they're cold.

I'm tempted to throw the rest away, but breakfast is the most important meal of the day—they've done research. And it's, like, set-in-stone research, unlike the research on egg yolks. One day they're upping your heart attack risk with each bite, the next they're giving you ALL the nutrients until your skin, hair, and nails shine like buffed glitter.

I watch the lake and drink my first quart of water. Scarlett and Amelia Grace have nearly paddled to where I can't see them anymore. I'm kind of bummed they didn't ask me to go with them, but I keep telling myself it's because canoes only hold two people.

Riiight. And our moms only drank a little bit of wine last night.

I take my plate to the sink and run back to the carriage house for my notebook before holing up on the deck again. I thought re-founding the SBDC would have felt better than this. If I have to plan out every minute, so be it, but I am going to have fun today.

8:00–8:30 Make and eat a healthy breakfast

8:30–8:45 Make a kick-ass To Do list

8:45–9:30 Stretch, run, stretch

9:30–11:30 Tennis

11:30–11:35 Jump in the lake fully clothed, because it's already sauna-level hot and you'll definitely need it (consider removing shoes first)

11:35–11:50 Quick shower/change

11:50–12:50 Make a lunch from Pinterest

12:50–1:45 Eat (ideally, not alone)

1:45–2:00 Call my reps

2:00–3:30 Go through SAT vocab flipbook while sunning on dock (take pictures in my new one-piece)

3:30–4:15 Swim to the corner of the lake and back

4:15–4:30 Take more pictures post-swim but only if hair
    looks like sexy beach hair
4:30–5:45 Shower and actually get cute this time
5:45–6:00 Attempt colorful eye shadow (One hue only is key!)
6:00–8:00 Some kind of dinner with our moms
8:00–10:00 Hang out (and by "hang out," I mean wait until
    it's a socially acceptable time to convince the girls to go
    find boys/a party)
10:00–10:30 Pray all five prayers back to back to back
10:30 Party!
Alternatively (if no party or unable to sneak out), sit on the
    deck while The Mom Show unfolds
(Consider making popcorn)
(Also consider taking video for purposes of bribery and
    next-morning humiliation)

I look over my schedule. It has all the makings for a really good day. Except.

Goals and wishes and curls of paper burning black.

I check to make sure I'm alone before turning to a blank page near the back. I put my pen to the paper. And I hesitate. If anyone saw this—

I think of Scarlett and Amelia Grace, paddling away from me in that canoe. Laughing. Sharing secrets.

Screw it. I need this.

I write down my goal, the one I wrote last night.

I want to get these girls to be my best friends by the end of the summer.

You can see why I can never show this to anyone ever. But they're going to keep asking, and what am I supposed to say? That I've always wanted to have a best friend, but I'm defective?

I already know how this goes. But this time is going to be different. *I'm* going to be different.

I write down my plan.

Befriend Skyler $\xrightarrow{\text{to get}}$ Amelia Grace $\xrightarrow{\text{to get}}$ Scarlett

I let out a satisfied sigh. I feel so much better.

I go back to my room and change into running clothes. Skyler's still in bed, so I try to be quiet. Then I go back to the main house and stretch on the deck. Two of the moms (not mine) are drinking coffee and showing signs of life.

"Did the girls get back from canoeing yet?" I ask them.

"I don't think so," says Val. "But I don't remember seeing them go either."

She looks puzzled and also like she might have a migraine.

"Okay. No worries. I run by myself all the time. It's, like, super relaxing."

The other mom, Amelia Grace's, makes a pity face. I find a path by the water and run until I can't feel my feet.

CHAPTER 16

Skyler

IN THE MORNING, MY JOINTS ARE LIKE RICKETY OLD houses. Knuckles wound tighter than spools of thread. Wrists ready to crack like peanut brittle.

I am lucky.

I have a sister who plies me with heating pads while I'm still asleep, so when I do finally wake up, the pain isn't nearly as bad as it could be, and also it smells like I'm sleeping in a field of wildflowers in the middle of Provence.

Another reason I am lucky: Today I have a plan. The excitement from making that impossibility pact last night still courses through me. This morning I am going to ask my mom about going to the doctor, and it is going to work brilliantly. I know because I've been practicing our conversation over and over while I snuggle under my blankets for just fifteen more minutes, and okay, maybe fifteen more after that. The other girls are gone when I get out of bed. They're not in the big house either. Huh. Well, that's okay. I really need to talk to my mom anyway.

I run upstairs to her bedroom.

Hey, Mama, I think I need to go to the doctor again.

Hey, Mama, I need to go see Dr. Levy.

Mama, I—

She sits on the floor, weeping.

My questions poof and disappear. "Are you okay?"

I rush over and sink to the ground and hug her, all in one motion.

"No." The word is garbled with tears. She sobs into my hair. "I scratched the shiplap."

Um . . .

"You're crying because of . . . shiplap?"

Perhaps this is not the best time to request changes to my medical care.

She shakes her head, strands of hair sticking to her tear-stained cheeks. "No. Because of your dad. I was moving the nightstand, and I scratched the shiplap. Two years ago, I texted him a photo of a shiplap accent wall and said, 'Wouldn't this look pretty at the lake house?' And the next time we came out here, he had already done it as a surprise."

The tears start fresh. "That man always did everything I ever asked him."

"Hey, it's okay. It's going to be okay." I hold her against me and stroke her hair. I can feel her breaking in my arms.

"That's what he told me when he asked me to marry him. That he was going to spend every day of his life making my dreams come true. How did we ever let it get this bad?"

Her questions make me feel young. And scared. I don't know the answers to them, but it doesn't matter. Sometimes it's important just to sit with people.

After a few minutes, she can talk in her normal voice again. Her eyes seem to focus on me in a different way.

"I'm sorry to be such a mess. Did you need something, baby?"

"Oh." I'd feel so selfish asking now. "I was just wondering if we had any brownie mix."

She cocks her head to the side. I am the actual worst at lying.

"I don't think so, but we can always run to the store later."

I give her one last hug. Try not to let the defeat show on my face.

"Thanks," I say.

I go back downstairs and out into the backyard and flop onto the grass. It is 9:00 a.m., and I am already a failure. I don't know how I'm ever going to find the silver lining in— Oh!

Is that?

I crouch down and pick up a squiggly orange mushroom. Give it a sniff.

It is!

I can't believe it's chanterelle season already!

You have to find the ones that smell like apricots. That's how you know. Because there's these other mushrooms—false chanterelles—that look all orangey gold and fluted like a chanterelle, but they smell like packaged hospital air. Also, they have gills when you flip them over (chanterelles never have true gills), but it's easier just to sniff them.

I run back inside for some supplies, and then I walk past mushrooms of all colors and sizes. Tiny crimson ones that look like fairy caps and white ones with tall translucent stalks. Fat brown ones of all different heights, arranged like a city in the crook of a tree. I also pass jack-o'-lanterns, another one that people mistake for chanterelles, but honestly, they're not even orange AND they don't smell good, so if you eat one thinking it's a chanterelle, you almost deserve the explosive diarrhea.

I spot a cluster of orange near the roots of an oak tree and scurry closer. They look promising. I cut one with my knife and lift it to my nose. Pure heaven. I cut all the ones around the tree and drop them in my basket. My fingers hardly hurt at all this morning, even when I grip the knife.

A confession: It's a knife specifically for cutting mushrooms, because I am that big of a mushroom nerd. Dad and I keep them here at the lake house because we get the best mushrooms up here, especially during rainy summers like this one.

I hope he's okay. I know, I know, I'm supposed to hate him and stuff. Scarlett always says I'm too easy on Dad. But I haven't forgiven him, I swear. I'm still mad, *really* mad. But I'm also sad. And confused. I just want to look him in the eyes and say, "Why?"

And then I'll let Scarlett punch him in the face.

When I come out of the woods, Ellie is standing on the dock, soaking wet.

"Did somebody push you in?" I wouldn't put it past Scarlett.

"Nah. I jumped."

With all her clothes on?

"I just played tennis for two hours," she explains.

"Fair."

131

"Whatcha got there?"

I blush. "Oh, um. Mushrooms?"

She comes closer. Peeks into my basket.

"I'm basically Katniss Everdeen," I say.

I'm sure she'll start making fun of me in three, two—

"Are those chanterelles?"

"They are! Ohmygosh, do you like foraging too?"

"Not exactly, but what I lack in knowledge, I more than make up for in my desire to eat fancy-ass food."

"They are the fanciest! Did you know they sell them in France for sixty dollars a pound? I've sold them to a restaurant around here before but never for that much."

"What are you going to do with them?" She leans to the side and wrings the water out of her hair.

"Oh." I feel some of the happiness leach out of me. "Usually, my dad cooks them. He's more of the chef. Somehow I always lose track and burn things."

Ellie smiles at me like I'm a stray kitten. "I can help you cook them."

"Are you sure?"

"Totally. I was planning on making something Pinterest-y for lunch anyway. I put it on my schedule and everything." It kind of just slips out of her mouth, and she gets this look on her face like she wishes she could put it back. I think it's a little odd that she schedules things like that, but she definitely didn't make fun of me for gathering mushrooms just now, so I'm going to roll with it.

"Well, great."

"Let me just change first." She gestures to her covered-in-lake-water self. "And, uh, hey, I'm going for a swim later if you want to come. I'm cross-training for tennis, but swimming is super low impact, so it could be really good for your softball rehabbing."

That *would* be a really good way to cross-train for softball. If my pain levels hadn't been so bad lately. I feel, if possible, even crappier about my failure to talk to my mom about going to the doctor. "Um . . ." How to say it without confessing A) everything about my illness, and B) that it is Day One and I am utterly failing on my pact. "I don't think so. But thanks!" I hurry to add when her face falls.

"Of course." She puts that sparkly smile back on and runs off to change.

Ellie meets me at the house later, and she actually seems to enjoy scrubbing mushrooms with toothbrushes (the worst part of the whole process). She also photodocuments every little thing until I start to feel like we're these glamorous celebrity chefs.

She makes pan-seared trout in one pan and something called beurre blanc in another. I mostly just keep her company.

"I think this is gonna be really good. I wish we had ramps though," says Ellie.

"Oh! There's a farmer's market in town. We could go tomorrow."

"YES! That is definitely something we should do. Also, we should pick some more of these, because I have a pickled mushroom recipe I want to try."

"Done and done."

"And so are these mushrooms."

I snag one out of the pan and pop it in my mouth.

"OMG."

"Right?"

They have this delicate peppery flavor—it's unbelievable. We sit on the kitchen counter, gulping down mushrooms and laughing. It's the first time I've felt really happy since I found out. And then I get the text.

Daddy: I hope you're doing okay. I love you.

CHAPTER 17

Amelia Grace

OUR PADDLES GLIDE THROUGH THE WATER. AT FIRST, we don't say anything. I just focus on matching her strokes.

Then Scarlett pauses. "Thank you," she says. "I had to get out of there. I can't with that girl."

"Aw, she's not so bad. I think she means well, anyway."

Scarlett wrinkles her nose in the direction of the house. "Maybe."

She checks her phone. "Oh!"

"Is everything okay?"

"Yeah. Sorry. I just realized it was time to text someone." She types something. "My boyfriend, I mean."

"You have to text him at a specific time?"

"What? Oh! No, it's not like that. Ew. I wanted to ask him about something, but I didn't want to text too early." She types and shakes her head and types again. "'What'd you do last night?' Does that sound normal? I want it to sound normal."

"I think it sounds normal?"

"Good." She puts down her phone. We start paddling again, but her phone pings.

"So, what'd he do?"

She almost drops her phone in the lake. "What?"

"What did he do last night?"

"Oh. 'Hung out with friends.'"

She texts a bunch more while nearly the full spectrum of human emotion crosses her face. Then she puts her phone down and starts paddling in earnest. We're almost far enough that we can't see the house anymore.

"Is everything okay?" I ask.

"Yeah." She nods too many times. "He's a really good guy."

I nod back. Of course he is.

"But. How do you know someone is The One?"

Her long red hair is flowing behind her in the wind like she's some kind of goddess, and I swear there are beams of light shooting off of her.

"Um . . ."

"It's a really big deal, you know? And it's only been five months, so why am I even freaking out over this? Except of course I'm freaking out over this because I freak out over everything because I feel like I have to figure out every single piece of my life RIGHT NOW or everything is going to be ruined forever. Will I marry Reese someday and what am I going to major in in college and what am I going to do as my Big Thing that changes the world?" She shakes her head. "It's weird. I'm weird."

"It's not weird," I say.

I try not to think about how it would feel to have her talk about me that way.

Scarlett dips her hand beside the boat and lets the lake water run between her fingers.

I would choose her in a heartbeat.

If she wanted that.

She turns around and looks at me, and I'm not ready for it, the sudden intensity of her eyes. I feel like she can read my mind.

"I'm sorry I haven't replied to your email yet," she says.

"Oh. No worries." I hope I sound casual, but not forced-casual. It's really not a big deal. Sometimes we'll have a flurry of emails and then not talk for weeks, but this had felt like the start of a flurry. And I know I could have texted her, but every time I pulled out my phone, I felt like she'd be able to sense the desperation in each letter. A pining S. An unrequited Y.

She looks apologetic. "I got really busy, but if I had known you were about to come out—"

"Oh, hey. That's okay. I, um, didn't exactly know I was about to come out."

"You didn't?"

"Nope." I shrug. "I guess it usually happens under better circumstances than getting caught making out with the church good girl. By the entire congregation. While dressed as angels."

Scarlett's eyes go wide. "Well, dayum." She says it with two syllables, like her mama, and she's right—a one-syllable damn will simply not suffice in this situation.

"Yeah."

"That's why you made the goal about being a junior youth minister, then."

"Yeah. I was finally going to get to be one this summer, but they took it away. After."

"I'm sorry, but that is a bunch of bullshit. You've wanted this for, like, ever, and you've been going to that church since before you could walk and you do all the mission trips, and—" She does not stop. She launches into a rant about Good Christian Bitches and drops the F-bomb at least four times and I am impressed by her lung capacity and her knack for colorful word choices and also how much she remembers from my emails. How much she cares about me.

Eventually, she has to stop and catch her breath. "Hey, who did you kiss?"

"Huh?"

"The girl you got caught kissing. Who was it?"

"Oh, um. Carrie. Sullivan."

"Oh." Scarlett nods. Again, more times than is technically necessary. "She's pretty. I remember seeing her in your Insta photos."

Neither of us is paddling. We're just kind of floating in this little cove that has no houses but extra squirrels. Scarlett shakes her hair like she's trying to focus. "So, what's the plan? How do we get you reinstated?"

"I don't know." I pick at a peeling sticker on my oar. "I guess the first step would be convincing someone else to be on my side. Pastor Chris—he's the youth minister, and it definitely felt like he was on my side when I came out to him. Like, just talking to him made me want to come out to my whole youth group. So I could see if he would help me. Or maybe I could convince my mom."

Her lips go tight. "Right."

"What?"

"Nothing."

"No, tell me."

"It just . . ." I swear her lips are twisting in on themselves. "Really sucks that you have to convince your mom."

"Oh." I can feel the face I'm making, and it does not feel good. "Yeah. It does suck."

"Is she that homophobic?"

"I want to believe she's not. I mean, how could Val be best friends with her if she was? She's always been religious, but ever since they got married seven years ago, she's been *really* religious. But my stepdad is terrible."

Scarlet's voice gets quiet. "Do you think she'll ever leave him?"

It's not something I could even begin to hope for. "I don't think she ever could. We were really broke when I was in fourth grade, and I think she feels like he rescued her or something. She doesn't even have a job because of him. She used to be a midwife, you know? And this one time, Mom said she missed being a midwife and maybe she might want to go back to it. And Jay was smiling and saying things like 'You don't need to work, sugar. I make plenty.' And 'They used to have you out all hours of the night. We'd never be able to have nice dinners like this.' "

Scarlett rolls her eyes.

"I know. And then he patted her hand and got up from the table, asking about was there any dessert. And Mom was saying, 'In the fridge.' And then she was like, 'Well, I know, but—' And he was trying to slide the coconut cream pie off the top shelf, but there was a Tupperware of chili on top of it, and he knocked the whole container of chili onto the floor."

"Do you think he did it on purpose?"

"No, but I think he uses his anger at unrelated things as a weapon. Or maybe a warning. Because he was like, 'God-*dam*mit. Who the fuck stacks Tupperware like that?' And he yelled it so loud, and Mom was up in a flash, cleaning it up. But my stepdad? No apology. No offer to help, even though it was totally his mess. He just sliced a big-ass piece of coconut pie and sat down in his recliner. And Mom never asked about the midwife job again."

"He is such an asshole."

"I know, but, like, I don't know what to do. I'm surprised he even let her come here for the summer, but it turns out he got a big welding job out of state. Every once in a while, she'll help out someone at church, like being a doula for them or helping them learn to nurse their baby, but not often enough. And being a youth minister isn't just a fun thing, it was going to be my job this summer."

"Hey, don't worry. I'll figure something out so you can have a job while you're here."

"No, Scarlett, you don't have to—"

"Don't worry. I'm not going to do anything ridiculous. You just convince whoever it is you need to convince."

I type up an email to Pastor Chris as soon as we get back. He's younger, and definitely more progressive than the older ministers, and who knows? Maybe this is the start of making our church more inclusive for all the kids who come after me. I have no idea if it's going to work, but just knowing I get to tell Scarlett and the other girls about it makes me feel powerful.

Hey Pastor Chris,

You probably heard about what happened at the play on Friday. I think you were in the audience. I'm sorry I won't be able to be a junior youth minister this summer. I've been looking forward to it for so long.

I was wondering if you might could talk to the other pastors and see about me starting in the fall when I get back. I know I would be good at this job. I'm great with kids, and I feel like I could help so much. Who I love doesn't change that.

Please let me know what you think.

Thank you,

Amelia Grace

I read the email eleventy billion times before I hit send. It's scary, putting your whole heart out there into the world like that. I hold my breath when I finally click the button.

JUNE

CHAPTER 18

Ellie

....

SKYLER AND I HAVE HUNG OUT EVERY DAY SINCE WE cooked those chanterelles. I totally maybe almost kind of have a friend! I'm so excited by how my plan is developing, I woke up early and did almost everything on my To Do list. Now Skyler and I are eating kiwi slices on the upper level of the dock while she quizzes me on my vocab. (I told her about my PSAT goal, and she didn't even call me a nerd! What is life?!)

"Assiduous."

"'Hardworking.' You know you don't have to do this, right?"

She smiles. "I know. But I'm trying to do one thing every day for my mind, body, and spirit, and I feel like this will count for mind. I already painted my nails blue for my spirit. And, like, I thought about the universe while I was doing it?"

"Oh! I love that idea. I try to pray every day for my spirit."

"That's so cool! Oh, and, um, pulchritude."

"What? Is that even real?"

"Yes," she says. "And you are never going to guess what it means."

"'About or pertaining to chickens'?"

"A valiant effort. It means 'beauty.'"

"Are you kidding me?"

"Nope." She slides the book across the picnic table.

"Huh. That is the ugliest effing word for beauty I have ever heard."

"Hey, think how romantic it could be: Her pulchritude was unparalleled."

"Her hair draped down her back in silky pulchritudinous locks."

"Pulchritude is in the eye of the beholder."

"Pulchritude is only skin-deep. Which is good because it doesn't respond well to antibiotics."

"Ohmygosh, ohmygosh, stop." Sky laughs so hard that tears leak out.

Scarlett walks up the stairs and onto the dock with Amelia Grace. She frowns at us, and we both go silent.

"What are y'all doing?"

"Nothing," we answer.

Certainly not talking about pulchritude. Haha, pulchritude. I snicker. Scarlett narrows her eyes like she's trying to figure out if I'm laughing at her.

"So, I was thinking about tackling the loft today," I say. "If you don't think your mom would mind."

"Knock yourself out. We're gonna go Jet Skiing."

She grabs a life jacket from the chest opposite our picnic table and looks at Sky expectantly.

"I think I'm gonna stay here," says Skyler.

My heart swells. I TOLD YOU SHE WAS MY FRIEND.

"Fine," says Scarlett.

I don't miss the sharpness in her voice and neither does Skyler, who looks epically guilty right now. Scarlett turns and walks down the stairs like it's whatever, but I can tell she's stomping in her head.

Amelia Grace watches her go. She does this awkward shrugging and blushing dance in front of us. "Um, so, I guess I'll just go with Scarlett."

She hurries to grab a life jacket.

"Hey, wait, I was going to ask you about something," says Skyler.

"Yeah?"

"Yeah, I have this friend, Zoe. We're in youth group together at my synagogue? I thought maybe I could introduce the two of you sometime."

"Oh," says Amelia Grace. "Ohhhhhh. Um, that's really sweet of you, but I think I'm okay on my own for now."

Skyler nods, all disappointed.

Amelia Grace runs down the stairs after Scarlett.

After their Jet Skis are well out of range, I lean across the table toward Skyler and lower my voice conspiratorially. "Does your sister know Amelia Grace is in love with her?"

"What?"

"You didn't know either!"

Sky cocks her head to the side. Wrinkles her nose. "I think they're just friends. Scarlett has a boyfriend. They— They're just really good friends."

"Hmph." I cross my arms over my chest. "We'll see."

I hear the buzzing sound of a motor on water and look up. Are they really coming back so soon? But, no. It's a boat. Not just a boat, I realize as it gets closer. A boy boat. A boat full of boys—THIS IS WHAT I HAVE BEEN WAITING FOR AND, OH, THEY ARE CUTE BOYS TOO.

I mean, it's cool. I'm just studying vocab in preparation for the day when I'm a senator or a Pulitzer Prize–winning journalist or a YouTube star, but also, sometimes I would really, really like to know what it feels like to kiss someone.

"Hey!" I walk to the end of the dock and wave—not like a pageant queen or like I'm flagging down a boat rescue from a deserted island. Just a casual, hi-you-could-come-over-and-talk-to-us-or-not-I'm-pretty-good-by-myself wave. I hear yells from the boat, and it turns in our direction. Boys are so much easier than girls.

"Skyler, get up here," I whisper. Urgently.

"Ummm."

(But she does it.)

"Hey, y'all," says one of the boys, the driver.

"Hey," I call back. I nudge Skyler's ankle with my foot.

"Hey," she says, looking literally everywhere except at the boat.

Another boy waves shyly from where he's stretched out on a towel on the front. He has blackish hair with super-red tips and those sporty shield sunglasses that wrap around your face. He opens his mouth to say something, but before he can, the guy next to him jumps up onto the front of the boat, King of the World style, and says, "What are you ladies up to?"

I shrug. "Just hanging out. It's pretty quiet around here."

"Oh, yeah?" He grins, and I shouldn't think he's hot, because he's the kind of guy who uses unnecessary hand gestures for the sole purpose of flexing his muscles, but whatever, he is. "Maybe you just don't know where to go."

I cross my arms. Smirk to show I'm playing his game. "And where's that?"

"Sandbar. Friday night."

"How do you get—"

"I know where it is," says Skyler. Still not looking at the boat.

"So, you'll come? Both of you?" says the driver.

"Sure," I answer for both of us.

The boy at the front whoops and does a backflip off the boat into the water and then climbs back up again. Tan. Blond. So freaking cocky. I am acutely aware that I am wearing a swimsuit as opposed to something that covers more of my body.

"Cool," says the driver. "Well, see you around."

"Bye," I say.

Skyler says nothing.

"Bye, Skyler," he says.

"Bye." Her cheeks go a little pink.

"Friday sounds like a good day to fall in love," I say as we watch the boat drive away. I pick up my vocab book like *nothing to see here, show's over.* And then I go for it: "And speaking of people being in love, which one of those boys on the boat are you in love with?"

"What?"

"The boat," I repeat. "You wouldn't look anywhere near it. Which means A) one of those boys hurt you, in which case I will be forced to kill him, or B) you like someone."

Skyler blushes to the roots of her hair.

"So, it's B." I grin at her. "Is it the driver? I have a very strong feeling it might be the driver."

She hides her face behind her hands. "I think he might be a jerk. Or the only person who gets me. It's a very fine line."

"Well, we'll find out Friday night!" I say with a shimmy. I close my vocab book. "So. You really up for helping me clean out the loft?"

A few minutes later, we are facing down the loft. It is . . . more cluttered than I remember. Maybe because it's daylight. I am not fazed. I Marie Kondo'd our entire house last winter break for fun. I move like a whirlwind, pushing the larger bins to the side, sorting the entire loft into "keep" and "throw away" and "donate." Skyler tells me what can go in which piles and gently puts items in a trash bag, almost like everything is made of glass.

"Hey, can you pass me that bag?" I ask.

She hands me the trash bag. "Here you go."

"Thanks, Sky. Do you care if I call you Sky?"

"I love it when people call me Sky." She grins like a Cheshire cat.

I giggle. "Why are you making that face?"

She leans toward me, chestnut hair sweeping forward like a curtain that will hide the secret she's about to tell. "Well, I really like being called Sky, but, like, I don't like to tell people. It's just, if someone thinks to do it, it lets me know they're special. And then they get to be in a secret club for awesome people."

"Um. I have always wanted to be in a secret club for awesome people."

HOLY CRAP, THIS IS SOME INNER-CIRCLE SHIT. FRIENDSHIP IS MAGIC.

I try to contain my chill as I reach for one of the last few things in the back of the loft.

"What is this? A vase?" I hold it up. It's not a very pretty vase. It's neon green and really long and—

"I'll take that," says Skyler. She trashes it fast.

I throw away a few pool noodles that are on their way to falling apart, and then we're done. Well, with the sorting.

"Do you think we should carry the bins down to the garage or what?" I ask.

Something like fear flashes in Skyler's eyes. "Um, let's wait until we have more people, in case they're heavy or something. I don't want to drop them."

"Sounds like a plan. Also! Do you know what this means?"

"What?"

"It means we can totally start on the magic portal closet now! I'm big on saving the best for last."

Skyler nods seriously. "Me too."

We approach the tiny nook that barely qualifies as a closet. If we squeeze, we can both stand in the doorway at the same time. It really is just candles and papers and a box of ancient cigars and stuff, but I can't shake the feeling I'm about to be sucked into another universe.

"What should we do first?" I ask.

"Candles?" says Skyler.

"Candles."

There are still some candles from last time on the over-turned crate in the middle of the loft. And I know we're supposed to be making the loft look all fancy, but it feels wrong to move any of that stuff. We made our pact there. It's kind of like the crate and the candle stubs and the bowl with the charred bits of paper are sacred.

We do, however, take all of the creepy-ass candles that are left in the closet and strategically position them around the loft so they make a rough circle of tea lights, fat white candles with petrified wax drips down their sides, and even a dusty wrought-iron candelabra that looks like it's straight out of *Phantom of the Opera.*

"Clearly, we should put this right in front of the little window," says Skyler.

"Obviously. How else are we supposed to summon the spirits?"

I go downstairs and grab some pink tea plates to put under the candles that don't have a holder (because only you can prevent lake house fires). Skyler is still rooting around in the closet. I find her turning the yellowed pages of an old book.

"Whatcha got there?"

"Journal entries?" She turns another page and then sneezes from the ensuing dust cloud.

"Anything good?"

"'Nick and I had sex for the first time last night. It was on the back deck of his house because his parents were out of town, and I don't know what to do because I couldn't stop thinking about someone else,'" Skyler reads aloud.

"Yeah, we're definitely saving that." I stack the other notebooks and papers and stuff and set them beside the crate like they're our holy books. Skyler adds Nick and his back-porch lovemaking to the top.

I take a look around.

"What do you think? I don't know about you, but my joy is seriously effing sparked right now."

"I think," says Skyler, "it's missing something."

She ducks back into the closet and grabs the rules for the Southern Belle Drinking Club. She tapes them to the wall inside the loft. I want to hug her so badly right now. I really do.

"It's perfect," I say. And then a realization slips like a slug down into my stomach. "Do you think we can really get the other girls to come back up here, and, like, do this thing?"

Skyler touches my shoulder. "I think being friends with my sister just takes time," she says. "You have to earn it."

CHAPTER 19

Amelia Grace

I FEEL LIKE I'M IN ONE OF THOSE HORROR MOVIES where the girls try to have a séance in their attic and accidentally bring a serial killer back from the dead. Or like I'm at an evening church service. One of those.

The loft is decked out with candles of every shape and size, wax melting slowly onto candelabras and pretty pink plates. The wooden crate is still there. And the bowl. But now the list has been tacked to the wall, and there are two stacks of old papers and books, and there's this feeling, like the kind you get when someone is standing behind you, just about to touch you.

"Whoa," I say.

Ellie grins. "Thank you."

"Y'all did a really great job up here."

Skyler looks pleased, and Ellie waves one hand like, *Of course, it was nothing, being a super-secret séance interior designer is one of my many hobbies.* I notice something unexpected in her hand.

"I thought we weren't smoking cigars." It comes out more judgmental than I mean it to.

"Oh." She looks at the cigar like she forgot it was there, and her eyes light up. "We're not. I just thought it would be fun to gesture wildly with it." She assumes the posture of a CEO. "What's the progress on those pacts? Darling, you absolutely must try this wine!" She punctuates each sentence with a sweep of her arm that would make Holly Golightly jealous. Then she giggles. "It's everything I could have hoped for. Hey, have you seen Scarlett? We told her to be here at ten."

"I know she's around here somewhere." I check my phone. 9:59. We play a hand of poker while we wait for Scarlett.

She finally arrives at 10:14.

"Hi!" says Ellie, waving her cigar like she totally wasn't freaking out about whether or not Scarlett was coming.

"Hi," says Scarlett. "What's the secret thing you need my help with?"

She glances from Ellie to Skyler, waiting, but Ellie just grins.

"In due time," she says. "First, I officially call this meeting of the Southern Belle Drinking Club to order."

She bangs her cigar against the wooden crate like a gavel. It breaks in half. "Oops. Oh, well. Any new business?"

We stare at her. And each other.

"Umm . . ." I begin.

"OMG, this totally makes me feel like Kristy from the Baby-sitters Club," Ellie says. "Maybe I should get a visor!"

Scarlett side-eyes her.

"What? Did you want to be Kristy? I'm really more of a Stacey/Jessi hybrid, so I don't mind."

"Oh! I call Dawn!" says Skyler.

Scarlett's side-eye changes direction, which is really a pretty impressive feat of extraocular muscles. "You are Mary Anne," she tells her sister.

"I don't even like cats! Or Logan!"

"Mary. Anne."

"Forty percent Mary Anne, sixty percent Dawn!" Skyler jockeys.

Scarlett lets out a long-suffering sigh. "I mean, I guess."

Skyler seems mortally offended. "You know what? You're Mallory."

"I am NOT Mallory," says Scarlett, just as Ellie says, "Ohmygosh, it's perfect! You have the red hair and everything."

"Nobody in their right mind would want to be Mallory. She's a horse freak and a whiner and the biggest mystery of the series is how she ever got mono." Scarlett smooths her hair. "I'm obviously more of a Claudia."

I check my phone to see if I've heard back from Pastor Chris yet. Nothing. I was really hoping to be able to report something tonight.

"Ames?" says Scarlett.

"Sorry, what? Do we still need a Dawn? I can be Dawn."

"*Ohmygosh.*" Skyler puts her hands on her hips.

I hold up my hands in surrender. "Or Kristy. She's good too. I always thought it was pretty cool how she started that little kid softball team."

I remember reading those books in fourth grade. Then everybody graduated to Harry Potter, and our preacher said Harry Potter was sinful because it was teaching kids witchcraft, and lots of the parents at church wouldn't let their kids read it anymore. Mom was different. She said she had to read the entire series herself before she decided. And she did, all 4,224 pages. She said she thought it was a spectacular exercise for the imagination and that I could keep the books. I thought it was really cool that she read them when almost none of the other parents did. And I'll never forget what she said: "Amelia Grace, it's always important to look at things for yourself and make up your own mind. Even the Bible. Even if the preacher's telling you something about it. A lot of people will tell you a lot of different things. That's why it's so important to read the Bible on your own, for yourself, every day, and to decide what you think about what you've read."

That was the year I read the Bible from cover to cover. A lot of people haven't done that, even the ones who go to church all the time and sew Bible verses onto pillows. It's hard to believe the woman who said those things is the same woman who's having so much trouble seeing me now. But maybe it's also why I should give her another chance?

"Ames." Scarlett nudges me again.

"Huh?"

"How's it going with the youth minister stuff?" asks Skyler. "You reminded me when you said, 'little kid softball team.'"

"Oh. That." I get the impression she's already asked at least once. "I emailed the youth pastor at my church . . ."

"That's awesome!" says Ellie.

"Well, I haven't heard anything back yet."

"That's okay. It's huge that you reached out!" Her smile is big and genuine. It makes me feel like I really have accomplished something.

"Definitely," says Skyler. "I'm still working up the courage to talk to my mom. I guess that's my update."

"Thanks. Actually, I think that's my next thing too. Talking to my mom about stuff."

"I'll go next!" says Ellie. "I've finally decided what my thing for the summer is going to be. This summer. I will. Be more authentic on social media."

Scarlett's eyebrows hover somewhere near the ceiling.

"Well, I guess it actually sounds pretty basic when you say it like that."

"Hey, knowing is half the battle," says Scarlett. "You change the world with your no-makeup selfies."

Ellie looks flustered. "No, what I mean is, I just feel so much pressure to be perfect all the time, and present this image, and it's not even the real me. So I wanted to talk about stuff like how I'm Muslim and how I love the fitness community but only when it's focused on being your best you. I used to be addicted to looking at all this super-unhealthy body-shaming stuff. And, like, I want to talk about how my perfectionism is so intense, it borders on anxiety at times."

"That's actually really cool," Scarlett says quietly.

Ellie blushes. "Thank you."

Scarlett suddenly looks like she's swallowed a firework. "I guess that leaves me then." She gulps, actually gulps, the way cartoon characters do.

We're so very quiet. More than quiet. There's an absence of the normal everyday movements that people make. It tells me the other girls are as frozen as I am.

"I want"—Scarlett looks like she'd rather do anything than tell us—"to have a healthy, grown-up relationship with my boyfriend and not let my past hold me back. So, yeah. I'm totally weak and stupid or whatever."

My first thought: I hate that she feels that way. For both the right and wrong reasons. My second: I hope he deserves her.

"No, hey, you're not," says Ellie.

Scarlett looks even more uncomfortable.

"Yeah, a healthy relationship is a totally normal thing to want," I say. Unless the person you want to be in a healthy relationship with is already in a relationship with someone else.

"You know what?" Skyler starts digging through the papers and books piled by the table/crate/altar of sisterhood. "I think we found something that could totally help. It's a journal. I think it's from one of the original Southern Belle Drinking Club girls and, hang on a sec, here it is."

She runs her finger down the page. And then she reads.

Nick and I had sex for the first time last night. It was on the back deck of his house because his parents were out of town, and I don't know what to do because I couldn't stop thinking about someone else. It doesn't make any sense. Nick and I are supposed to get married and have kids and stuff. We've even talked about it. Which I guess is weird because we're only nineteen, but sometimes you just know. At least, I thought I knew. And now there's this other guy, and he's not like anything I ever planned. How do you know? Really know? It's like there's this whole alternate future unspooling in front of me, but I don't know if I'm supposed to reach for it or run.

"Wow," says Scarlett. She's eyeing the book, but her fingers are clenched tight into fists on top of her legs.

"Here." Skyler hands her the journal, and Scarlett's entire body lets out a sigh of relief.

I stare at the journal in her lap, and I get this prickly feeling on the back of my neck. "Wait. You don't think this was our moms, do you? Like, the club and the journal."

Ellie flinches beside me.

Scarlett snorts. "Nah. The notebook paper would have, like, biodegraded by now."

Sky nods. "Plus, our mom never dated anyone named Nick. Did either of your moms?"

Ellie and I shake our heads.

"We have a lot of repeat renters in the summer, long-term ones too. It's probably from one of them," says Scarlett.

"Yeah, sounds like that's definitely what happened. I think we can adjourn now," says Ellie.

We blow out the candles, leaving wisps of smoke rising to the ceiling like wishes.

CHAPTER 20

Scarlett

....

I THROW MY ARMS AROUND REESE'S NECK. "YOU
came!"

He grins. "Of course I did. I can't go a whole summer without seeing you."

"It's only been a couple weeks."

He pulls me closer so his hips are against mine. "It felt like
a lot longer," he whispers in my ear.

"I know. I've been kind of lonely without you."

"Aw. Well, it's a good thing I'm here to rescue you." He
kisses me on my forehead and then my mouth. "Hey, remember how you used to eat lunch in the bathroom?"

I purse my lips. "I don't think that's particularly funny."

"And then I asked you to Winter Formal, and suddenly
everybody started treating you different?"

He twirls me around on the porch, laughing when we
almost fall over. Then his face grows serious. He strokes his
fingers down my scars. "And you haven't given yourself one of
these since you met me."

"Yeah. I guess not." I feel weirdly defensive right now. I try
to shake it off. "Hey, c'mon, I want you to meet everybody."

I grab him by the hand and pull him inside.

"This is Reese!" I tell Aunt Val and Aunt Neely and Amelia Grace as we pass through the kitchen.

"This is Reese!" I tell everyone on the back porch, even though Mama and Skyler already know him.

Reese says hello and shakes hands with everyone, and he's perfect and charming and Southern. He's so good at talking to people, so easy in a way I'll never be. I'm really very lucky to have a guy like him.

"We were just about to eat lunch," I tell him. "But I thought it would be fun if you and I took a picnic basket and rowed out to the little island."

"Yeah, that sounds perfect," he says, grinning.

"Awesome!" I say, which is uncharacteristic of me, both the awesome part and the talking with exclamation points in my voice part.

I go change into my bathing suit and pull on an off-the-shoulder shirt and a pair of shorts. Short-shorts. The kind I really only wear over a bathing suit. I grab the picnic basket I made from the counter.

"Have fun," says Amelia Grace, her brown eyes focused on the cantaloupe she's cubing.

I meet Reese back outside. His eyes travel up my legs and then he realizes all the moms are watching so he tries really hard to look everywhere in the world that is not my legs. I snicker at his misfortune.

"You ready?" I ask.

"Yep." He follows me down to the dock but stops me just before we get in the canoe. We're in a mom-free zone, so he can look all he wants. "You look hot. And beautiful. And hot." He kisses my nose. My mouth.

"Thanks," I say, blushing. Compliments turn me into Sky, I swear. I tug at the ends of my cutoffs. "I don't usually wear shorts this short."

"Well, you should, because you look amazing. And hot. Have I told you how hot you look yet?"

I giggle. "You might have mentioned that."

His fingers trace the seams of my shorts and stray to the exposed skin of my legs. And then to the skin just under my shorts. He moans. "You're killing me. Are you sure you don't want to go for a drive or something after lunch? Or now? We could go now."

"Reese!" I pretend-whack him with the picnic basket.

We get in the boat and paddle out to the tiny island that isn't too far away from the house. I love how small it is, smaller than the house even, with a big rock just perfect for laying out. Sky and I used to pretend to be explorers here when we were little. Reese and I tie up the canoe and clamber up the rock. He helps me lay out the blanket and unpack the snacks. My hands shake a little as I pull a sandwich out of a plastic bag. If it was just me and Sky, I would have taken off my clothes already. We always have our picnics in our bathing suits. That's kind of the point of going all the way to the rock. We'd stuff ourselves with chicken salad and then, when the heat became unbearable, we'd jump into the water to cool off.

It all feels different today. I think about eating my lunch in my clothes. And then I decide that A) that is a bunch of BS, and B) tan lines are my nemesis—it doesn't matter that I slathered myself in sunscreen. And I pull my shirt off. Reese nearly chokes on his ginger ale. Oops.

"Sky and I usually lay out," I hurry to say. "I don't want to get tan lines."

"Yeah, I mean, that's a great idea," he says.

He takes off his shirt too, and I've seen him like that before, but it still throws me off. We eat our lunch, awkward-quiet, Reese racing to finish his sandwich. I see the way he's watching me, and oh, I suddenly get why he's in such a hurry. I pop the other half of my sandwich back in the bag and zip it shut.

"I'm not very hungry," I say. (Truth: I am nervous as all hell, and I don't think I'll be able to eat a bite until after he's gone.)

We put everything back in the basket, and it's like this unspoken thing that we both know exactly what is going to happen next. He lies me down on the blanket and kisses me.

"Winston-Salem's not really the same without you," he says.

"Thanks." I smile. And then, "Seems like you guys are getting by though. Seems like you're hanging out with Carter a lot."

Dude, why do I do this to myself? It's like my mouth has its own separate nervous system and its hobby is to give my brain the double middle finger. Often.

"*Scarlett.*" He's annoyed. I did that.

"You're just on her Instagram a lot is all."

"Because we're *friends*. I'm allowed to have friends. I'm a good guy. You know you don't have to worry about me around other girls."

"Yeah. I know." I wish I could convince my stomach that he's a good guy. Every photo I see of him with Carter feels like a gut punch. Isn't there some saying about trusting your gut? That's probably for regular people with regular guts though. Not damaged people like me. "I'm sorry," I say.

I really am. He's so easy to be with. It's more than I deserve.

He has to be the one, right? When you find someone who's better than you, you're supposed to keep them forever.

"It's okay. I love you." He takes my hand in his. "You're amazing, Scarlett. Don't worry about Carter. Or anything else." His eyes flick to my scars. "I know everything's really hard for you right now with your parents and stuff."

"Yeah, my dad's been calling my mom, and I'm freaking out because—"

"Shhh, you don't have to worry. I'm going to take care of you."

I bristle. I was trying to tell him something. But then I think of the pact I made. I don't need to bring all my damage into this relationship. So instead I say, "Thanks." And I scoot closer to him on the blanket and snuggle my head against him.

He snakes his hand around my back and tugs at the strap of my bathing suit where it's tied around my neck. Pulls the top down around my waist. It makes him catch his breath, which feels like a victory. I don't have a coltish, fitness model body like Ellie or muscles on top of muscles like my sister, but my boobs are pretty gigantic. And Reese has a way of making me feel beautiful. Like I can't contain myself.

"I brought a condom," he whispers.

"Oh."

"We don't have to use it. I just want you to know that we're ready. For whenever you decide you're ready."

"I'm not. Yet," I hurry to add.

"That's okay. I'm pretty excited about these Other Things we were talking about."

He grins and pulls my bathing suit the rest of the way off. We're hidden well enough by the trees that I don't think anyone will see us, but I'm still feeling jumpy. After a few minutes, I forget that I'm nervous, and everything is *Yes, do that* and *Ohmygosh, more of that.* We do not have sex. Still, what we do is enough to make me blush for the. Entire. Time. I guess I'm also blushing because my body wants more, and I don't think it's a good idea for me to want that. Yet. Maybe. I sigh. Why does being close to him scare me so much? Isn't it normal to want to do everything once you've found your person?

And even if I decide I do want to . . . have sex (See? I can't even think it without feeling funny. That can't be a good sign), I have no idea what I'm doing. I thought about talking to Sky. It would be good to get advice or something, or at least to tell her I'm thinking about it. To have someone else in this with me. But I can't. She's too innocent for that kind of stuff, and I don't want her judging me.

Afterward, I put my bathing suit back on, and we jump in the lake because it is HOT AS BALLS this summer. Sometimes his leg will brush against mine, and I feel flushed all over again thinking about what we just did.

When he kisses me goodbye, he whispers, "Today was amazing. I don't want you to feel like I'm rushing things, so just let me know when you're ready. I know a lot of guys would take advantage, but I'm not like them. I'm one of the nice ones. But, like, I still have needs and wants and stuff, so let me know."

I feel like I'm supposed to know.

I wish I knew.

But I just . . . don't.

CHAPTER 21

Amelia Grace

I WATCH SCARLETT AND HER BOYFRIEND WALK down to the dock talking/laughing/touching.

Something clicks inside my brain, a bright, painful falling into place.

Scarlett Kaplan-Gable does not like girls. She likes boys—*this* boy—with the floppy blond hair and the broad shoulders. Seeing them makes it real.

I hate his face.

I hate the way he touched her wrist just now.

I am embarrassed it took me so long to figure it out.

I ask Skyler to pass the chicken salad sandwiches.

I ask her, "So what's the name of that friend you were talking about?"

She nearly drops the entire tray of sandwiches in her lap, she's so excited. We make plans for her to casually-not-casually bump us into each other at the sandbar party on Friday.

I eat my last sandwich triangle in one big bite.

Sometimes you have to stop waiting.

It takes me a second to realize Val's wife, Heidi, is talking to me.

"Hey, Amelia Grace, would you be interested in a part-time gig while you're here? Painting and building bookshelves and stuff? This third trimester is kicking my butt, and I could really use some help getting the house ready for the baby while Val's at work."

"Sure. I'd love that."

"Fantastic. Scarlett mentioned you had a ton of experience doing Habitat for Humanity builds."

I grin. "Power tools are my friend." My gaze is drawn to the lake where Scarlett disappeared with her boyfriend. Then I realize Heidi is still looking at me. "I'm also really into interior design–type stuff too, so if you need any help there, I've watched pretty much every Netflix show about it."

Heidi laughs. "Sounds perfect. Could you come over tomorrow?"

"Definitely."

Heidi smiles at Val, and Val reaches over a bowl of chips to squeeze her hand. For a second, they're in their own world, just the two of them. It makes my heart catch.

My eyes dart to Mama. She's not frowning, didn't even flinch. In fact, she's looking at them the way anyone does when they're happy for their friends. Maybe a summer at this lake house really is what we need.

My phone buzzes. An email from Pastor Chris! I can't open it fast enough. I can't wait to—

Dear Amelia Grace,

I am so disappointed that you won't be one of our junior youth ministers this summer. You know I think you would do a fantastic job. I've prayed on it a lot, and I really feel like God is calling me to defer to the wisdom of the church elders here. I hope you will search your heart because it would be wonderful to have you back in the fall. Please let me know if you ever need someone to talk to.

Love in Christ,
Pastor Chris

So, that's it then.

The church doesn't want me.

God doesn't want me.

Skyler nudges me, but I have no idea what she just said. I shrug, confused, but she grins. "I was just asking if you want to come to Wednesday night church with me tonight."

"Oh. Um, I think I'll stick around here, but thank you."

She frowns. "Are you sure?"

My mom frowns too and tries to pretend like she's not listening, even though CLEARLY SHE IS.

"Yeah. Thanks though."

The thought of going to church right now, any church, is enough to break me. I picture the people there, judging me and turning me away because I don't fit in the way I am. I get up from the table because I feel like she might keep asking and I don't want to talk about it.

"Okay. That's cool." Skyler glances in Mom's direction.

Wait. Have they talked about this? I go inside and put my plate in the sink. Is Skyler, like, in league with my mom or something? I don't know why the thought of it bothers me so much.

"Hey."

Speak of the devil. Mom stacks her plate on top of mine.

And hovers. Conspicuously. Between the crowd of people and the Kaplan-Gable family crisis, I've been pretty good at avoiding her up until now.

"Are you sure you don't want to go to church with Skyler? She seems like a really sweet girl."

Here we go.

"She is. It's just—"

I'm feeling an extreme disconnect from church and God right now.

I didn't even pray before falling asleep last night—haven't prayed in days—which is super weird for me, because I'm normally the poster girl for praying without ceasing. When I'm worried about a friend. Every time an ambulance goes by. Whenever I see a really beautiful sunrise.

I feel like I have to figure some things out, and I feel like a strange church is maybe not the best place to do that. I don't want to be in a place that doesn't want me.

"I don't know," I finally say.

"Well—"

"Hey, have you talked to anyone from church since we've been here?"

Mom looks puzzled. "I've talked with your stepdad."

"I mean, have you tried talking to any of the pastors or anything. About me. I tried emailing Pastor Chris, and he said I can come back in the fall, but it sounded like there could be . . . conditions."

Mom puts her arm around me. "Everyone is really excited to have you back in the fall. But the church elders have made their decision on qualities they're looking for in a junior youth minister." She holds me tighter. Waits for the information to click.

"Oh." But. "Is that what you really think?"

"It doesn't matter what I think. That's what the church thinks. Everybody's allowed to have their own opinion, baby girl."

It's time for me to walk away. You have to protect your heart.

"Amelia Grace, wait," she says.

And then her phone rings. My stepdad. I can tell by the pained look that crosses her face.

"You should probably get that," I say.

She does.

She answers in a voice that is softer and more hesitant. "Hello?"

I turn the corner. Stop to listen.

"I'm sorry I didn't pick up before. Amelia Grace and I were eating lunch, and I just wasn't paying attention."

He says something back, but I can't hear what.

"I know. I'm sorry. I don't want you to worry."

I walk back to the carriage house because I don't want to hear any more.

CHAPTER 22

Skyler

....

AS I OPEN THE DOOR TO THE CARRIAGE HOUSE, I hear my sister asking someone, "Are you okay?"

"I just tried to talk with my mom about the youth minister stuff," says Amelia Grace.

I think about turning around and leaving, but my medicine is in the fridge.

"How did it go?" Scarlett asks.

I listen as I walk up the stairs from the garage, but I don't hear Amelia Grace say anything back. When I get to the top, I see them beside the coffee table, hugging.

It isn't about the way they're hugging. It's about the way they jump apart when they see me see them hugging. Amelia Grace's cheeks are pink. So are my sister's.

"Sorry," I say. "I just came up to get my medicine."

"You're fine. We were just talking," says Amelia Grace. "Actually, I need to go check on something."

She's down the stairs and out the door before I can think of a reply.

"Hey," I say to my sister.

"Hey."

We stand there in the room pretty awkwardly for two people who used to share a uterus.

"I need to talk to you about something." I wasn't going to do this, but between what Ellie said and what I just saw . . .

"Okay."

"Okay, what?"

"Okay, what do you want to talk to me about?"

"Oh, that." I pretend to be very interested in the countertops.

"Sky?"

"Do you like Amelia Grace?" I blurt.

"*What?*"

I shrug.

Scarlett takes a couple seconds to recover the power of speech. "That's ridiculous. I mean, I'm dating Reese."

"Yeah, I know. I guess I just thought—"

She narrows her eyes in that way that makes it impossible to tell anything but the truth. "What?"

"Nothing. I guess I just wanted to make sure is all." I nod. "So, you don't like her." I nod again. "Good."

She raises her eyebrows like I am a weird sort of train wreck she can't puzzle out.

"Well, because that means it's okay if I set her up with my friend Zoe."

Her eyes go wide. "Yeah. Of course. Totally."

She is saying it is fine, but her hands can't seem to stop moving. Adjusting her ponytail. Scratching her elbow. Finding her pockets, and only then finally being still.

"Okay," I say.

"Okay," she says back.

"Well, I guess I'll do it at the party this Friday then."

"Yeah, that sounds brilliant. I mean, go for it."

"Okay."

"Okay."

Scarlett takes a book and a cup of coffee out onto the little deck, and I pull up my messages with Daddy on my phone.

Daddy: I hope you're doing okay. I love you.

I've been doing this for days now. This time, I finally reply.

Skyler: Thanks. Love you too.

My finger hovers over the call button. I lock my phone and put it back in my pocket.

I should try talking to my mom again. Today. Now. Or after I do some research on juvenile arthritis treatments, because it's always good to be prepared before making your case. I get out my tablet. Biologics definitely seem to be the thing right now. I find so many stories about people saying they switched from pills to injectables. I guess what hits me when I'm reading all the posts and watching the videos is that most people had to try more than one thing before finding something that worked for them. The fact that my meds aren't working doesn't mean my joints are irreparably broken.

I feel hopeful. More hopeful than I have in a long time.

And then I read a story about a girl who plays softball just like me. With arthritis. And she makes it work.

And I feel like maybe I could make it work too. I'll just be so chill, and I'll ask about the meds and I won't even tell either of my parents about the softball part, especially not my dad. Not until I can figure out if it's doable.

"What are you doing?" asks a voice from behind me, Scarlett's.

I snap my laptop shut. "Nothing."

"Uh-huh. Looked like you were researching arthritis meds." She crosses her arms. Waits. She's really good at the intense waiting.

Ugh. "So what if I was?"

She frowns at me, more concerned than grumpy. "Your meds aren't working, are they?"

"They're working fine," I say quietly.

I can't look her in the face, and she sighs.

"Skyler, I can tell they're not. I've seen how much trouble you're having lately. Why don't you just tell Mama?"

"It's not that easy."

"I can tell her if you need—"

"No!"

My sister's eyes widen. Great.

"I just need to figure out some things before I talk to her. I want to finish researching other types of meds first."

She does not look convinced.

"It's really important to me that I do this myself," I tell her.

"Okay." She holds up her hands. "I won't tell her."

"Thanks."

I feel like I can finally breathe again.

There's a reason why I have to be careful. A day three years ago. I was thirteen and I was going to fall in love with Jason

Greenly. I remember that seemed like the most important thing in the world, that I fall in love with him.

At the county fair. Just as the lightning bugs start to come out. With balloons and clowns and roller coasters in the background. Maybe we'd be on the Tilt-A-Whirl or eating cotton candy, though probably not both at the same time because I may've still been waiting for my first kiss, but I knew enough to know it probably doesn't happen after someone vomits. Anyway, I'd orchestrated the whole thing flawlessly.

A plan to accidentally-on-purpose run into him at the perfect summer activity? Check.

Confirmation that he would be at said activity after weeks of low-key Instagram stalking? Check.

Falling-in-love hair? Double check.

I scoped out the fairgrounds for Jason and messed up my loose curls (courtesy of my best friend, Paige, and her curling iron), just to make sure they were still properly windswept.

"It's really hot out here," Scarlett said.

"You know what's good when you're hot?" my dad said. "Cheerwine funnel cake."

She wrinkled her nose. "Ew."

My dad just laughed. "Are you sure you're my child?"

He pushed his sunglasses on top of his head, Croakies with his fraternity letters on the sides. So, okay, having my family along was not originally part of my fall-in-love-with-Jason-Greenly plan, but when I asked if I could go to the fair with some friends, Mama and Daddy got all nostalgic like, "Wouldn't it be fun if we went as a family instead?" And I couldn't very well say no.

It'll be fine though. County fairs are made of magic. One

time, my parents took us when we were, like, seven years old. And I convinced my dad to play one of those grabby machines where you never win anything. And he won not one, but TWO sparkly unicorn stuffies that had clearly spent their whole lives subsisting on jelly beans and edible glitter, just waiting to be our best friends.

So, you see? County fairs operate outside the usual laws of the universe. I was basically expecting all the magic of a rom-com, a Disney movie, and an early Taylor Swift song rolled into one. I may not have worked up the courage to talk to Jason at school, but I knew it would all work out. When you're trying to fall in love with someone, double unicorn magic is exactly the kind of magic you need.

My sister let out a long-suffering sigh. "How much longer are we staying?"

"Are you kidding? We haven't even ridden all the rides yet!" I also hadn't seen Jason yet, but I was sure I'd run into him any minute.

"And I'm serious about that Cheerwine funnel cake," Daddy said.

"Oh! Funnel cake stand! Right there!" I pointed with more vigor than was technically necessary and slapped my dad a high five (again with the vigor).

Scarlett crossed her arms and stomped along beside me. *Honestly, how hard is it to be happy when you're about to eat fried dough?*

Dad and I left Mama and Grumpzilla at a picnic table while we waited in line. To pass the time, we had the Great Funnel Cake Debate: Cheerwine vs. Classic. I am Classic all the way.

"There's a ten-minute wait while we make another batch of classic batter. That okay?" asked the woman at the counter.

"Absolutely," I said. And then, because my dad just would not stop snickering at this recent development, I added, "Classic is one hundred percent worth it."

The woman cocked her head to the side as she took our money. This only made my dad laugh harder.

"Hey, thanks for saving my spot," said a voice from behind me.

Jason Greenly slid into the line beside another guy from eighth grade.

"You almost didn't make it in time," said his friend.

Jason. Greenly. Was. In. Line. Behind. Me.

I did not look at him. I prayed my dad would stop laughing. Now-ish.

Dad and I shifted over to the order-up window. Jason ordered his funnel cake—classic. I knew I liked that boy.

My dad leaned toward the funnel cake shack and inhaled deeply. "Do you smell that?"

"Yes," I said.

It was the smell of true love.

Okay, fine, it was the smell of frying batter along with the faintest hint of manure wafting over from the 4-H competition, but from that moment on, I would forever associate the two.

I heard Jason's friend order next, not that I was eavesdropping. He chose a Cheerwine funnel cake, and do you know what that meant? Ding! Ding! Ding! No wait for batter. Which meant he and my dad got their funnel cakes lickety-split, and Jason and I were left waiting at the order-up window. Alone.

Double unicorn magic FTW!!!

I glanced at Jason. Glanced back at the order-up window. Shifted my weight from one foot to the other. Glanced at Jason again. Right. I guess double unicorn magic can only take you so far.

I opened my mouth. It seemed to take 500 percent more effort than usual. "Did you get classic too? Um, funnel cake?" I finally asked.

"Huh? Oh, um, yeah."

He was looking at me. He was looking RIGHT at me. This was happening.

"They said it would be a little while on the batter."

"Oh," he said. He clicked the power button on his phone. Crap, was he checking the time until he could get away from me? "I can't be late for the sheepdog trials. My little sister's hoping for a blue ribbon, and she'll kill me if I miss it."

"Aw, I used to love going to the sheepdog trials. I haven't seen it in forever." Thing no. 141 my sister could not be convinced to do.

Jason smiled. Something about the way his lips curved up at the sides made me think he was the kind of person who believed in little-kid magic too. Or at least who wouldn't laugh at me for it.

Jason's friend was back, grabbing his elbow. "Jason, c'mon, man. We're gonna be late."

"I'm still waiting on my funnel cake," Jason told him. And then added: "His sister's competing too."

"Dude, just leave it. My mom'll kill me if I'm not there."

Jason wrinkled his nose at the order-up window. Glanced over at me, but then quick as could be looked at the ground, so I wondered if he even looked in the first place.

Mama squeezed past in my peripheral vision, and my

sister was right after her, hissing something about how she wanted to go home. I ignored them. If I could just hold on to this moment—

"Hey," Jason said, his eyes lighting up. "Do you—"

Yes. Yes. Whatever it is, the answer was yes.

But before he could ask and before I could answer, my sister started saying, no, *screaming*: "I JUST STARTED MY PERIOD! I'M BLEEDING THROUGH MY SHORTS! I CAN- NOT STAY HERE ANOTHER MINUTE!!!"

Jason's words died in his throat. I could feel myself turning red while I watched Jason and his friend turn even redder. Something about the way he looked at Scarlett and then back at me told me he knew she was my sister. I wished like anything she wasn't.

"Order up!"

The lady behind the counter rang the bell and slid two classic funnel cakes in front of us. Jason took his like a stunned robot, and he and his friend walked away. I opened my mouth to say bye, but nothing came out.

I took my plate back to our table, cheeks still flaming. Mama told Daddy we needed to go.

It was over.

I placated myself with bites of funnel cake as I walked. It didn't taste as good as I remembered, but I would eat until I puked before I shared it with my sister. I've always been okay with the fact that she's cooler and more mature and she needs more of Mama and Daddy's attention. Heck, I purposely tried to balance things out by never needing anything and being super-extra bubbly. But sometimes I needed things too.

It was supposed to be magic that day.

It *was* magic, before my sister got involved. Scarlett walked a little closer and leaned into me. "I'm really glad we're leaving," she said. "This was the worst fucking day."

I looked at her. Really looked. Of course she couldn't see anything outside of herself. "Why do you always have to do this?"

"What?" Her voice was confused, hesitant.

"This is the perfect day. We're at a carnival." I gestured around me, arms flailing wide. "Why is it so hard for you to just be happy?"

I was being mean and really asking at the same time. I didn't understand it.

"Carnivals—" she began, with her I-am-better-than-everything-and-everyone, I-accept-no-personal-responsibility tone.

WRONG. "No, you know what it is? You're a ruiner," I said. And I saw the hurt flash in her eyes, and it felt good, so I said it again. "You ruin things. That's all you're good for."

I walked away because I saw our van. I walked away so I could leave her there. But it didn't take more than a few steps before I wished I could take it back. The anger had evaporated, and in its place was a queasy, shameful thing. I crawled into the backseat and lay across it with my face down so she couldn't see me cry.

Later that night, I woke up thirsty. It happens when I cry a lot. I tiptoed down to the kitchen for a glass of water. The light was already on, and Scarlett stood with her back to me. Maybe she got thirsty like me. I stopped, mapping out an apology in my head. It had to be good because we almost never fought and never like this. While I was thinking, she pulled out an old steak knife. Maybe she was hungry, I thought. That would have been good. This apology would really go a lot better with cheese.

My sister didn't get any cheese. She stayed right where she was and dragged the knife across the inside of her forearm, a couple inches below the elbow.

My mouth opened in a silent gasp. I was just about to lunge at her, pull away the knife, make her stop. She set it down on her own and stared out the window. I couldn't stop staring and I couldn't speak and I couldn't walk away. I started crying. Why would she do this?

You're a ruiner. You ruin things.

I shook my head because I didn't want it to be true, but I knew it was. I did this. There's a reason I have to be the easy, happy, shiny one. And there's a cost when I fail.

CHAPTER 23

Ellie

MOMMA DRIVES US THROUGH THE MIDDLE OF NO-
where to get from the lake house to my tennis tournament in
Charlotte. At least it's a shorter trip from the lake house than
it would have been from DC. There are people who play tennis,
and then there are people who Play Tennis. Being the second
kind means you spend a lot of your weekends driving all over
the place to find people as talented (read: obsessed) as you. We
pull into the parking lot of the athletic club.

I feel different than I usually do at tournaments. They're
not as scary as they used to be. Riley and Autumn and Emily
Rae. I have friends now. Well, a pact to get friends. That's
almost the same thing. Potential friends. Future friends.

So when I see Autumn standing on the sidewalk by her
mom's car, I wave to her. "Hey, Autumn."

"Hey," she says back. She looks smaller without them
standing next to her. She shifts her weight to her other foot
and holds her tennis bag between us protectively.

"Do you want to walk up and get changed?"

"I'm waiting for my *friend*," she says.

Okay, ouch.

I nod awkwardly. Before I can think of a way to respond, Emily Rae arrives.

We walk to the locker room. Autumn and Emily Rae in front. Me by myself. There isn't really room to walk in threes on this sidewalk. I try to walk close enough to Autumn and Emily Rae so I'm part of their conversation.

"Hey, wait up!" a voice calls from behind us. It's Riley.

Okay, perfect. Because now there's four of us, so we'll walk two and two and I won't have to be by myself. I turn to walk with Riley. Only, she's not there. Because the sidewalk has somehow shifted, and now there *is* room for three, and Riley and Emily Rae and Autumn walk squeezed in together, and I follow behind them, alone. Again. I feel like there's something about me that if I'm in a group of people, I'm always the one who gets left out.

The three of them chatter their way to the locker room and drop their bags on a bench.

"So, who do you think's the player to beat from Academy South?" I ask, sliding my bag off my shoulder so I can set it next to theirs. "I think Marjorie is looking—"

Emily Rae cuts me off. "Well, it was really great seeing you." She gives me a huge, toothy smile and squeezes my shoulder. "We're going to get changed now."

"Um, yeah, um, okay." I mumble and move away from them, feeling scolded and scalded. How can someone sound like they're being so nice when they're actually being the meanest?

I feel shaky as I change into my tennis skirt. I feel shaky as I walk to the courts. I don't feel shaky when it's time for my second match and I have to play Emily Rae.

I square up on the court across from her. Feel the weight of my racket in my hands. One more win, and I get to move up to the semis. I am inches away from greatness, and this girl has made it clear she's not my friend.

The match begins. Point for me. Point for Emily Rae.

I pump my legs to sprint after a ball. I just make it and send the ball flying back over the net with a satisfying thwack. Emily Rae misses it.

I'm up. Thirty–fifteen. Forty–fifteen. I send the ball flying. Let's finish this. Or let's hit it directly into the net.

"Crap!" I yell just as Emily Rae yells, "Come on!"

You're really only supposed to yell "Come on" when you do something good, but she's the kind that also yells it when someone screws up. Whatever. I'm not letting her get in my head like that.

Forty–thirty. I wait for her to serve the next ball. I slam it back. I am going to make her eat that last "Come on." I attack the court like if I hit the ball hard enough, run fast enough, it'll erase my mistake.

Emily Rae slices the ball to the back of the court. I shouldn't be able to get it. But I do. I run for it, whipping my racket through the air, sending it whizzing back. The ball jets past her racket. There's no way she can return it. I squint as it hits just inside the line.

Emily Rae holds up the finger signal for out.

"That was in! I freaking saw it!"

The words bubble over before I can stop them. The people on the courts nearest us turn to stare.

You don't do what I just did. Tennis is a sport of ethics and trust, and people have to make their own calls all the time, especially if the refs are short-staffed and it's the earlier matches, and you trust that they're honest. It's what you do.

And I just called Emily Rae Fuhrman a liar.

"Ex*cuse* me?" she says, eyes flashing.

I should back down, apologize. But all I can see in my head is her ferocious smile as she tells me the Southern sunshine equivalent of "Kindly fuck off."

"IT WAS IN." I set my racket on the ground in what I think is a calm way, and it makes a loud noise and bounces into the net. Oops.

Suddenly, *everyone* is staring. At us. No, at me.

I attempt to rein it in. "Can we get a line judge over here?" I ask calmly.

There's nothing he can do about the current call, it's not like tennis has instant replay, but he can watch for her cheating in the future. Which, of course, she doesn't, now that a line judge is watching.

We get through the rest of the match. I advance to the next round because I beat Emily Rae. It's a cold win. Not the glorious explosion of victory you see in a sports movie. But I'm proud of myself for standing up to her.

CHAPTER 24

Amelia Grace

....

"THANKS FOR TRUSTING ME ON THIS," I TELL HEIDI. "I think it's gonna look really great."

"I can't wait to see the finished product," she says. Her stomach growls. Audibly. She laughs. "I'm gonna take that as a sign that I should go make lunch for us. You up for a break in about twenty minutes?"

"Sure thing. I just want to get the doors on these cabinets."

Heidi leaves, and I get back to work. The bookshelves are coming along really well. There's this one wall of the nursery with a big window looking out onto the lake, and I'm putting a built-in bookcase on either side with cabinets for storage and a window seat in the middle with drawers underneath for more storage and an eensy connecting bookshelf in the triangle-shaped span of wall over the window. The whole thing looks like one cohesive piece, and I'm in love with it. I can't wait to show Heidi the fabric options I'm thinking of for the window seat.

I attach the last cabinet door and brush my hands off on my shorts.

"Gorgeous," I say to no one in particular.

I head downstairs for lunch, passing photos of Heidi and Val on the stairwell. I stop in front of a big one of them on their wedding day. They both have on white dresses, but Heidi looks like a wood sprite and Val has on a leather jacket. They're so happy.

I don't think I want to wear a wedding dress when I get married. And then I realize: I've never thought about getting married until today. Being in their house and hanging out with Heidi—it makes me feel different things. I imagine myself in a house like this, in a photo like that. The girl next to me in the photo starts to take shape.

"Hey there."

I jump.

Heidi is standing at the bottom of the stairs, watching me in a way that makes me feel like she's been there for a while. Long enough to see me gazing sappily at their photo.

I blush. "Hey, I was just coming down."

I head past Heidi and into the kitchen.

She looks at me with eyes that make me feel like I can't hide anything (she's definitely going to be a good mom, that one). "Amelia Grace, do you—"

"Want a sandwich? Yes, I'm starving." I grab a plate and take a ludicrously big bite so I don't have to answer any questions.

After I leave Heidi's, I go to the carriage house, and then it's shower/dinner/SBDC. We don't have a full-on meeting, we just play cards for a little bit while we wait for it to be optimal Sneak Out to Parties time. Which is good, because I'm not really ready to tell everyone how badly things are going on the youth minister front. Just being with the three of them makes me feel better though. More hopeful. I'm meeting a girl tonight, I tell myself. Zoe, her name is Zoe, and it's going to be awesome. All I have to do is survive this card game and then sneak out of the house and steal a boat. What could possibly go wrong?

Skyler

I still haven't talked to my mom, yet. I know. *I know.* I was totally going to and I had all the research done and everything, but it feels like it's always the wrong time. Like things are so fragile, and I'll be the one to send the house of cards crashing down.

But then I saw her smiling after dinner, and it was definitely one of her real smiles, not one of her putting-on-a-brave-face smiles, and I feel like tonight is the night. Plus, I'm going to see that boy at the party tonight, and I want to be able to tell him, hey, I'm working on doing a thing that's just for me, and I have something to look forward to now, and by something to look forward to, I definitely mean softball, not you.

I dance into the kitchen, where Scarlett is telling Mama that we're all pretty beat so we're going to turn in early. Perfect! Scarlett knows I want to play softball again, and she can back me up if I need help.

"Hey, Mama, I need to tell you something!" I say brightly.

I'm totally nervous, but whatever, "Fake it till you make it" is a thing.

"Oh, good! You're both here," Mama says, setting down a wine opener. "I need to tell you something too."

Um, well, okay. I was hoping to get it out fast like ripping off a Band-Aid, but she seems like she's in a really good mood, which can only help my situation.

"What is it?" asks Scarlett. Skeptical. Always skeptical.

"Your dad and I have been talking, and he's going to come out tomorrow evening, and we're going to go to dinner and talk."

She's smiling so brightly, and her eyes shine like glass. Maybe that's why she can't seem to see the face my sister is making.

"A date," Scarlett says. "You are going on a date with the man who cheated on you and destroyed this family."

Mama's shine shatters. "Scarlett—"

"No. You know what? I have tried to be supportive, and I have tried to keep it together, but if you're hell-bent on fucking up all of our lives, I can't do this."

"Scarlett Elaine Kaplan-Gable."

"You can quadruple name me all you want—"

"Have a little respect—"

"Not for him!"

"He says he's sorry. He'd do anything to make it right."

"I literally can't even with you!"

I get upset when people yell at each other. Always have. I get upset when I'm trying to say something important and nobody listens. I get upset about a lot of things, but I tamp them all down because I have to be the strong one. I can't let this send Scarlett spiraling.

I put my hand between them like I'm waving a flag. "Scarlett and I are going to the carriage house. We can talk about this later when you've both calmed down."

I wrap my arm around my sister and walk her out of the kitchen. She seems like she wants to yell eighty billion things over her shoulder at Mama, but she mostly complies.

"Skyler, you can let go of me," she says as I pull her across the grass.

"Okay, but if you turn around, I will drag you into the carriage house by your feet."

She doesn't try to turn, but she does do a lot of yelling. "UGH! Can you believe them?!"

"Nope," I say. "Not even a little bit. But we are going to a party tonight and we are going to have fun and you are going to blow off steam and everything is going to be okay."

I'm not totally sure if she's listening to me. She seems pretty transfixed by her phone.

"Scarlett?" I say.

"Let's go to that party."

CHAPTER 25

Ellie

"SHH! YOU'RE BEING TOO LOUD."

"Well, I can't see anything!"

"Ow. That was my foot!"

"Sorry!" Sky whispers.

It was my foot, and honestly, I don't even care. You know why? Because I'm just sneaking out of the house with my new friends to go to a party, no big deal.

"*Y'all!*" hisses Scarlett. I didn't realize that word could have such authority. "We are about to have to slip under the porch where our moms are sitting and drinking wine, and this time we don't have Journey for cover, so I need you to get it together."

We do. We try reallyreallyreally hard. We slide along the house with our backs to it and we don't make a sound.

Our moms' voices carry down to us. My aunt Adeline is telling a story in her loud, Southern drawl. "Skyler came out just fine, but the doctor had to REACH INSIDE ME and pull Scarlett out. Let me tell you how fun that was."

Skyler mimes vomiting into the bushes, and I try not to giggle.

Then, Momma chimes in. Something about second-degree tears and thirty-seven stitches and not letting my dad anywhere near her after, and—

"Ohmygosh, did she just say 'vagina-specific PTSD'?"

It comes out, I can't help it. I clap my hand over my mouth while Scarlett shoots laser beams at me with her eyes.

Sorry, I mouth.

We all stand there, frozen, but luckily the moms don't seem to have heard me. They've moved on to talking about these things that are like maxi pads but they turn cold when you shake them, and OMG PLEASE REMIND ME TO NEVER HAVE CHILDREN EVER.

We tiptoe under the porch, right underneath them. I can tell by the way the other girls are grinning that they feel as badass as I do right now. It's not like Momma never lets me go to parties (when I actually get invited to one), but I definitely have to confirm that there will be a parent there and that there won't be any drinking. Skyler and Scarlett have the same rule, and Amelia Grace's mom is even stricter. So, secrecy.

There's a pretty rough stretch where we have to go right across open grass, and Amelia Grace does a secret agent–style forward roll, but the lights are off at the dock and there are more than enough shadows to hide us. We can't take the real boat, unfortunately—it would make too much noise—but I feel like a lot of CIA operatives use paddleboats in all their most harrowing maneuvers.

We pile into the paddleboat. Quiet as a mouse, stealthy as a dying elephant. Seriously, I thought we were going to tip this thing for a hot second. And then Skyler and I take the foot pedals, and she teaches me how to handle the rudder, and we sail off into the moonlight to a Gatsbyesque floating party.

This is seriously the best night of my life.

Scarlett

I am so angry, I could set things on fire with my mind. Why is she doing this? I get that you don't get to choose if someone cheats on you, but you do get to choose how you respond to it. Ideally, with a rage level that could melt glass.

I resist the urge to kick the paddleboat, mostly because Amelia Grace is sitting next to me and I want her to think I'm a nice person.

Mama came over to the carriage house and tried to talk to me more before we snuck out. She said Daddy'd be staying at an Airbnb in town, but she also said we'd "see how it goes," and just, fuck no. I am not staying here if there's even the slightest possibility that he's staying here, so I told her I'd sleep over at my friend Kayleigh's house so I don't have to see him. She said that was fine, but she looked super wounded about it. Then she asked me if I'd been cutting, and just, fuck all the way off. No, I haven't. Not that you're helping matters.

I get out my phone and text Kayleigh about tomorrow. I should probably text Reese too because tomorrow is our six-month anniversary, and he was going to come out here and we were going to go to Los Lobos, but now I don't know. Also, I have an Instagram update. Carter. And Reese. Having milkshakes at the diner. And they're with a group of people just like last time, but you know what? I don't care. Between that and my parents, it's all too much. Because all I can think is *Carter plays softball and sings in school musicals and is student council treasurer. And she doesn't have any scars. Why would he want someone like me when he could have a girl who floats on clouds?*

Kayleigh texts back that they're not at the lake this weekend, but I can use their spare key and stay in the guest bedroom anyway. I type back, thanks. And then I'm staring at the picture of him and Carter (Really? Do their faces need to be that close together? And who takes selfies with other people's boyfriends anyway?), and I don't know what comes over me, but I dash out a text to him:

Hey, can you pick me up from my friend Kayleigh's house tomorrow? I'll send you the address. It's empty right now, but I'm gonna stay in their guest room so I don't have to see my dad when he comes over.

I hesitate before I type the next line.

And you should spend the night.

Skyler

Sandbar parties make me think of some fantastical world lived entirely on boats and in starlight. The party shines like a beacon even from a long ways out. But as we get closer, it starts to take shape. Boats and people and music and lights and shadowy spaces to fall in and out of love.

Scarlett

I don't get why everyone freaks out over sandbar parties. It's really just a bunch of boats tied together and people drinking PBR while calf-deep in lake water.

Ellie

This sandbar party thing is totally and completely fabulous, and I am taking approximately one million pictures for my Instagram feed, of which I will post maybe two (it's important not to look thirsty). Also, there is no place in the world more perfect for a first kiss. I'm certain of it.

Amelia Grace

It's kind of weird the things rich people do for fun. I mean, the party looks cool, don't get me wrong, but still. Weird.

Skyler

We finally get close enough for someone to reel us in and tie off our paddleboat. Ellie is pinging with excitement beside me. The tricky part is getting from our tiny boat onto a big boat, but some guys pull us up without anyone landing in the water.

The second Ellie is on semi-solid ground, she starts craning her neck in every direction.

"What are you doing?" I ask.

"Looking for you know who."

"Voldemort?"

"No, your boat driver."

"Oh." I feel like I have swallowed a lot of hot chocolate very quickly.

Ellie leans into me. "Do you see him yet?"

I shake my head. "No. Wait, yes! Okay." I whisper to Ellie, "He's standing over there by the giant ice block thing. Look. Don't look! Sorry. I mean, he's right there, but don't look like you're looking."

Ellie whistles. "He certainly isn't lacking in the pulchritude department."

"Shh. What if he hears you?"

"He's not gonna know what it means."

I glance over again. He appears to be drinking from the ice block.

"So, what do you want to do?" I ask. "It's your first sandbar party."

"Um, creepily watch while you hit on your boat-driver man, obviously."

I look again. His face looks so much less tight and guarded tonight. I think about how good it would feel to go over there and talk to him and escape everything that happened with Mama and Scarlett.

"I definitely need to introduce Amelia Grace to my friend Zoe first."

Amelia Grace

I should probably find Skyler so I can find Zoe. But Scarlett was like, "I need a drink. Stat." And she doesn't like beer, so I felt like it was my duty to hop from boat to preppy, white guy–filled boat with her looking for something that wasn't PBR or Corona. We somehow ended up on a dilapidated pontoon boat with three girls wearing ultra-short jean shorts and cowboy hats.

"Hey, y'all!" yells one, hugging me like we're long-lost sisters. "Y'all want a drink?" Drank.

"If you have anything that's not crappy beer, I will give you my firstborn child," says Scarlett.

"We got sweet tea vodka, and we're getting shitcanned!" hollers another girl. She swings the bottle over her head.

Scarlett flashes a wild grin. "Sounds good to me."

They pour her a shot and hold their glasses toward the moon. "To gettin' shitcanned!"

Not drunk/wasted/plastered/tipsy/tanked/sloshed/intoxicated/hammered. Shitcanned.

And I know it's weird, but I feel the biggest flood of relief. I can breathe in a way I couldn't when we were on those blinding-white speedboats with the boys in polos talking about playing golf and getting lit. I am among my people.

Ellie

So far, we're one for three. We have successfully located Sky's boat-driver boy, but we still haven't found Zoe or any boys I might be interested in kissing. I keep an eye out though. Some friends of Skyler's offer us drinks. My stomach tightens at the thought of being the only person not drinking, of people noticing, but the cooler has nonalcoholic options too, and Scarlett's not around to show off for, so I crack open a can of grapefruit LaCroix. Well, technically it's pamplemousse-flavored because that's what it says on the side and that's the French word for "grapefruit." I don't know about you, but it makes me feel at least twice as fancy.

I pull out my phone. Take a sip of my drink. Mmmm, pamplemousse. The best part is how LaCroix fills you up even though there's no calories. Maybe it's the bubbles or something. I know we've only been here for, like, twenty minutes, but I really want to check Insta and see if my floating party post has a gajillion likes yet. 2,044. Not bad!

But then a Discord notification pops up. It's a DM to me and Riley. From Autumn.

"Hey, Sky, I have to take care of a tennis thing. Can I catch up with you in a minute?"

Skyler smiles at me. "Sure."

She heads off toward another boat, and I stop and lean against the railing of this one and pull up my phone again.

Autumn: Hey, I wanted to talk to y'all about Emily Rae.
Riley: What's up?
Autumn: I had kind of a weird thing happen when I was scrimmaging with her the other day. Ellie, what really happened at the tournament?

My first feeling: Ohmygosh, someone else finally sees it too. And Autumn of all people. She's Emily Rae's best friend.

My second: Autumn DMed ME. I feel warm down to my toes. I've always wanted to be part of a private Discord gossip chat. I'm flooded with this weird sort of giddiness as I type my reply.

Ellie: She lifted her finger to say it was out when it was definitely in.
Riley: But everybody can make mistakes like that every now and then.
Autumn: But with Emily Rae, it's more than that. Right, Ellie?
Ellie: I mean, yeah. It just happens too much. And too, like, obviously.
Autumn: So, you agree that she's cheating?

It's hard to come out and say it so strongly, even though I know it's true. But, you know what? Yes. I don't need to be friends with stupid Emily Rae and her stupid lack of integrity.

Ellie: I think she's the biggest effing cheater I've ever played tennis with.

Scarlett

I throw back another shot and decide it would be a good time to check my phone again.

Oh! He's texting. I watch the three little dots at the bottom of my screen. And watch them. Ohmygosh, I have never seen him take this long to send a text in the entire history of our relationship. Is he writing a novel? Finally, a text!

Does this mean what I think it means?

Ha, I think I broke his brain because it took ten minutes of typing to produce that sentence. I snicker into my fist, thinking of him sitting there with his phone, typing and deleting and deleting and typing. But when it's time to text back, I hesitate.

Yes.

He texts me back, again with the long pause.

Three smiley face emojis.

That is it. I mean, they're the kind with the really big grin, but I all but told you I was going to have sex with you, and you can't even reply with actual words?

You're in charge of planning the date, tho, I text.

This time I don't have to wait for a reply.

Already on it. It's going to be perfect.

I smile. I'm doing it. My parents' relationship may be falling apart, but I am making this work. I look up from my phone to see Ellie clambering over the railing. Also stumbling. Oops, and almost falling. I rush over and hold out my arms so she doesn't face-plant. She grabs my wrists.

"Thank you," she says, smiling.

As she lets go, her eyes remain on my forearms for a second too long. Widen in a way I've seen too many times before. I brace myself, but she doesn't ask me how I got them or try to offer any weird advice.

"That could have been bad," she says, before going over and saying hi to Amelia Grace.

It is maybe a little bit possible that I should give her another chance.

Amelia Grace

"How you doing?" I ask Ellie.

Scarlett and our new friends are doing another shot behind me.

Ellie shrugs. "Good, good. I'm, uh—" She glances at her phone, then shoves it in her pocket, fast. Stands up straight. "I'm looking for my first kiss."

"*Really?*" I ask.

She blushes.

"I didn't mean it like that. I just meant. You seem like someone who would have had a first kiss already. I also did not mean that to sound bad." Geez.

"No, you're okay." She smiles. "I've just been really focused on tennis and friends and . . . tennis. You're also not really supposed to go around kissing people if you're Muslim, so there's that too. And there's definitely guys I think are hot, and sometimes it's fun to wonder if today is the day I'll meet someone and that thing that happens for people will happen for me, but for now I'm just happy being me."

"Oh. Well, I think that's really cool."

She grins. "Thanks."

We look out at the lake, bats swooping across the sky every now and again to snatch a mosquito.

"Hey, Amelia Grace?"

"Yeah?"

"Has it ever happened for you? That thing that hits people?"

I watch Scarlett laughing in the moonlight.

"Yes."

Ellie

I have completely lost Skyler. I hop from boat to boat to boat trying to find her. I'm just wading through the water in the middle in case she's hanging out there.

My phone buzzes in my pocket. And then again. And again. I try to focus on searching for Sky, but it. Will. Not. Stop. Vibrating.

I type in my password. I expect the onslaught of pings to be coming from my DM with Autumn and Riley.

But they're all coming from the main tennis server.

Oh, no. Oh, no no no no no.

Someone has screencapped our DM convo and posted it to the General channel.

Autumn: Oh, hai, just wondering how some people can be such sore winners:

Ellie: I think she's the biggest effing cheater I've ever played tennis with.

I click to view the replies.

Autumn: Bitch should know I always get receipts. 🔥 🔥 🔥

Underneath are the screencaps of the rest of our conversation.

Stephanie: WOW. Just wow.

Macy: Holy. Shit.

Holy shit is right. I feel like I can't breathe right now. Autumn is Emily Rae's best friend. I know this. How could I have been so stupid? I keep scrolling. I can't pull myself away.

Emily Rae: I just think teamwork is SO important and seeing comments like these after knowing how hard we've all worked to build team unity is really hurtful and wrong. Thank you so much to everyone who has reached out to me personally. It's been a pretty freaking terrible night, but your messages are the thing getting me through it. I love my academy girls ♥ ♥ ♥

Her post has dozens of likes. Almost everyone at the academy. And then the replies:

Stephanie: We love you so much, Em! I'm so sorry this is happening to you.
Macy: this is so fucked up but we got your back gurl! #strongertogether
Autumn: Emily Rae for President!!!
Riley: Here for you, Em ♥

That's the one that almost breaks me.

Skyler

I find Zoe on my way to find Amelia Grace.

"Hey!"

"Hey!"

We are the kind of friends who squeal when we see each other and hug extra tight.

"You have to come with me to find my friend!" I say.

Zoe shrugs happily. "Okay."

She follows along behind me as we hop from boat to boat. I love how easygoing she is. And how cool she always looks in her sundresses and gray hair (but not old-people gray, the cool kind). Also, she likes science and she's really funny. So she's basically perfect for Amelia Grace, right?

We find her on a rusty pontoon boat at the edge of the

party. A girl in a camo bikini top helps us onto the boat. I run right up to Amelia Grace.

"Hi! This is Zoe!"

I stand there while they blink at each other. I'm sure they'll start falling in love any second now.

"I'm Amelia Grace," says Amelia Grace.

"I'm Zoe," says Zoe. "Oh. I guess she already said that."

"OKAY, I HAVE TO GO FIND ELLIE NOW, BYE," I say.

I am nothing if not stealth.

Amelia Grace

"Well, that was awkward."

The girl I just met, Zoe, does this laugh/blush combo. She has a really beautiful smile. "Yeah," she says. "How do you know Skyler?"

"Oh." How to explain this without telling her all the things? "Our moms are best friends, so we're staying at the lake house with them this summer." There. The low-drama version. "And you go to church with Skyler, right?"

"Synagogue," says Zoe. "Skyler and I do Jewish youth group stuff together in the summer, but I think she goes to a Christian church sometimes too."

"Oh, right." I kind of remember that.

Neither of us says anything for a second. Zoe tucks her hair behind her ears but then pulls it back out and kind of fidgets with it.

"Hey, so, I just got new shoes and my feet are killing me," she says. "Do you, uh, want to go dip our feet in the water?"

She glances up at me, quick like a rabbit. Her cheeks turn pink again.

Ohmygosh, she's nervous. A girl. Is nervous. To be around me. It makes me feel special and interesting and kind of like I might throw up.

"I'd love to," I say.

Scarlett

Amelia Grace is talking to Zoe. Not that I care. I look around, but my sister has already vanished, so I don't even get the pleasure of telling her how much it doesn't bother me.

Why did she even ask my permission anyway? I'm in a relationship. And I'm pretty sure I'm straight.

Zoe and Amelia Grace go to the back of the boat and dangle their legs in the water. I don't know why I'm watching.

They look cute together, like they're supposed to be a couple. Their bodies arc toward each other, even though they're just talking.

I pull out my phone to text Reese again.

Ellie

Do I apologize? Take it all back? Or do I stand by my initial (and entirely true) assertion that Emily Rae is, in fact, a big effing cheater?

I feel sick. I sit and watch as the replies keep coming. I am every academy girl's Friday night. Come one, come all, there's carnage and it's fresh.

I type things and delete them. Type and delete. Nothing I say can fix this.

I can feel my blood pressure rising. And then I see Skyler coming toward me, and it hits me. I have real friends now. Well, one real friend, at least. Why am I doing this to myself?

I type out a response, one that is more concerned with expressing the honest contents of my heart than making people like me, and this time I hit send.

Ellie: Friendship is important. Team unity is important. But so is integrity.

I'm sorry for what I said and how I said it. But I think it's important that we examine ourselves and how we're playing to make sure we're being our very best, in all areas.

My fingers have barely finished moving when the replies start coming in.

Autumn posts a GIF of a garbage truck. On fire.

Autumn: Actual footage of Ellie's apology.
Macy: just when you thought it couldn't get any worse

Stephanie: Nice, nice. Way to double down with your trash-fire apology.
Autumn: Right? Pretty sure real apologies don't contain the word "but."

"Hey!" Skyler is bouncing in front of me. "I don't want to brag, but I think Zoe and Amelia Grace are totally going to fall in love with each other tonight!"

"That's awesome!" I squeal. (Well, attempt to squeal. It's hard to summon a true squeal while you're staring down an internet drag.)

"Right?!" Sky squeals enough for the both of us and gives me an excited hug. Then she blushes. "Sorry. I just really love hugs."

I realize my fake smile is probably not the greatest right now. "Ohmygosh, me too!" I rush to say. "Totally a hugger."

I glance down at my phone again. My post has two likes. Sadia and Heather. And a lot more replies.

Emily Rae: Saying friendship is important after writing what you did is really crazy in this context.
Autumn: You wouldn't know friendship if it bit you in the ass.

Skyler starts acting all fidgety. "Oh! He's here again!"

We've somehow ended up back on the boat with the ice luge where boat-driver boy is the once and future king of all the shots. I watch her watching him. He's stumbling this way.

I think about the messages eating up my phone. They're wrong. I CAN be a good friend.

I gently push Skyler so that she runs into the boat driver.

Skyler

"SKYLER!!!!" Boat Driver yells and spins me around in an almost-hug.

"Hi!" I say when he puts me down. And then, I don't know, there's something about his excitement that unleashes something in me, and I just blurt it out. "Guess what! I'm going to start playing softball again!"

He frowns and cocks his head to the side. Right. I guess I didn't exactly connect the dots for him. I check to make sure his friends are still in the background by the ice thing before I go all, *Remember that offhand thing you said that changed my life?*

"During the Great Canoe Rescue, remember?" I say. "You were talking about how having something to look forward to can get you through?"

The blankness is still in his eyes. Oh, gosh, he has no idea what I'm talking about. I would like to melt through the floor of this boat now. Or apparate. Apparition should really be a thing.

"Shit, I can't even remember two hours ago."

It is then that I realize how much he's slurring his words. And also that he smells like a distillery.

"Oh," I say.

"I'll see you around," I say.

"Wait, Skyler, wait. Don't go." He wraps a sloppy arm around me. "I'm sorry. I'm just like, I'm just like, so crossfaded right now."

A tan boy with bright red highlight things in his hair grabs

Boat Driver by the elbow. "Sorry, I'm just gonna collect him." He says it to me, but he glances at Ellie.

"Wait, noooo." Boat Driver hangs on to me like a sleep-deprived kid.

My sister appears out of nowhere, and I have never been more grateful to see her.

"This party sucks. You wanna go?"

"Yes, please," I say, removing his arm from my person.

"Wait," he slurs. "Where you going? You know what?" he calls after us. "You're so serious all the time. You should smile more."

Scarlett flips him the bird without even turning around.

Sometimes I love my sister so much it's hard to put into words.

CHAPTER 26

Skyler

TODAY, WE BREAKFAST LIKE FRENCH PEOPLE. BRIE and croissants and honey and preserves and fresh berries and café au lait. It makes me feel the absolute fanciest. Scarlett would probably feel fancy too if she wasn't so hungover.

The moms are still inside, so it's just us girls rehashing the party from last night.

Amelia Grace pops another raspberry in her mouth. "Zoe wants to go to Duke, did she tell you that? And she wants to major in physics."

"That's so cool," I say. I already know both of these facts about Zoe, but honestly, it seems to be giving Amelia Grace such joy just to say Zoe's name, and, hi, I'm not going to crush that.

"She's going to be away at some kind of serious science camp for a while, but she said she'd text me when she gets back."

"That's awesome!" Not to brag, but I totally made that happen.

I go to squeeze some honey over my brie, but I can't get it open.

"Hey, Ellie, can you get this for me?"

"Sure!"

She seems really excited to help, and she does it in half a second, which is good because no one notices, but bad because it means it was easy enough that I should have been able to do it myself.

"Ughhhh," says Scarlett.

We all turn to look at her.

"Sorry. My head hates me this morning. Also my stomach." She lays her head down on the table.

Ellie nudges me. "How did things go with your boy? The conversation looked . . . interesting."

"Who are we talking about?" Scarlett is like a wolf that's smelled blood.

"Just a guy," says Ellie.

"The one you flicked off as we were leaving," I add.

"Ew. That guy?" Scarlett tears into him. Viciously. Sometimes I hate how sarcastic she is. And other times she uses it to eviscerate someone who totally deserves it and it's my favorite thing about her.

She pretends to fall off her chair. "I'm sorry. I'm just like, I'm just like, so crossfaded right now." It is honestly a spot-on impression. And it makes me feel at least 50 percent better about thinking that I shared a connection with that loser.

"What's 'crossfaded'?" asks Ellie.

And at that exact second, our moms arrive.

"Crossfaded?" says Mama, pulling up a chair.

"Umm . . ." My eyes go big. Crossfaded is getting drunk and high at the same time, such that you are "crossfaded."

My sister clears her throat. "Crossfaded is kind of

like a mixture of balayage and ombré, such that your hair is crossfaded."

"Oh, that sounds gorgeous," says Heidi, who came over with Val to have brunch with us this morning.

"Yeah, I'll have to ask for it next time I go to the salon," says Mama. "You girls are the best at keeping me up on my style."

We try to hold in our giggles, but Amelia Grace is even worse than me, and she has to play it off by pretending she's having a coughing fit.

"Are you okay?" asks Heidi.

Amelia Grace nods. "Hey, did you show Val the bookshelves yet?"

Val gets all excited. "They are AMAZING. I thought you were just going to assemble some Ikea stuff. I can't believe you built those out of nothing so they'd be just perfect for the room. I feel like there's a word for that."

Amelia Grace grins. "Bespoke."

They chatter on about nursery ideas before Heidi sets down her fork and groans. "I am SO hungry, but then I eat, and it's like there's not enough room for any food because the baby is taking up ALL the space."

"When are you due?" asks Aunt Neely.

Heidi pats her belly. "Four weeks."

"You know Neely used to be a midwife?" says Val.

"I think that's so cool," says Scarlett. Just as Heidi says, "You don't do it anymore?"

"Sometimes I'll act as a doula or a lactation consultant for women at church who need help, but that's about it these days."

Heidi's eyes light up. "Oh, we're still looking for a doula.

And I know there are some ladies on my mom board who need lactation help."

They launch into a discussion about breastfeeding, all of the grown ladies, but also my sister who has seen every episode of *Call the Midwife* at least twice and who asks Aunt Neely if she needs an apprentice. The rest of us take it as our cue to leave as quickly as possible.

I go swimming with Ellie, slow and easy, not pushing. After, my hands are feeling so good that I decide to do some practice pitches against the net my dad set up out back. I do it when the moms go out for lunch at Los Lobos, just to be safe. I don't want them to see me, or worse, for Daddy to see me when he comes for their date. Throwing feels good. I don't need my family. I don't need some new cute boy. I just need me.

I'm still up in my me-and-only-me feelings as I'm walking down to the dock to dip my feet in the water before dinner. I slip off my shoes and pad across the weathered boards in my bare feet. That's when I see it. A rock in the leftmost corner, right where the dock ends and the water begins. I swear it wasn't there yesterday.

There's a blue piece of construction paper underneath folded in half. I pick up the rock. SKYLER, the paper says. So I open it.

Skyler,

I'm really sorry about what happened at the party last night. Well, about what my buddy, Andres, told me about the party last night. I actually don't remember a whole lot. This is probably not helping my case.

Look, I know what you must think of me, but I swear I'm not like that. If you want to give me another chance, there's a party at Nate's house tonight—it's the big blue one off the corner of Horseshoe Island. I promise it won't be like last night, just some people playing pool and stuff.

Please be there?

Bennett

CHAPTER 27

Ellie

I THINK ABOUT CHECKING DISCORD. I KNOW, I know, I said I wouldn't. But I'm out here on the dock all alone with my lunch, and my phone is calling to me. I wonder how many likes Emily Rae's posts have now. I type in my password. Flip to the Discord app.

You know what? I don't need to do this. I take a picture of my avocado on toast and post it to Instagram instead. #healthy eating #goals

There. That's better.

I bite into my twelve-grain toast with avocado spread. Isn't it weird how food just *tastes* better when you know it's so good for you?

I hear footsteps on the dock.

"Whatcha doin'?" Skyler sits down next to me.

"Oh. Um. Just posting my lunch to Instagram."

Her eyes light up. "Oh, is it for your goal?"

My g—? *Right*. That goal. "Um, not exactly." I start blushing, I can't help it. "But that's a good point. I should get started on that."

"Do you need any help?"

"Totally!" I don't actually know what I'm doing, but she looks so happy at the idea of helping that I jump at the chance.

"Cool. So, what do we do?"

Good question. Despite what Scarlett thinks, my Be More Authentic campaign is going to consist of a lot more than no-makeup selfies. Anyway, I already do those.

"I'm not even totally sure yet," I admit. "I've already made some changes. Like, I used to spend all this time on Insta, just looking at photos and thinking about how to do workouts better and eat healthy, but it's hard because fitness bleeds into thinspiration and body goals and then I started looking at all this thigh gap and pro-ana stuff."

"Pro-ana?"

"Pro-anorexia." I note the flash of surprise in Skyler's eyes. Will she still like me after I tell her this? "Not that I was ever anorexic. I wasn't. I don't think. I just felt like I was going down that path, you know? So, a couple years ago I said I'm not allowed to count the calories in my food anymore or track everything I eat in a spreadsheet or even weigh myself. And I unfollowed anyone who talked about stuff like that too. I only let myself look at the stuff that focuses on fitness in a positive way now."

"Wow, that's really amazing that you did that."

"Thank you." I duck my head the way she would. I don't know why I feel so shy about being praised for this. I really am proud of myself. It wasn't an easy thing. "So, I guess now what I want to do is put stuff out there that helps people who are going through the same stuff that I went through. I mostly post stuff about how to eat healthy and get better at tennis—and I definitely do it in a positive way and not a shaming way," I rush to add. "But I still feel like it's not totally honest. It doesn't show how hard it was to go from the girl who weighs herself five times a day to the girl who's trying to look at food in terms of what makes her feel the best for playing tennis."

"Well, maybe that's what you say on social media."

"What do you mean?"

"I think you should tell everyone what you just told me. And we could take a series of pictures to go with it. Like, maybe you smashing a scale with a sledgehammer and you playing tennis and stuff like that. I feel like just being honest can be really powerful. Sometimes I get so caught up in trying to pretend everything is perfect. I feel like it would resonate with a lot of people."

I smile. "That would be really cool."

We sit there for a couple minutes, and then Skyler looks at me slyly. "Can I show you something?" she asks.

She passes me a blue sheet of paper, and I read it. I have but one response:

"We have to steal a boat."

"*WHAT?*" Skyler looks confused. Or scandalized. Probably some of both.

I sigh, like, *This is totally and completely simple, how do you not get it?*

"To see your boy tonight? You are obviously giving him another chance after that letter."

"I didn't say I was going to give him another chance." She tries to make her face hard. It's kind of cute.

"Uh-huh, remind me what his name is again?"

Sky pauses. "Bennett."

And there it is. The tiny smile that steals over her face. She can't even say it without looking totally smitten.

"Yep. That settles it. Definitely stealing a boat. How far away is this Horseshoe Island?"

"Far," says Sky. "We can't just paddle over in the paddleboat. We'd have to take the pontoon boat."

"Okay."

"So, we can't just take a pontoon boat! They are not exactly quiet."

I point at the dock. "What about that other boat? It looks like a James Bond boat."

She shakes her head. "Speedboats are definitely not quiet."

"Okaaay." This was an unexpected hurdle but not unsolvable. "So, we wait. The moms will go to bed eventually and then we'll take a boat."

"I don't know," says Sky.

But I do. Tonight is going to be brilliant.

I'm at least half right. The aunts do go to bed. Well, three of them do. Skyler's mom still isn't back from her date with Skyler's dad yet.

"Do you think your mom's going to shack at your dad's Airbnb tonight?"

"*Ew.*" Skyler makes a face.

"I'm just asking! So I can figure out our plans. Based on the amount of cleavage she was showing, I think we can assume yes."

It takes some (read: A LOT) of prodding, but eventually we're on the pontoon boat and ready to begin our life of crime. Scarlett is on some clandestine date, and Amelia Grace is wiped from building stuff for Heidi and Val, so it's just me and Sky tonight.

My phone vibrates in my pocket, but I ignore it. I don't have to check Discord to know what's happening to me on there right now. And you know what? I don't care. I have a real, live friend right in front of me, and I am going to prove what a great friend I am by helping her steal this boat right now so she can meet up with Bennett and fulfill her destiny.

Skyler

I guide the boat in carefully so I don't bump any of the dozen other boats that are tied off outside the party house. It hurts, but I manage.

"Are you feeling okay?" asks Ellie.

"What? Yeah, I'm fine," I reply automatically.

"Okay. Just checking." She gives me the kindest smile.

I feel warm all over. It occurs to me that "Are you okay?" is a thing people always ask my sister. It feels good to have the focus on me for a second.

There's no room to tie off at the dock, so we have to tie off to another boat, which means blocking that boat in, but there are a lot of boats blocked in tonight. I can always move it later.

This lake house is huge—four stories and four porches, each filled with people with cups in their hands. We'll see just how different this party is.

The instant we walk in, Bennett spots me and stops what he's doing. It makes me feel important.

"Skyler!" he calls across the room, tripping over an

ottoman to get to me. Trouble standing already? "Hey!" he says, with a goofy grin. "I'm so glad you're here. We were just about to play Don't Blink."

"Is that a drinking game?" It's not that I'm anti-drinking or something. We totally drink wine at Seder and when we do Shabbat dinner and stuff, and sometimes I even drink at parties, but I really didn't like the Bennett I met at the sandbar party. I just know I'm not meant to date a frat-star douchebag in training, you know?

"What? No. It's like Werewolf."

Ellie and I stare at him blankly.

"Oh. Um, Mafia? Assassin? Cops and Revolutionaries?"

Still nothing.

"Capture the flag. Have you heard of that one?"

"Ohhhh," we say in unison.

He looks relieved. "Yeah, it's just like a really fun group game for parties and stuff."

I look around this "party" in a new light. No keg. No ice luge. A couple of guys doing a dramatic reenactment that involves repurposing throw blankets as capes. A girl sitting cross-legged on the floor reading a book. There's a guy in the corner drinking from a wineglass, but he is definitely wearing a beret.

My eyes light up. "Ohmygosh, this is a nerd party."

Oops, I just said that out loud.

Ellie choke-coughs. "I'm just gonna go get something to drink," she says, leaving us alone.

(Sometimes it's hard to watch people crash and burn that spectacularly.)

"I think you just called me a nerd." Bennett smiles, and I try to remember to think straight.

"Oh, I definitely did. You are a nerd, and this is a nerd party." I look around the room again, bouncing in place a little, because I'm so pleased.

He cocks his head to the side. "And that's . . . a good thing."

I grin. "Definitely a good thing."

If he says he reads fantasy, that's it. It's over. I am kissing him and I am never coming up for air.

We're only talking for about a minute when Ellie comes at me with wide eyes and a hand cupped over her phone.

"Your mom is home, and Momma put her on the phone because you're not answering yours, and she wants to talk to you."

Not where I saw this evening going.

I put the phone up to my ear. "Hey, Mama."

"Where in the damn hell are you?"

I pull the phone back from my ear a bit. "Ellie and I just took the boat out for a moonlight cruise. Did you have a good date with Daddy?"

"That is not what we're talking about right now. I can't believe you took the boat without asking. We were worried sick. You better get your ass back home in the next ten minutes or I'll— Wait, have you been drinking? Don't come if you've been drinking. I can pick you up. Well, I can't, but your aunt Seema can."

I roll my eyes. So it was a good date. I know I should be as panicked as Ellie right now, and a part of me is, but honestly, we're not doing anything really bad right now (other than grand theft pontoon boat), and I'm kind of used to Mama being lax about curfews and stuff for me since I'm the good one. "I'm sorry I didn't ask first, but, well, the truth is I really wanted to go to this party. There's no drinking. We're about to play a capture-the-flag kind of game. Is it okay if I stay? It sounds kind of fun."

Bennett smirks at me, and I roll my eyes.

"Um, no. No, you cannot stay. People who sneak out of the house like cat burglars do not get to stay at parties."

"Oh. Um, okay."

Bennett's face falls, and I realize this is the least stressed-out I've felt since I found out about Daddy. I need this.

"You know what? There's, um, a really big boat blocking us in. Two big boats. And, uh, I don't think we'll be able to leave for a good while."

Ellie's eyes go, if possible, even wider. I hold my breath. Wait for what's next.

"Skyler?" Mama says icily.

"Yes, ma'am?"

"You get home as soon as you can."

Ellie leaps into the air. "HOLY TACTICAL NEGOTIA-TION SKILLS! Wait. Did you definitely hang up the phone?"

I nod.

"HOLY TACTICAL NEGOTIATION SKILLS! That was the best thing I've ever seen. You are a golden goddess of covert ops, do you know that? You should be a spy. Or a fashion buyer."

"Thank you." I hand back her phone and do a little curtsy.

"All right, it's time to play some Don't Blink!" yells Bennett.

People start to gather. Apparently, that's a thing that happens when Bennett yells.

"Okay, so! There's Runners and there's Statues. The Runners start in the kitchen, the Statues go hide. If your room is dark, you can tag a Runner and freeze them. But if a Runner turns on the light, the Statues freeze until they're alone again. Statues stay frozen if The Doctor tags you with his glowstick."

"Hey, now!" yells somebody in back.

Bennett explains the rest of the rules, and then he explains them two more times because there are so many questions.

"It's really easy once you get the hang of it, I promise. Okay, if I tap your shoulder, you're a Runner. Everyone else is a Statue. Except Nate." He hands the boy from the kitchen a glowstick. "You're The Doctor."

"Allons-y!" yells Nate.

Bennett taps Ellie's shoulder and then mine.

A pretty girl and the boy with the beret run up the stairs panting. "We turned off. All the lights."

"Excellent." Bennett waits for the Runners, including Ellie and me, to get to the kitchen. Then he flips off the living room lights. "Let the games begin!"

Ellie leans into me. "Do you actually know what you're doing?"

"No. Do you?"

"Nope." She grabs my arm. "Don't leave me."

At first, I just think she's being funny, but it's actually pretty scary walking around a house in the dark. The living room lights get flipped pretty quickly, but it's empty. The Runners split up from there. Upstairs, back deck, bedrooms. Ellie and I follow a guy and a girl down the stairs to another living room (honestly, how many of those do you need?).

"Split up and find the lights," the girl whispers.

Ellie and I veer left along the wall, feeling our way in the darkness. I feel like I can hear someone breathing, so I creep faster. Who puts light switches so far away from the—?

"Ahhhhh!!!!!" Ellie screams next to me, and my fingers find a light switch, and I am never going to be able to sleep again.

The room floods with light. There's a boy standing next to her, his hand comically frozen on her shoulder.

"Are you a Statue?" she asks.

He nods and removes his hand, but other than that, remains frozen. There's another Statue in the corner, near the curtains.

"Troy, we need you!" calls a voice from upstairs. The Runner Boy (Troy, apparently) bounds back up the stairs two at a time.

"I'll stay here so they can't turn off the lights," the girl calls after him.

She gestures at Statue Boys 1 and 2. Right. And Ellie is stuck here too, which means I get to go down to the bottom floor. Alone. In the dark. What kind of sadistic horror movie fanatic thought of this game?

I make my way over to the last set of stairs. They creak, because of course they do.

The bottom floor is darkest of all. I can make out a pool table and some easy chairs and, oh, holy shit, those are footsteps and they are coming my way. I run toward the other wall, because I clearly picked the wrong side, and my heart is pounding out of my chest, and I flip the switch just in time. A girl with curly brown hair skids to a stop in front of me.

Whew.

She's the only one down here, but I guess I should check the bedrooms too. I go to the back of the den and open the first door. Oh, it's not a bedroom, it's just the laundry room. And it's empty. I step inside so I can pull the light cord just in case when two hands grab me from behind.

"Fudgesicle Ripple!"

The person behind me laughs. "Did you just say 'Fudgesicle Ripple'?"

Bennett. My pulse races for reasons that have nothing to do with being scared.

"What? No. I'm pretty sure you're hearing things."

"Shhh," he whispers. "You'll give away my hiding spot."

"Yeah, well, you deserve it," I whisper back. Turns out whispering can feel incredibly sexy.

I take a step closer and poke him in the chest. "This game feels like being in a horror movie."

"Now that you mention it, I have a confession to make. Do you want to know what I am?" His eyes twinkle mischievously.

"Oh, for sure."

"Say it. Out loud."

Wait. Is he . . . ?

"Say it!"

Oh em gee, he totally is.

I match his seriousness. "Vampire."

"Are you afraid?" He makes a brooding face that is the exact right mix of wannabe-sexy and constipated.

"Only of how much I hate glitter."

He bursts out laughing. "Oh, man, I was doing such a good job of keeping a straight face."

He looks suddenly serious. Real serious. Not the pretend-vampire kind.

"I'm really glad you came. I, uh, didn't think you would."

I smile at him, then stop. "Hey, what was going on yesterday at the sandbar party? It's not that I'm against drinking, but like—"

"I'm really sorry about that." He picks at his fingernails. "I, uh, got off the wait list and into art school that night."

"Are you serious? That's amazing."

"Thanks." His smile should really look happier. "It would be, except that my dad told me he's not going to pay for it, and then I told him I was going anyway, and it got . . . bad. I guess I just needed to blow off some steam, but apparently the ice luge is not my friend."

"Oh, Bennett, I'm really sorry."

"Me too." He tries to shake it off. "But, it's fine. I'm still going to go, and it's still going to be great. But, yeah. He's pretty unsupportive. That's why I was out on the lake the day we met, so at least something good came out of it. I'm mostly sorry about what happened at the party though. With you."

There's a pause. Not awkward, but not exactly comfortable either. There's too much electricity in the air for that.

He shifts his weight to his other foot, and when he does, his shoulder bumps the door slightly and it closes an inch. We both stare at it for longer than is normal or wise, wishing it would just swing shut all the way.

"Well, I'm glad I'm getting to know the real you," I say.

"Wait, how do you know Sandbar Me isn't the real me?"

I cross my arms. "I much prefer the vampire version."

And then I do it. I slide my foot over so the door shuts a little more.

His eyes go wide, but he tries to play it off. "You do, huh?"

"Mmm-hmmm."

His chest is rising and falling so quickly, and I see a muscle tighten in his jaw, and then his shoulder bumps the door again. This time, on purpose.

I feel like I'm not me right now. I'm an entirely different girl who is powerful. And sexy. And brave.

A girl who deserves an escape. I smile at Bennett as I put my entire palm to the door. And then I push it closed.

The laundry room goes entirely dark, but Bennett has no trouble finding me. His hands push me and my hands pull him against the door (the door that is STAYING EFFING CLOSED), and his lips are on my neck and my collarbone, kissing fire all over my skin. And I grab his face and pull it to mine, and oh. I didn't know kissing could be like this. Feeling full and like you'll never get enough at exactly the same time. And our clothes are on, and I'm thinking how much fun it would be if they were off, but also, this kissing. I think it could sustain me for the rest of my days, and maybe our clothes could just stay on as long as our lips never have to—

"SKYLER KAPLAN-GABLE AND ELLIE JOHNSON."

Is that . . . my mom?

I pull away from Bennett. He looks every bit as confused as I do.

"Hold on," I say.

I rush toward the back deck.

What is happening right now?

I hear it again, like the voice of God, except this time it's Aunt Seema.

"WE KNOW YOU'RE IN THERE. COME OUT NOW."

I throw open the door. My mom stands next to Ellie's mom on the back of the speedboat. And they have a bullhorn. This is mortification at its most extreme.

Aunt Seema hands the bullhorn back to Mama.

"WE'RE HERE TO COLLECT YOU SINCE YOU'RE BLOCKED IN. OH, LOOK, THE BOAT ISN'T BLOCKED IN ANYMORE." She pauses dramatically. "GUESS YOU CAN DRIVE HOME NOW."

Passes the bullhorn to Aunt Seema.

"WE ARE GOING TO KEEP TALKING UNTIL YOU COME DOWN HERE, *JAMEELAH ROSE JOHNSON AND SKYLER KAPLAN-GABLE*, SO I SUGGEST YOU HURRY."

I run back inside. Scurry past Bennett. "Gotta go. Sorry!"

"ADELINE, DON'T YOU HAVE A JOURNEY CD ON THIS BOAT SOMEWHERE?"

I run faster.

Ellie is right in front of me, scrambling down the stairs to the dock.

"What in the world is happening right now?" she asks breathlessly.

"They've come for us."

Because she's half turned around, she almost barrels over a lanky boy with slicked-back hair the color of red lipstick. He starts to say something to her, but we're kind of busy, so she doesn't notice.

We tear down the dock, waving our arms.

"Stop! Holy crap. Please, stop!"

Aunt Seema clicks the bullhorn off and holds it at her side.

"Follow us home," says Mama. "We'll talk about this there."

I knew the lecturing would get really bad after they separated us. Not that it wasn't bad before they separated us. But now that my mama has me alone in her bedroom, she breaks down crying.

"How could you do this to me?" She flings the words from where she's lying on the bed, broken.

"Mama, I know it was wrong to take the boat without asking, but we didn't even do anything bad. It was a nerd party with games and stuff. I didn't even drink anything."

"It's not about that." Again with the flinging of the words. She's just so wounded and I don't get it.

"What's it about, then?"

"You lied to me."

I wait and let the words sink in. Scarlett's been caught lying about a million times. About things that are actually a big deal. I don't understand—

"I just found out the person I built my entire life with has been lying to me," she says, like it costs her dearly to explain it. "I can't handle anyone else I love being dishonest with me right now. Especially not someone I trusted as much as you."

Oh. Oh, I get it now, and it hurts, this newfound understanding.

I feel guilty and awful and a little bit sick.

And the worst part? This isn't the most important thing I'm lying to her about. Not by a long shot.

CHAPTER 28

Scarlett

REESE PICKS ME UP AT THE FRONT DOOR OF KAY-leigh's house. It's just across the lake from mine. He's holding a bouquet of pink and yellow roses that almost cover his face, but between the flowers I can see his smile is a little shy. It would be sweet—*is* sweet—but all I can think about is Daddy maybe showing up with roses and Mama maybe acting like it makes a damn bit of difference.

"Hey, beautiful. I brought you something." He passes me the bouquet and kisses me on the cheek.

"It was so sweet of you to bring me flowers." I bury my face in the roses and sniff till I'm dizzy in hopes that it'll help me forget. "I love them."

He takes me to Los Lobos, which is normally my favorite lake restaurant. Reese devours his blackened shrimp tacos. I pick at my enchiladas.

"Is your food okay?" asks Reese.

"Yeah, it's great. I just ate a gigantic lunch," I lie. *Should I really feel this nervous?*

He strokes one of my legs under the table. "You look so hot

tonight. It's been killing me watching you, knowing we get to be alone all night."

I laugh nervously.

"Are we—? I mean, are we definitely—?"

He can't finish the sentence, and despite what I texted him, I'm unsure. "Maybe."

I smile—coyly, I hope. Reese shifts around his chair like he is physically incapable of holding still.

I'm feeling less bold by the time we leave the restaurant. Every time I start to calm down, Reese does something like touch my hand or stare at my legs and another adrenaline rush shoots up through me like a solar flare. Should I really feel this nervous if this is the right thing to do? There's this part of me that always wants to hold something back from him, but I tell myself my hesitation is all me. Sex is normal. It's something happy, normal people do.

Before I know it, he's pulling into Kayleigh's driveway, and we're getting out of the car, and I have no idea what happened to the last twenty minutes. Reese, on the other hand, seems more excited with each passing second.

And then we're walking down the hallway to Kayleigh's guest bedroom, and he's shutting the door behind us.

"Um, so this is Kayleigh's guest room. My house is just—"

He kisses me mid-sentence. "I love you," he says. "You're the best girl ever, you know that?" He pulls me into his arms. "I can't believe this is really happening." He groans. "You're so hot. That *dress*."

He takes a step back so he can see me better, his eyes undressing me before his hands do. He pulls off my dress, and when he sees the pink lace bra underneath, he groans again. And then it's almost like he's waking up from a dream.

"Hold on a sec." He rushes over to where I set the roses on the dresser, pulling the petals from two of them and scattering them over the bed. "There. What do you think?"

"Um." I know he's speaking English, but my brain feels so sluggish. "Yeah, it's great."

He smiles. "I know you want tonight to be special. And it will be."

"Okay," I whisper. I wonder if he can hear how fast my heart is beating.

He kisses me, his lips warm and soft against mine. I'm already jittery, and the kiss makes my head spin.

Through the window, I can see lights winking at us across the lake. I think of my parents, and my hands automatically clench into fists. I pull Reese tightly against me. And then everything starts to happen so fast. Our clothes are coming off, and we're on the bed, and I can barely concentrate on what's happening with all the nervousness and excitement. I try to focus on Reese's body, which isn't hard because he's really freaking hot and I'm really freaking attracted to him. If I can pretend like all we're going to do is fool around, I can enjoy myself.

I want this, I tell myself. I want to stop being the damaged girl everyone worries over and be the kind of girl who has sex with her boyfriend and has everything turn out perfect and wonderful. If we do this, things will feel right. For one night, I just want to feel like Carter or one of the other shiny girls at school.

But we're in a car without brakes, hurtling toward an

232

unknown destination. And when we finally reach it, everything comes to a screeching halt.

It hurts a little, but I was expecting that. I wasn't expecting everything else. I feel too much emotion. Everything is entirely too much. Sometimes in a good way, sometimes in a bad way, but always overwhelming. By the time it's over, there are tears streaming down my cheeks.

"Scarlett, what's the matter?"

"I'm fine," I rush to say. "Sex is just a really emotional thing, you know?"

I feel like if I tell him everything—that I'm worried this doesn't actually change anything about me or us and I'm scared I did this for the wrong reasons but also there were parts of it I kind of liked and that made me feel powerful or something—he won't understand.

"Of course it is." He's saying it in this soothing voice, but I saw that flash of a look on his face. He gently wipes my tears with his thumb. "I love you so much."

"I love you too," I say, a fresh bunch of tears building.

"I'm gonna take care of you. I've got this."

Reese calms me down. Strokes my hair and whispers how much he loves me. Time passes, I don't know how much, and he falls asleep, and it's safe to start crying all over again. How can he look so calm when I think I might explode?

In the morning, Reese and I kiss goodbye. I think we are different people now. No, we've always been different, but now I see it, because otherwise why would he be able to smile like a Cheshire cat when I feel like everything inside me is broken. I wanted this. A part of me definitely did. But it didn't make me feel the way I thought it would, and I'm mad at myself for thinking any different. I'm still me. I'm just a me who's had sex.

I do not stay for breakfast. I drive to the lake alone.

My dad's car isn't out front, so I figure it's safe to go inside. I climb the steps to my mom's bedroom. She's sitting up in bed, reading a book, and she looks really actually happy. Dad's side of the bed is still made up, show pillows and everything.

Mama sees me. "Hey, sweetie." Her smile falters. "Are you okay?"

It was supposed to make things right.

"I'm sorry I yelled at you before," I whisper.

That's all I have to say to make the tears start falling again.

She waves me over, a tiny gesture that completely undoes me. And I crawl into the bed with her and snuggle underneath her arm like I'm eight years old again and I sob like she can make it all better.

Skyler

THERE IS BROKEN GLASS INSIDE OF MY KNUCKLES. That is the only possible explanation. Because the pain wakes me up, and my hands are gnarled like claws, and I can't do anything, can't get out of bed even. I am lying here, and I am crying, and I am thinking that I am so lucky that I have a sister who is going to bring me handwarmer pads any minute now.

And then I realize. Scarlett isn't here. She's on a secret anniversary date with her boyfriend. A second, far worse, realization: The handwarmers aren't coming.

I think about giving up. The pain is like a pulling and a twisting and a metal rod prying my hands apart at the joints.

I try to pull down my blanket.

I wonder if it would be better to be dead.

"Oh please, oh please, oh please." Hot tears down my face. A voice that isn't my own.

What if I don't survive this? I feel like this could really possibly be the end of me.

"Sky, are you okay?"

A sheet of brown hair sweeps through my peripheral vision. Ellie. Oh, thank goodness.

"Can you get me my heating pads?" I say through clenched teeth. "They're in my duffel bag. No. The other zipper. The front one."

Ellie digs around until she finds them. Every word costs me.

"What now?" she says. Calmly, but I can tell she's freaking out.

"Microwave for two minutes."

She runs, doesn't walk. I hear the microwave whirring. Help is coming. Just hold on.

It beeps, and she's back in an instant.

"Put them on my hands. Please," I add.

The heat is instantaneous. The relief takes time. I try not to hiss or whimper. This is already so embarrassing. I can't stop the tears though. It's like they're leaking out of me, 100 percent out of my control.

After about half an hour, it occurs to me that Ellie is sitting in bed with me stroking my hair. I finally feel good enough to sit up.

"How are you feeling?" she asks.

"Better," I say, even though the pain is definitely still a six at least. "Thank you for helping me."

"Of course," she says. "What's, um, the matter? If it's okay to ask," she rushes to add.

And she's looking at me so intently, like nothing in her world matters more than this. I feel like we've reached the point where I can tell her, even before she had to help me, I mean. "I have juvenile arthritis," I say. "Scarlett usually puts heating pads on my hands before I even wake up in the morning."

Something clicks behind Ellie's eyes. "But Scarlett's not here."

"Yeah."

"Gosh, I never even noticed her doing that."

"I think she was tucking them under the covers. I can't believe you saw it when it was that bad. It's so embarrassing."

"No." Ellie says it with a firmness that both startles and comforts me. "It's not embarrassing at all. It's totally okay, and I'm happy to do it anytime."

And I'm grateful for her, I really am, but I can't live like this. I'm telling my mama today.

Ellie

I think I'm finally understanding what this friendship stuff is all about.

Skyler

I head to the main house, strong, resolute. Mama is in the kitchen, crying to my aunt Val. But she's always crying. I've been waiting and waiting, and there is never a good time. I might as well walk through the door and tell her anyway.

"I feel like I'm drowning. With my marriage and worrying about the girls and Scarlett's issues and Skyler's arthritis."

I stop outside the doorway where she can't see.

"Jimmy was a good partner in a lot of ways. Well, before. But watching her suffer after that game was one of the worst days of my life and one of the lowest points in our marriage. He can't handle the hard stuff. And it makes me wonder if he's really the right person for me if he could handle something so important so badly."

Aunt Val is saying something back, but I'm already on my way out of the house. So, that's it then. Telling her is not an option. It could very well be the thing that keeps my parents from getting back together. I can't go the rest of my life with that kind of guilt hanging over me. I already have enough.

But based on how bad the pain was this morning, there is one thing I am certain of: I am going to the doctor. This week. Tomorrow. And I'll do it my own damn self if I have to.

I look all over the lake house until I find Ellie.

"I need your help with something," I tell her.

CHAPTER 30

Amelia Grace

I'M ONLY HALF LISTENING AS ELLIE CALLS OUR MEET-
ing to order because my phone vibrates with an email
from Zoe. She's having fun at camp, and how are things
going here?

"What are you looking at?" Scarlett bumps me with her
elbow, and I hide my phone screen, quick. I don't know why I
don't want her to see Zoe's email.

"I'll go first!" says Ellie. "Sky helped me with the post on
Instagram of me smashing a scale, and I'm feeling deeply
proud of myself."

She snatches an olive out of the bowl on the table and
tosses it into her mouth. We huddle around her phone. "I'm
tired of letting my worth be defined by a number," Ellie reads.
"A scale is just a thing. It shouldn't have that much power over
my life. A couple years ago I decided I wasn't going to weigh
myself anymore. It hasn't been easy. But today I'm slaying
my dragons."

I have chill bumps, and I squeeze her shoulder, and she
and Sky tell us all about how they made the post. Scarlett tells

Ellie she thinks the post was "really brave" and Ellie blushes to the roots of her hair. Then she catches my eye from across the circle. "How about you?"

"Things didn't go very well with my youth minister," I say quietly. "I think I need to do some research and Bible reading and soul searching before I try talking to anyone else." I haven't even touched my Bible since we got here.

Skyler's face lights up. "Oh! You can come to church with me on Wednesday if you want!"

"Um, I'm okay. Thanks."

I may be ready to read my Bible, but that doesn't mean I'm ready to face people like Mrs. Bellcamp.

Her face crumples. "Why not?"

"Skyler," hisses Scarlett. "Why are you being like this?"

"Things aren't great with me and church right now," I say. "Because of how people responded when I came out. I heard back from my youth minister, and it seems like the only way they'll let me back is if I don't like girls."

Ellie scoots closer, holding my hand.

"Bullshit," says Scarlett. "You're not actually thinking about it, are you?"

"No. But, like. I feel so unwelcome there, and that's why I need to think about things more before I try going to another church."

I can see it click in Skyler's mind, and her eyes open wide. "I'm so sorry. Your mom said you loved church and were really going to miss it while you were here and that I should invite you, and I was only trying to help. I'm really sorry. I promise I would never try to push my religion on people."

She means it. I can tell.

"It's okay," I say.

"Also, I thought you were Jewish," says Ellie.

"I am. I go to youth group stuff and High Holidays at my synagogue, and sometimes I go to church. Plus, I have Lake Church and Home Church. So, like, there's four of them."

"And you . . . ?" Ellie says to Scarlett.

She shakes her head. "I'm agnostic. Sky goes to enough church for the both of us."

"That's really nice that your family is cool with you being different that way," says Ellie. "I go to our masjid—mosque—at home, but I'm not sure if there are any around here."

"Oh, if you end up finding one, I'll go with you," says Skyler.

Scarlett touches Ellie's shoulder. "Don't let her steal your religion. She collects them."

"I don't know what you're talking about. Just because I'm interested—"

"Pretty sure it's cultural appropriation."

"Wait. Is it? I'm really sorry."

Scarlett snorts. "I swear half the reason you dated Jonah is because he's Buddhist."

"Buddhism is awesome! Someday I might raise my kids Buddhist!"

"You are only proving my point." Scarlett crosses her arms. "Also, what did you need help with?"

"Huh?"

"The whole reason I'm here is because you and Ellie have some sort of secret plan afoot, and I'm nosy as hell. Spill."

I force myself to pay attention because these are my friends and this stuff is important to them, but what I'm thinking is that Scarlett hasn't gone yet. She's going to talk about her big date. I can't decide what's worse: hearing about it or wondering about it.

"Oh," says Skyler. "I need you to call my doctor and pretend to be Mama."

Scarlett almost spits her wine across the room. "What?"

"I need to see Dr. Levy, and every time I try to ask Mama, she's so stressed out, so I figured I could just go myself. It's no big deal."

Scarlett's lips purse in a way that suggests it is, in fact, a very big deal. Based on how squirrelly Skyler looks, I'm inclined to agree. But Scarlett simply says, "Okay."

"Okay?!"

"I'll do it."

"Thank you!" Sky hugs her, and she looks pleased and a touch embarrassed by the public display of sisterly affection.

"Also, it's your turn to share," says Skyler.

Scarlett makes a face. "Um, pass?"

"No passing!" yells Ellie.

"We're here for you," I say.

Scarlett nods, and her tough girl persona falls away. I feel like I can't breathe.

"Something happened with Reese, and I'm still trying to figure it out. Is it okay if I talk about it next time?"

"Of course," Ellie rushes to say. "You tell us whenever you're ready."

I can't shake the feeling I've dodged a bullet.

CHAPTER 31

Ellie

THE SMASHING THE SCALE POST I MADE WITH SKY
has more likes than any of my other Instagram posts ever. By
double. And the comments. I can't believe how many people
are connecting with what I wrote.

Love this post!

Thank you for sharing this!

Wow, this is really powerful and inspiring.

😍😍😍😍😍

And yes, I am a teenage girl on Instagram, and I wore workout pants and a tank top in the post, so I'm getting the usual
creepers and mouth-breathers with their "Hey ur hot," and
"How old are you? You seem like an old soul. DM me." But for
every one of them, there are five girls telling me: "I went through
the same thing." And "Your post made me realize that I need
to work on my relationship with my body." And "I smashed my
scale today too, and I'm not getting another. Thank you."

I'm working on another post now, one about tennis. Sky
just took a billion shots of me playing so we could get the perfect picture. She scrolls through them while we sit on the dock
and eat nectarines.

"What do you think of this one?" She pushes her phone in front of me.

I'm right in the middle of a serve, and every muscle in my body is flexed, and there's a look of pure determination on my face. It's #strongisbeautiful if I've ever seen it.

"It's amazing," I say.

But my face must be giving me away because Skyler frowns. "What's wrong?"

"I'm worried about the posts. I mean, it's not like people don't post stuff like this. There were definitely people like that who were inspiring for me when the recovery was the hardest. But."

Sky doesn't say anything. Just waits till I'm ready. I love that she does that.

"But I guess I feel like, did I really have anorexia? Because I'm not sure I did. And then, do I really deserve to be making inspirational recovery posts or is it fake?" It's easy to pretend about cold eggs or doing yoga on top of a cliff, but these are my very most vulnerable and important parts. If someone doesn't like them, it means something.

"Hey, of course it's not fake. If it's your real story, it doesn't matter that it's not exactly the same story someone else had."

Relief washes over me. "I think that about a lot of things. Not being enough."

Not anorexic enough. Not Indian enough. Not Muslim enough.

"I think you should do it," says Sky. "If you think it would help you and if you think it would help other people. And Ellie?"

"Yeah?"

"I think you're enough."

I almost start crying. I can't even get out the words "thank you," so I take her hand and squeeze it tight. After a couple minutes, I type up a caption and post the photo.

Tennis is one of the most important things in my life. It's a big part of why I knew I had to change the way I was thinking about food and eating. Not having enough energy for a two-hour tennis practice? Yeah, that's not gonna work for me. Sometimes I wonder what it must be like to be a guy. To just worry about playing tennis, instead of having to worry about what you look like, what you're wearing, if you're fat or skinny—all while trying to be the best.

My legs are bigger now than they were two years ago. Because I'm stronger.

I have so much more energy, and my tennis is taking off in ways I couldn't have dreamed of.

I'm focused on what my body can do. Not what it looks like or how much it weighs.

And I'm only just beginning to learn what I'm capable of.

Skyler and I sit at the picnic table side by side, staring out at the lake, and I think about my Other Goal. And then I think: I've done it. Even if nothing ever happens with Amelia Grace and Scarlett hates me forever, this thing that's happening with me and Skyler, we're becoming the kind of friends I've grown up my whole life hearing about. And the things I've been telling myself? I'm wrong. I'm not some kind of unfriendable person. I just told Skyler some of the biggest, darkest things about me, and she still likes me. She might even like me more. And I don't need to do stupid stuff like pretend to be Emily Rae to make people like me. Maybe I could just be me.

Amelia Grace

Today I'm painting butterflies for a 3-D art installation. When I put them all together, it'll look like a kaleidoscope of butterflies flying out of a jar and across the nursery wall. (Skyler told me "kaleidoscope" is the official name for a group of butterflies.) Maybe I should go to church with her. I don't know. I feel so breakable right now.

Heidi sits across the room folding impossibly tiny clothes into dainty stacks.

"Hey, Heidi?"

She keeps folding. "What's up, sweetie?"

"Has my mom . . . told you anything about me?"

"Oh, honey." She sets down the onesie she's holding and comes over to sit by me. "I am so sorry about what's been happening to you." I feel bad because it looked like kind of a lot of work for her to get up and sit back down. "Your mama and Val have been having more talks than you know. Honestly? I thought I wasn't going to like her very much, but I think it has less to do with her personal beliefs and more to do with fear. I think she's going to come around."

That's not something I can really hope for, but it means the world to me that she and Val are trying.

Heidi squeezes my shoulder. "I need you to know that there is absolutely nothing wrong with you. You are such a beautiful soul, and it's the people around you who are wrong."

"Thanks." I say it so softly because if I don't, I'll start crying.

"I'm from a really small town too, and I'm sure some of

them are great, but mine was a lot like yours." She takes a deep breath and holds it. I can see her strapping down the memories in her brain so they can't roam free. "I met Val in college." Her smile lights up her whole face. "Life after small towns is pretty great."

I can't help spinning futures in my head. It's like she looked inside my brain and told me the thing I was most desperate to hear. Someday, somewhere, I could imagine being all my pieces at once. Queer and kind and messy and creative and earnest and Christian. That reminds me why I started this conversation in the first place.

"Did you go to church a lot, like me?"

"I did," she says quietly.

A flare of hope. Right in my chest.

Then I realize Heidi's smile has gone brittle. "I don't really do church anymore."

"Oh. I'm sorry. I didn't mean to—"

"It's okay. It just wasn't for me."

She squeezes my shoulder again. I look around the nursery at the life she and Val are making for this baby.

It still makes me swell with hope, but I can't help but wonder. Did Heidi not care about going to church anymore, or did she have to give up one of her important pieces? And I worry. About what it would be like to live in a world where I don't hide myself. That it won't be everything I hoped it would be. I hope that I can get there without it costing me any of my important pieces.

CHAPTER 32

Skyler

THIS IS OFFICIALLY THE MOST DISHONEST I HAVE ever been.

I dial Dr. Levy's office and pass my sister the phone. She sits up straighter—shoulders down, chin high, back like a ruler. As if adopting Mama's posture is the first step to mimicking her voice.

I count the rings. One, two, thr—

"Hi, there. This is Adeline Kaplan-Gable. I'm calling to make an appointment for my daughter Skyler to see Dr. Levy this week," my sister says in a clipped Southern voice. Wow, she really can sound a lot like Mama. "Yes. Yes, she is." Yes, she is what?! My eyes are wild, I can tell, but my sister just shakes her head like, *Don't bother the grown-ups while they're handling things.* "We wanted to talk to Dr. Levy about other treatment options. We feel like her current medication is just not working out. No, our insurance info has not changed. Wednesday at two o'clock would be perfect. Thank you so much, Irene."

She hangs up.

"Wow," I say. "That was just—WOW."

"Right? I'm not gonna lie, I'm feeling pretty damn pleased with myself right now."

I do that laugh thing where the laugh comes out your nose instead of your mouth. It's funny seeing her this way, all confident and beaming.

"Well, thank you. I couldn't have done it without you."

"You definitely couldn't," she says, bumping me with her hip.

This time when I laugh, it's the full kind. I should feel guilty. For lying and for going behind my parents' backs. Maybe I would if I didn't need this so much.

Before I know it, it's Wednesday and my sister is driving me to "the mall over in Columbia," aka my clandestine doctor's appointment.

"You're terrible at lying," she says.

"I know."

"If she asks you directly whether Mama's okay with this, you're basically screwed."

"*I know*. Hey, I thought you were supposed to be coaching me in your dishonest ways. How is this helping?"

Scarlett flips her red hair over her shoulder and turns into the parking lot of Dr. Levy's office. "Because," she says, "it's important to play to your strengths. Okay, so Dr. Levy is going to be asking you stuff, and you're going to be turning red and acting all shifty because that's what you do."

"Again. Not sure how this is helping."

"Because you need to use it. It's like this—"

She coaches me right up until it's time to walk in for my appointment. She even goes inside with me, saying hello to

Dr. Levy's receptionist, Irene, and settling down in the waiting room with a *Teen Vogue*.

But in the exam room, I am alone.

At first, it's easy. One of the nurses takes my vitals and makes small talk with me. She has unicorns on her scrubs and she smiles a lot.

Then Dr. Levy arrives. "Hi, Skyler, how are you feeling?" She beams at me. She's very beamy, Dr. Levy.

"Good," I say, because it's really hard to say anything other than "good" or "fine" when someone is smiling at you like that. I give my head a little shake. "I mean, not good. That's why I'm here. I don't think my meds are working. I know we had talked about biologics before, and I know I was the one who said no because needles are really freaking terrible, but . . . I wanted to revisit that."

"Of course. Of course." And then she realizes it. I can tell because her spotlight smile dims down to more of a feeble house lamp. "Skyler, where's your mother?"

"Right. Well." My cheeks go hot and my eyes cut sideways and, for gosh sakes, why can't I stop touching my hair?! Also, I'm annoyed that Scarlett was so right. But not so annoyed that I won't take her advice and use my nerves to my advantage. "My, um, my parents are in the middle of separating right now, so my mom's not actually staying in Winston-Salem, she's out at our lake house, and uh, she was hoping I could bring the forms to her and she could sign them and give them back." I duck my head and look at the floor like Scarlett taught me. "She's—she's not doing so well."

Dr. Levy touches my shoulder. "I'm so sorry to hear that." She asks me about my pain levels and how much worse it's been and for how long. Then she nods. "I can send the forms to Adeline, but I can't send the prescription for the biologic to the pharmacy until she signs them, okay?"

"Thank you," I say.

I feel gross. Like my soul needs fifty showers and also some bleach or some kind of super-advanced cleaner you can only buy on late-night infomercials.

But underneath that, hope. And it's more powerful than anything else.

I walk out of the office with my forms and my plans and my dreams of a pain-free future. Pull my sister out to the parking lot by the hand and squeeze her to me tight.

"Thank you," I say into her hair.

She pulls away, all flustered. "It's fine, Sky."

"Well, thank you anyway. It's a really big thing that you did for me."

I can feel the tears shining in my eyes. My face is basically the living embodiment of a Hallmark movie right now.

"Well, you're welcome," Scarlett says, still clearly uncomfortable. "But I don't see why you can't tell our parents and make an appointment the regular way."

I try to meet her eyes. I have to force myself—it's like I'm scared she'll be able to look into them and see the truth. "I just can't."

Amelia Grace

I can't stop thinking about my talk with Heidi. I sit at the coffee table in the carriage house and surround myself with papers and books and Scarlett's tablet. I don't even notice when Ellie comes up the stairs.

"What are you doing?"

"Oh, um."

Truth? I was reading this story in Genesis that always comes up when people talk about the Bible and being gay. God is going to destroy Sodom and Gomorrah because the people there are grievous sinners, and two angels come to Lot's house and break bread with him. All the men of Sodom show up at Lot's house and demand that he bring out the two men so they can have sex with them. I remember my preacher taking an extra-long pause after reading that part. He wanted it to sink in how bad those men were, men who wanted to have sex with other men.

But the Bible never actually said that. And I couldn't help but look around at the faces in the pews and wonder why I was the only one who thought having sex with someone against their will was the real sin here. And then Lot, he's supposed to be our hero, and this guy is all, no, wait, take my virgin daughters instead. You can do whatever you want with them. Why aren't we talking about *that*? Why aren't we acknowledging that, hey, there was a lot wrong with the way things were back then, and maybe we don't need to be following every verse to the letter of the law unless we want to be cool with slavery and incest and stoning people who wear cotton blends.

That seems like an awful lot to unload on Ellie right now, so instead I just say: "Reading. And, um, looking for stuff online about being Christian and gay."

Some of the websites hurt, and you just want to close them and give up. But others . . . I don't know. Maybe it's too much to hope for. Especially after my talk with Heidi.

"Oh, yeah?" Ellie's eyes are big and fearful, like she's scared she'll say the wrong thing.

"Yeah. I'm worried there aren't churches that believe the same thing as me."

She seems genuinely puzzled. "I don't know where *you're* from—sorry, wait, that sounds judgey. I'm just saying that there are, like, seven churches near me, and five of them have pride flags."

"Wait, are you serious?"

"Yes."

Wow, that's, I mean, that's really incredible.

"I've heard of things like that and I know they exist. Theoretically. But growing up where I did, it's really hard for me to picture it in real life."

Ellie scoots some papers over so she can sit next to me on the couch. "I get that. It's harder to find LGBT-inclusive mosques too. But. I just can't believe Sky would take you to a place where you'd feel uncomfortable. She's a really good friend."

"Yeah."

She's right. Skyler is a good friend. And based on the things she says, it's hard to picture her at an intolerant church. But sometimes it's hard to picture me and Mom there too.

"Hey, I don't want it to seem like I'm pushing you to go," says Ellie. "If you don't feel right going, then don't." She squeezes my hand. "I just don't want that to be the reason why."

"Me neither," I tell her.

I hope she's right. Because I feel like there are only so many chances for me, and I don't think my heart can take it if she's wrong.

CHAPTER 33

Scarlett

....

I broke up with Nick. Nothing happened with the other guy. Yet.
Not that Nick believes me. He was so pissed, I was scared he
might pick a fight. But I want things to happen. So many things.
I'm scared that I left Nick without actually knowing if anything will
happen with this new guy, but I'm more scared of what would have
happened if I'd stayed. Because I have all these big dreams, and
yes, they include someday being a wife and a mother, but that's
not the whole of them. I don't think Nick understood that.

I'm curled in an easy chair in the living room of the big house,
half reading the journal Skyler gave me and half eavesdropping on the conversation our moms are having on the deck as
it drifts through the open windows. Apparently, my parents
have been on another date. This time a lunch one, and this time
they didn't even bother to tell me first. And I know my sister is
probably all Team Parent Trap, but I'm not. When someone
treats you badly, you can't expect they'll ever change.

I need to make sure these dates aren't leading anywhere.
Which requires me knowing exactly what's happening.

"So, how was it?" asks Aunt Seema.

Mama's eyes dart over at me for a sec. "Good. His apology spiels are really improving." She lowers her voice. "I'll tell you everything after the girls go to the movies."

Mmm-hmmm. That means it's probably worse than I feared.

The other girls are ready now, so we get our purses and head to Ellie's mom's van. Skyler and Ellie get inside, my sister taking the driver's seat because Ellie's only fifteen.

"So, Amelia Grace and I aren't coming," I tell them.

"You aren't?" Skyler asks.

"We aren't?" Amelia Grace asks.

I can feel my cheeks getting red. I don't blush often, but, being a redhead, I am a super blusher.

"No. We're going to stay here and figure something out. It might be SBDC- related. Can you cover for us?"

"Yes," says Ellie too quickly.

"Okay," says my sister.

"Cool. Don't drive away till I give you the signal."

Amelia Grace and I go back to the house.

"Hey, I just forgot something upstairs. I'll only be a sec," I call.

"Okay," comes the mom chorus from the back deck.

I make the "wait here" motion to Amelia Grace as I run upstairs and then back down. Open the door, wave to Ellie and Skyler, close the door. As they drive away, I sneak down the hallway.

"C'mon," I whisper.

"What're we doing?" she whispers back.

"We're finding out what happened at that lunch."

We tiptoe into the living room. Everything in the lake house is open floor plan, which means the only really good place to hide while spying on the back deck is inside the massive yellow velvet curtain that Mama pulls shut whenever we have movie night. It's giant—we're talking covers-the-whole-back-wall-of-windows-at-once, used-to-belong-to-a-theater-company huge. I pull Amelia Grace inside with me. It makes me think of being seven years old and hiding with Skyler.

Luckily, the windows are open, and our moms aren't exactly quiet.

"Did you go back to his Airbnb with him?"

"He wanted me to."

"When was the last time you—?"

"Too damn long ago."

Ew.

The song on their old-people playlist changes, and they all go quiet. I don't know why. It's just some old country song about this girl and she's seventeen and drinks strawberry wine and she likes some boy who's way older than her and honestly sounds like kind of a tool.

"Do you know I didn't realize this song was about losing your virginity until I was in college?" says my aunt Neely.

Ew. Is it really?

But the other moms laugh.

"Oh, Neely, are you serious?" says Aunt Val.

"Isn't it weird how a song can bring back a memory for you?" Mama's voice slides through the window, Southern and low. "I am physically incapable of listening to this song without thinking about losing my virginity."

I grab Amelia Grace's wrist and make big desperate eyes

like, OMG IF I HAVE TO LISTEN TO MY MOM TALK ABOUT LOSING HER VIRGINITY WITH MY DAD, I WILL NOT SURVIVE IT.

"Same," says Aunt Val. "Even if it wasn't the heteronormative stuff of country songs." Her voice goes softer. "Hey, whatever happened to Nick Ellison?"

Wait. WHAT? Nick, as in, *I had sex with Nick on his back porch* Nick?

"Oh," says Mama. "I'm friends with him on Facebook. He's not married to Kathy anymore. His new wife seems nice, and they have a couple of kids together." Mama pauses. "She's a butterface."

The aunts laugh and squeal, but all I can think is *Holy hell, our moms are the OGs of the SBDC.*

"You just had to get that in there," says Aunt Seema.

"Does that mean you still have feelings for him?" asks Aunt Neely.

I press my face so close to the window they'll see my nose if I'm not careful.

"Ugh. No." Mama laughs. "I just really enjoy being petty about my exes."

Exes, plural? Are there more because I don't think I can handle more? Also, something in my chest definitely loosened when she said no, and I don't even want to think about what that means for how I feel about her and Daddy.

"You know, I actually ran into her at a baby shower last year? She was sloshed. Who needs three glasses of white wine to get through a dang baby shower?"

Aunt Neely clucks her tongue. "Bless her liver."

The four of them cackle.

Mama speaks again, and she sounds serious. Thoughtful.

"Sometimes I wonder if I made the right decision picking Jimmy all those years ago. I mean, how could I not after what happened? But I know without a doubt Nick wouldn't have been the right choice. He wasn't terrible or anything, he was perfectly fine, but somehow our relationship still felt like work most of the time. With Jimmy, it was just so easy. *Being myself* was easy. I felt like we made each other better than either of us was on our own. It was like magic. And I know it isn't magic anymore, and I don't know when it stopped being so, and the fact that I didn't even catch it makes me scared we'll never ever get it back again."

She stops talking. Why has she stopped talking? I need to know more about this magic. I feel like it could be the key to knowing what to do about me and Reese. And then I realize. She's crying. And suddenly I'm crying too.

"Nothing about him cheating on me and how bad things are now can erase that we used to have it. I didn't build my life around a lie. I know that. And yeah, I feel completely pathetic sometimes for thinking about staying, but you know what? If there's a chance of getting back what we had, I'm going to take it."

She dissolves and so do I. Outside I hear the sounds of chairs scraping and tears muffled into shoulders, and beside me, Amelia Grace takes my hand and I squeeze hers so tight. The curtain wraps us up like a blanket fort, safe. And we just stare at each other, holding hands, our eyes telling each other all the important things because we can't make a sound.

Are you sure you can handle it on your own?

You haven't given yourself one of these since you met me.

Hey, remember how you used to eat lunch in the bathroom?

I know a lot of guys would take advantage, but I'm not like them. I'm one of the nice ones.

Well, it's a good thing I'm here to rescue you.

I think about Reese. About the pact I made amid a circle of candles. And I think about what Mama said about magic. Maybe it is worth staying for. And maybe it's also worth leaving for.

CHAPTER 34

Amelia Grace

I DON'T WEAR A DRESS. THERE'S A PART OF ME THAT wants to because it's a new church, and you only get one chance to make a first impression, and I've been taught my entire life that church means dresses and white shoes from Easter to Labor Day. Instead, I wear black pants and a black vest and black shoes, even though it is June 21. All kinds of sacrilege up in this outfit.

At the lake house, I am confident. But once Skyler and I are in the parking lot staring up at the church, not so much. It's a white country church with a steeple and a bell. It looks just the way churches usually do.

You need to get your life right with God before you come back here.

My feet don't want to move. What if they can tell from the moment I walk through the doors? What if I'm not welcome here? I walk up the path with Skyler, a half step behind like it'll make a difference. She waves to everyone in the entire world. People smile at me just for being friends with her. No one makes the I'm-judging-you face, though a few of the smiles I get seem a smidgen concerned. I try to relax my face and shoulders and hands and breathing. Skyler and I sit on the left side of the church, midway from the front. That's when I notice.

There are these two women sitting a few pews in front of me. Just sitting. But I can tell.

And it makes me wonder, what is it about two people that tells you they're together? I mean, if they're not holding hands or touching each other or something obvious. Is it that they're sitting just an inch inside each other's personal bubbles? Is it that her head is tilted ever so slightly?

The minister comes to the front and starts talking. Surprise no. 1: She's a she. I nudge Sky, even though of course she already knows. She giggles silently. Surprise no. 2: her sermon. She talks about how people can have two kinds of attitudes. The first: The church doesn't do this thing that I want, so I'm going to leave. The second: The church isn't doing this thing that I want, so I'm going to be the person that makes it happen. And then she starts talking about how people have started ministries at the church related to Black Lives Matter and Pride Week and making lunches for kids who need them, and where am I right now? Is this real?

"If you want things to be different, you have to make them different. We're here as a community to make each other better and to make the world better, but we have to have people who feel so passionately about things that we're willing to step up and suggest ideas and change how things operate. We're going to have a Sunday school series starting at the end of July on what the Bible has to say about being LGBTQIA+. Karen Michaelson is putting it together. She's been dedicating so much time to this, and it's going to be wonderful. Please reach out to her if you have an idea for another series after that."

I'm pretty sure my mouth is hanging open, and I keep looking at Sky, like, waiting for her to be shocked, but no one in the entire congregation bats an eyelash. This is their normal, and it is so mind-blowing and extraordinary, and they don't even know it. They've grown up in a castle at the top of a beanstalk, never realizing that everyone else lives on the ground. This is it. This is what I've been looking for. I knew there had to be people out there who believed the same way as me.

And then the sermon is over, and the pianist starts to play "Great Is Thy Faithfulness," and it's one of my favorite hymns, and it reminds me, that, yes, this really is a church. On Earth. In reality. The two women a few rows in front of me stand. And only one of them is holding the hymnal, but she's having trouble finding the hymn, and the woman beside her laughs as she helps her turn the pages, and for a split second they are holding the hymnal together, one hand on either side. In that moment, I see a different future. Or, no. It whacks me in the chest so hard I gasp.

Sky puts her hand on my shoulder. "Amelia?"

"Excuse me. Sorry," I whisper.

I slide past her and walk as fast as I can down the aisle and out the back doors of the church. I'm crying before my feet touch the grass.

I find a bench surrounded by mountain laurel. I put my head in my hands. After a few seconds, I feel movement beside me. Skyler puts her hand on my back.

"I'm sorry. Was it something she said?"

I shake my head. "No, it was fine." I try to figure out how

to tell her all the things I'm thinking, and the tears threaten to spill over again.

"Hey, it's okay." Skyler hugs me to her shoulder, and I hug her back like she's my lifeline. This entire day feels like a lifeline.

"I didn't think it could be possible," I say into her hair.

It's scary to have that much hope dropped into your lap all at once.

CHAPTER 35

Ellie

THIS IS IT. MY FINAL INSTAGRAM POST IN THE SERIES I've been working on. Also the one that makes me the most nervous. People can be pretty terrible to Muslim women on the internet. I make Sky sit beside me as I write it up. She squeezes my shoulder when I finish, and her eyes are a little red and so are mine. I didn't understand that it would feel like this, when I spent all those years wanting what my momma and her friends had. I didn't realize friendship could be a thing that makes you feel like you've been cracked wide open, but in the best possible way.

Thank you so much for all the responses I've been getting to this series of posts. I've been overwhelmed by your kindness and insight. Today I wanted to share a picture that my cousin took of me during Eid a few years ago. I chose this photo because I'm wearing my hijab. I don't wear one all the time, but I do wear it when I go to our mosque.

  Most people don't guess that I'm Indian and Muslim. It's something that I can choose to tell. Sometimes I feel guilty about that, especially when I see how differently my brother and I get treated at the airport or when Momma is exhausted from dealing with people who think being Muslim means she can't be a feminist. I'll never know what it's like to live life from Zakir's perspective or Momma's. Passing = privilege, and I know it makes my life easier. Sometimes I feel like it means I'm not enough. Like I have to work harder to prove that I belong. I try to get each of my momma and nani's recipes just perfect and I fast during Ramadan and I do and feel a million other big and little things. I know my family loves and accepts me, so it's not that. It's hard to say where the pressure comes from. But I feel it, every day. Like the world wants to make me feel like everything would be so much easier if I would keep my mouth shut and be one thing or the other. Just go along with it when people think I'm white or assume I celebrate Christmas. Don't make waves.

I feel like I'm fighting just to take up space. Like I'm too much and not enough at exactly the same time.

I am Jameelah Rose Johnson. I love tennis and cooking and photography and making lists. I am Indian. I am Muslim. I am American. I am a feminist. I used to have issues with food and my body and I'm working really hard on it.

I am enough. And so are you.

I click share.

CHAPTER 36

Scarlett

....

I GET UP FROM MY DECK CHAIR AND STRETCH. "I have to go into town to run a few errands. I'll see y'all later," I tell the other girls.

Amelia Grace stands too. "Oh! Is it cool if I come with you? I have to pick up some paint at the hardware store, and I don't know if my mom will be back by then."

"Sure."

We go to the carriage house to get our stuff.

"Oh. Are you sure you don't mind running a ton of errands with me?"

"No way. It'll be fun! Let me text my mom so she knows I have a ride."

We take my mom's car, and we hit the hardware store, the boat store, the gas station, and the fabric store. I take forever choosing quilting supplies because, hi, I can't pick until I've touched all the fabrics at least twice.

"Thanks for being super patient," I say.

"It's fine." She grins at me. "I have a lot of feelings about fabrics. Are you sure you don't want to do your quilt in *Game of Thrones* characters? Or Grumpy Cat, maybe?"

"Ha."

Our last stop is Target, and I text Aunt Neely as we walk in.

Almost done. At Target now. Can I still come shadow you today?

She texts me back almost immediately.

I would love that! Also, can you pick up a nipple shield while you're there?

Um. I look at Amelia Grace. "Do you know what a nipple shield is?"

"What?" She almost runs into a display of greeting cards. "I'm sorry, you can't just ask people things like that while they're walking."

"Your mom told me to bring her one."

"Oh, how's that going anyway? The shadowing?"

"Awesome! There are two little babies who can totally drink milk now because of me. Well, mostly your mom, but a little bit me."

"That's really cool. Oh!" She holds her phone up. "Found it!"

Turns out nipple shields are thin and plasticky and are shaped about how you might expect but with four holes at the top.

"Where do you think we find one of these?" asks Amelia Grace.

"I don't know, but we better figure it out because I would rather die than ask that dude at the customer service counter."

She busts out laughing, and so do I. It's been like that all day—laughing, singing songs along with the radio, putting our hands out the window to feel the breeze. I feel lighter and funnier and smarter and braver. Like being myself is a good thing, the best thing.

Running errands usually sucks, but with her it's easy. Like magic.

CHAPTER 37

Ellie

TODAY IS THE GREATEST. I HAD SO MANY PEOPLE reach out to me after my newest Instagram post. I never realized how alone I felt sometimes until I had all these other people telling me how they felt alone in exactly the same way. And not just Indian girls or Muslim girls, but queer girls and disabled girls too. I don't even bother looking at the likes—it's not about likes anymore. I've had more life-changing talks about invisible marginalization in one week than I've had in the rest of my life combined. I'm just coming back from tennis with my new trainer, who is AMAZING. After our practice, I was so full of energy that I had Momma drop me off at the end of the road so I could jog all the way home. Things are finally coming together. With tennis. With the girls. I open the doors to the carriage house and take the stairs two at a time. I think Scarlett is actually starting to like me now. At breakfast this morning, she even—

"I have been looking everywhere for you!"

"Whoa! Hi!" I manage to stop myself from barreling into Scarlett, but only just. She looks happy. And excited, deeply, intensely excited.

"What's going on?" I ask. (Somewhat skeptically.)

"We need to have an emergency club meeting! Tonight! No, a sleepover! On the dock!"

This is the moment I have been waiting for.

Okay, but did an alien come and switch our brains?

"That's fine with me," I say. "But what brought this on?"

Scarlett flashes her most mischievous smirk. "Just be at the dock tonight. You'll see."

What. The crap. This is more than I ever could have imagined. The entire upper floor of the dock has been transformed. Four air mattresses have been positioned geometrically to make a space in the middle for a coffee table topped with candles. Each mattress is made up with a colorful sheet and a quilt, and there are brightly patterned throw pillows and cushions lining every railing, so all you see is a swirl of color and softness.

"This is amazing," I breathe.

"Right?" says Scarlett proudly. "Ames did it."

Amelia Grace grins.

Skyler sets two trays on the coffee table. "And I made mini pizzas and Mary Berry's Viennese Whirls."

"Also amazing. Um. But why are we doing this?"

"Apparently, my sister has some big giant secret to tell us."

Scarlett clutches her chest like she's been wounded. "It is so much more than that."

She sits on the mattress with the red and orange spiderweb-patterned quilt, back straight like a queen. We rush to find our own spots. Whatever this is, it's going to be good.

"The original Southern Belle Drinking Club?" She leans forward. "It's our moms."

"What?!" squeals Skyler.

"It's true," says Amelia Grace.

Scarlett cocks her head at me. I am clearly not reacting as expected. They're gonna figure out I knew. Are they gonna be mad at me?

I duck my head. "I know."

"Wait, seriously?" says Scarlett.

"I was worried you guys wouldn't want to do it if you knew it was our moms."

"That's probably true."

"How did you find out?" asks Skyler.

"My mom had a bunch of pictures and stuff in our attic."

"Pictures like these?!" Scarlett plunks a photo album down on the coffee table and ceremoniously flips open the cover.

"Wow, that is an intense amount of flannel," I say.

"I would actually wear those overalls though," says Sky.

I point at a photo of our moms dressed up for going out. "Yeah, and Aunt Adeline is rocking that choker."

Scarlett snorts. "And that scrunchie."

"Okay, okay, okay, but *why* would you ever want your jeans to be down around your hip bones?" says Skyler.

"Pretty sure you can't bend over in those." Scarlett sighs as she turns the pages. "So much blackmail material in such a thin book. Okay, but this is important, y'all. I thought we could do a dramatic reading."

"Um, yes. That is definitely a thing we should do," says Amelia Grace.

A fact about Scarlett: She can sound exactly like my aunt Adeline.

Another fact: It is hilarious.

"The party was pretty boring, so we started playing Hey, That's My Name," reads Scarlett. "So, Seema goes up to this guy, and he's all, 'Hey, I'm Jack.' And she's all, 'Oh, wow, that's my name! It's short for Jacqueline.' And Neely had to be Kyle, which could easily be her real name except that she can't lie worth a damn and she couldn't stop giggling. But then I met this guy I actually kind of liked, only his name turned out to be Trevor. TREVOR. So, I had to be Trevor for the rest of the night and possibly the rest of my natural life because Val will not stop calling me that."

"Ohmygosh, ohmygosh, we are going to hell in a handbasket," giggles Skyler.

Scarlett makes a big show of stretching her arms across the backs of several pillows. "Hey, at least this handbasket has comfy throw pillows."

She reads some more, and I laugh so hard I have to run back to the carriage house to go to the bathroom for fear I might literally pee my pants. While I'm there, I grab my pillow. Momma's friendship bracelet is underneath, and I grab that too.

"Can you help me put this on?" I ask Skyler when I get back to the dock.

"It's really pretty," she says as she fastens the blue threads around my wrist.

This is it. The moment I know I've accomplished my goal for the summer.

We stay up past midnight digging through their journals and reading the good parts out loud. Our moms come out to the deck to drink wine and talk, but I don't think they can hear us. Skyler pulls a photo out of the album and looks at it—the one with all four of our moms, chins resting on their hands, lying on the floor of what I now know is the loft.

"That one's my favorite too," I say. "Momma has a copy of it."

Sky holds up the photo of the four smiling teenage girls, and behind it, our moms are sitting at a picnic table, forty-something years old, still laughing, still best friends. I feel like I can see our whole lives spreading out before us. We come visit each other in college, crashing in each other's dorm rooms. We go to concerts and on road trips and we mend each other's broken hearts and we're bridesmaids in each other's weddings. And we're there for each other when one of us gets a phone call that makes her legs go weak. We're there for all of it.

CHAPTER 38

Skyler

....

TURNS OUT, IF YOU SHOVE A FORM IN FRONT OF MY
mom while she's talking to my aunt Seema, she will sign practically anything. I feel a guilty sinking in my stomach at how
easily she trusts me, but mostly I try not to think about it. A
quick fax later, and Dr. Levy has called my prescription into
the pharmacy near our lake house and I am picking it up.

I have them, my new meds.

I did this, myself.

I feel powerful.

Well, at least until I pull out the syringe. I take my sweet
time cleaning a patch of skin on the top of my leg with an alcohol wipe like Dr. Levy taught me. And then I remove the cap.
Why did it have to be needles? The way the light glints off
them all menacing, and the thought of them fishtailing around
under your skin, and the way the bore always looks So. Freaking. Huge. I'm like 90 percent certain there's no medical need
for it to be that large.

I try not to look at it as I get rid of the bubbles.

And fail.

Ohmygosh, why didn't I get Ellie or Scarlett to do the injecting part? They both offered. But Past Skyler was all, Noooo, I have to do this all by myself. It's more meaningful that way. Plus, I have to prove I can take care of myself. Just me. Alone. Present Skyler is holding the syringe with shaking hands and feeling less than thrilled about Past Skyler's decisions. "C'mon," I say. "Do it for Future Skyler, the one who gets to play softball again."

I take a deep breath and pinch a fold of skin around the injection site. I avert my eyes.

Wait a minute, how am I supposed to see where to inject if I'm not looking?

I de-avert my eyes. Focus on the spot on my leg.

And BOOM.

I push in the needle, quick like a dart. Let go of the fold of skin. It stings, but I push the plunger, slowly, because that's what the doctor said, but slowly is no good because slowly means I have time to think about the needle and the fluid and how it's flowing into my skin like a worm—

I remove the needle. Place it in the sharps bin the pharmacist gave me. Try to ignore the hot, creeping, light-headed feeling spiraling through me.

I did it.

I pass out on my floor.

"HEY YOU GUYS, I DID IT."

Scarlett and Amelia Grace look stunned. Well, I guess I did just bust onto the dock, screaming at them.

Scarlett raises one eyebrow like she's trying to pretend I didn't just scare the bejesus out of her. "Did . . . what?"

"My injection." Ugh, really people, get with the program. "I just did it. Like, by myself."

I'm eight feet tall right now, not even kidding.

"That's amazing!" says Amelia Grace.

Finally.

"Wow, and you were cool with the needle and everything?" asks Scarlett.

"Um, well, I may have kind of fainted after."

"Skyler!"

"BUT I DID IT."

"I told you you could ask me." Her eyes look almost hurt that I didn't.

"I'm sorry. I know. I just." How to say this so that it makes sense? "It was really important that I do it myself, you know?"

Scarlett nods, but there's something underneath it that I can't quite place. "You don't have to do everything yourself," she says quietly.

I squeeze her hand. "I know." There. We good? Can this please be about me right now, seeing as how I just injected myself with a REAL. LIVE. NEEDLE. I need someone to be unequivocally happy for me.

"Oh! Where's Ellie? I totally have to tell Ellie!"

Amelia Grace shrugs. "Carriage house?"

Mmm, probably not, seeing as how I was literally just passed out there, but I'm taking no chances!

"Let's go check!"

First, we all go to the carriage house, and Ellie is not there. Then I run over to the main house and check every room and even the closets, and Ellie is not there. And then I run back to the carriage house, and Ellie is still not there.

"Where is she?!" I am exasperated. I am desperate.

Scarlett and Amelia Grace just shrug. Ugh. So much shrugging from them, on this, the biggest day of my life.

"Oh! She always writes down her schedule in that planner-journal thing!"

Scarlett grabs it from the top bunk. "Let me see." She flips some pages. Her face goes funny and she snaps the book shut. "Nope. I don't think it's in there."

"What? Of course it's in there. It's always in there. Like, down to the last minute and everything." I grab for the journal, but she holds it out of my reach.

"Sky, I really don't think you should—"

"What? Does it say something embarrassing like she's getting a bikini wax? Just let me see it!"

I have to jump for it, but I grab the journal out of her hands.

"Skyler. Please don't." She says it all monotone like she knows it's useless. I'm already flipping the pages.

Schedules for homework and fitness plans and detailed itineraries for each day and— Oh. That's why Scarlett didn't want me to see it.

Befriend Skyler $\xrightarrow{\text{to get}}$ Amelia Grace $\xrightarrow{\text{to get}}$ Scarlett

And underneath that, a list of things. About me.

"What are you doing?" asks Ellie.

She's standing in the doorway.

Ellie

Oh, no. Oh, no no no no no. Sky is holding my notebook, why is she holding my notebook? There's a sinking feeling in my gut.

"What are you doing?" I ask. At least, I think I ask it. There's a ringing in my ears right now, and it's hard to know.

There's this one page, and it would be so very bad if she saw it. She winces as she hands me the notebook. She's already seen it. I feel like I'm going to throw up. How am I supposed to get her to understand?

"It's not what you think," I rush to say.

She shakes her head and her eyes are so damn sad. "I thought you actually liked me."

She crosses her arms over her chest and walks out of the room with her head down.

I think about running after her, but it's like I'm frozen. "Sky," I call, even though I know it's too late.

She doesn't turn around.

My feet finally start working, and I chase her down the stairs. Touch her shoulder. "Sky, wait."

"I really don't want to talk about it right now," she says softly.

I watch her walk across the grass to the main house. The other girls have come downstairs now. I look to Scarlett like she'll know what to do.

"You really fucked up," she says. "Also, I'm sorry. I was the one who opened your journal. I was trying to figure out when you'd be home, because Skyler was so excited to tell you about her arthritis stuff. I didn't know . . . what was in there."

She's less angry than I thought she'd be. More disappointed? The weird thing is, I don't really care. I mean, I *care*, but I care so much more about Sky and her ducked head and sad eyes right now. How do I get her to believe that I really like her? That I always wanted to be friends with her and that she wasn't just a means to getting the other girls to be friends with me? That she means everything.

"I didn't mean it the way it sounds," I say.

I just meant it like, Scarlett is the hardest. Not like Scarlett is the best. But are they somehow connected in my brain? Isn't that why I always try to be friends with girls like Emily Rae? No. I shake off that thought. That entire tennis academy is a trash fire.

"Good luck convincing her of that," Scarlett says. "She's sweet, but she's stubborn as all hell."

She leaves too, and Amelia Grace starts to go after her, but then pauses.

"You have to try," she says. "Maybe we have a meeting and you explain everything?"

"There's no way they're coming to a meeting now."

"Maybe if I ask them," she says. She squeezes my elbow before she leaves.

It's the only thing that's keeping me going.

JULY

CHAPTER 39

Scarlett

WHEN REESE COMES TO VISIT, WE TAKE OUT THE pontoon boat, which is good because I could use a break from the girls after Notebookgate. We putter around on the lake until he finds an inlet with no houses, just trees. He keeps trying to take off my clothes, and I keep trying to talk to him. They say this is what you're supposed to want. A boy. Solid boy. Nice boy. Handsome boy. A boy who doesn't have any cracks in him yet but will date you in spite of yours.

"How was the new Zendaya movie?" I ask.

"It was all right." He goes back to kissing my neck, pulling down the strap of my tank top.

"Did Carter like it?"

He jerks back, surprised, but recovers quickly. "I told you, you don't have to worry about that." Kisses me on the lips. Unties the top of my bathing suit. "There were other people there, and I'm only interested in—"

"But she's *always* there. And she's always right next to you." I scoot away from him and pull my bathing suit back up so it covers me. There's only so naked I'm willing to be right now.

Reese sighs. "So, I can't help but notice you don't seem very interested in having sex with me." Something about the way he says it sounds like an accusation.

"What does that have to do with you hanging out with Carter?" Is he trying to say—

"Nothing," he says, like I'm the most exhausting person on the planet. "It's just an observation."

I am all hard edges and exposed nerves. "An observation you felt the need to mention right in the middle of talking about Carter."

"You have to stop being so sensitive. I'm allowed to have thoughts about things. I'm a really nice guy. I would never cheat on you with Carter."

Am I really making something out of nothing right now? I don't think I am.

Before I can say anything, he's talking again. "Most guys would be pretty annoyed right now. They'd feel like having sex and then not wanting to have sex is a lot like a tease."

Something inside me snaps. "Isn't that exactly what you're saying right now?" My voice isn't the sweet one I find myself slipping into whenever he's around. It's sharp. And he flinches.

"What? No. I'm just saying that's how *most guys* would feel. You're really lucky you're with a nice guy like me."

This is not magic. This is, in fact, the opposite of magic.

"I think we should break up."

"*What?* Scarlett, calm down. You don't have to threaten to break up with me."

"Who says I'm threatening?"

"Scarlett, chill, I'm sorry, okay?" His face is sweet. Sincere.

The face of someone who always gets their way when they ask for things.

"I really think this is the best thing." I say it gently.

"Please don't do this."

He tries to take my hand, but I don't let him. And the sweet, sincere mask falls away.

"Wow. Okay, sure. I can't believe you'd break up with me right after we have sex for the first time, but of course that's something you'd do."

"What's that supposed to mean?" Even though I'm not sure I'm ready for the answer.

"You have all this baggage and shit, and I've been trying to keep things normal, but it's like you don't even know what that is. And I've always been cool with that, and I've never tried to make you feel bad about it because I'm a good person. But you're never going to find someone else as good as me who's willing to put up with someone who has as many problems as you."

He's angry, I tell myself. He's angry, so he's lashing out to try and hurt me like he's hurting.

But I don't know if I believe it.

We don't share one last heartfelt hug. Or say something wise and kind about the future. We get ourselves back to the house, and he peels out of my driveway without looking back. When something's toxic, you have to get away as fast as you can.

I've never told him about how I worry I'm broken. I mostly just tried to hide the broken pieces whenever he was around. That's the scariest part of all this. That he named my secret, dark fear without me ever having to tell him.

It's how I know everything he said is the truth.

I've known it for a long time now.

It started and ended with McCloud Harris.

The start: her walking up to me in eighth-grade English and telling me she loved my teal underliner. She had the longest, blondest corn silk hair—the kind of girl people's eyes followed down the hallway. I couldn't believe she was talking to me. Before I knew it, we were hanging out every spare second, listening to the angriest music we could find while we complained about all the people ruining our lives. Our parents. Our teachers. The other girls at school. And her boyfriend, Billy. Oh, man, did we ever tear that kid up one side and down the other. Except sometimes we didn't. Sometimes she would tell me about how they would kiss in Billy's basement. And I would watch her lips as she told me what it felt like to press them against his. It made me feel like there were fireworks inside me with no place to go. I had never kissed a boy before, that's probably why.

Then one day she broke up with him. I remember feeling weirdly happy and also disappointed at the same time.

"You can do so much better," I told her. "Billy Sanders is the actual worst."

I did my very best to eviscerate him whenever we hung out. She was my only girlfriend unless you counted Sky or Ames or something. I wanted her to know I was on her side.

The end: her fourteenth-birthday party. We were going to go to the county fair with all our friends, and then we were going to have a sleepover in McCloud's family room and watch all the stuff on Netflix our parents wouldn't let us see and maybe even sneak out.

Then four days before the party, she came up to me after school. It was weird because she wouldn't look me in the eye.

She said, "My mom says I can only invite four friends to my party."

A volcano bubbled inside me, ready to spew rage about how unfair her mom was.

Then she said, "So, um, I'm sorry you can't come."

Wait. *Me?*

I was so shocked I just sort of said, "Okay."

All my feelings came after. I put them in an email to Ames.

The next day, I saw McCloud holding hands with Billy. She didn't meet my eyes then either.

And I heard her giggling and telling Anne Florkowski, "Well, it's not like I could invite her. I want this party to be really awesome, and she's so negative. Especially about Billy."

Anne nodded conspiratorially. "She's a total fun vampire."

So, that was it. There was something wrong with me that made McCloud and the other girls not want to be my friend. I shouldn't have let so much of my darkness show around her. That was stupid.

I went home that day, and I knew biting my lip wasn't going to be enough. I kept tossing and turning in my bed, replaying everything. Eventually I snuck down to the kitchen and got a knife. The sharp ones scared me, so I picked a dull one for cutting steak. I ran it across my forearm until it made a straight red line, not quite bleeding. I ran it across my arm until McCloud disappeared.

Afterward, I put a Band-Aid over it and hoped my parents

wouldn't notice at breakfast. They didn't. What they did do was laugh with my sister over Saturday morning pancakes while they told me they were taking us to a county fair that night. THE county fair. And there was no way I was getting out of it.

Some things you should know: County fairs smell terrible. And they're always hot as balls. And dusty. And the rides look like they'll collapse if you so much as breathe on them funny. I don't see why anyone would ever want to go.

I decided it was important to share these thoughts with my family. "It's *really* hot out here."

"You know what's good when you're hot?" my dad said. "Cheerwine funnel cake."

"Ew." Cheerwine tastes like Coke mixed with over-sweetened cherry cough medicine.

My dad laughed at me. "Are you sure you're my child?"

Which is something he never, EVER says to my sister.

I sighed. Loudly. "How much longer are we staying?"

Maybe if I complained enough, we could leave sooner. Like, before I ran into McCloud.

"Are you kidding?" my sister said. She and my dad went off about everything they love about county fairs, culminating in gratuitous high-fiving. I wish I was joking, but that's how my sister is. Her soul is made out of cotton candy and lilac petals and fresh-cut peonies and soap bubbles and silk pajamas. It's pretty and delicate, but I kind of get the feeling it would melt and disappear if I dumped enough water on it.

She and my dad decided we're, like, contractually obligated to go to this funnel cake stand Sky spotted, so Mama and

I grabbed a picnic table. I took advantage of this opportunity and laid my head down.

"I really don't feel well," I said. "I think it's the heat."

Mama patted my arm. "We don't have to stay too much longer. Don't put your head on the table. It doesn't look sanitary."

I rested my head on her shoulder instead. Moms really go for that, especially once you're older and don't snuggle much anymore.

"Aw, sweetie." She touched my forehead. "You don't have a fever."

My eyes flicked to the order-up window, where my sister was doing some sort of weird little shy person dance. Then they flicked to the line for the haunted house. McCloud. Was there.

I watched as she and Anne and three other girls who used to be my friends laughed and sipped lemonade slushies. Billy had missed the joke because he was too busy trying to rub McCloud's arm without her dad seeing. (Spoiler alert: He failed. Miserably.) I narrowed my eyes. What did she see in him?

Mama followed my gaze. "Oh, look! It's the Harrises. We should go over and say hi."

"I really don't want to." I said it fast and through clenched teeth.

"Scarlett Elaine, what is the matter with you? You love McCloud."

"Mama, *please*."

McCloud still hadn't seen us, but all she had to do was turn her head. I was begging and my face was desperate. Mama got up from the table, and she didn't notice. If she dragged me over there, it was going to look so bad. Like I was trying to use Mama to crash the party and shame McCloud into asking me to the sleepover.

"I'm just going to say hi to Mrs. Harris. You can stay here if you don't feel like going over there."

She started walking toward the haunted house. I grabbed her arm just as she was squeezing past Sky.

"I need to go home. I need to go right now!"

"Scarlett!" she hissed.

A burst of inspiration hit me. "I just started my period! I'm bleeding through my shorts! I CANNOT STAY HERE ANOTHER MINUTE." I screamed it as loud as I dared. Contorted face. Flashing eyes.

Her face softened. "Why didn't you just say so, sweetie?"

I looked at my feet. "I was embarrassed."

You know who else looked embarrassed? Skyler and the two boys standing next to her. Like, the embarrassment equivalent of being mortally wounded. Whatever. Better them than McCloud. I risked glancing at the haunted house again—did that line never move?!

"Order up!"

Skyler walked back to our table silently, her cheeks as red as Cheerwine. Mama and I followed.

Mama touched Daddy's shoulder. "Babe, we need to go."

He scrunched up his face. "But—"

She bent down and whispered a lot of things in his ear. His face turned white. "Yep. We can go."

And then it was over. We were walking away, and McCloud and her stupid friends and her stupid boyfriend never had to know I was there. I took one last look at her over my shoulder. Watched her bump her hip against Anne's. That's where I would have been standing if they didn't find me so catastrophically wretched to be around.

Sky walked along next to me, eating her funnel cake with dainty fingers. She didn't offer to share any.

"I'm really glad we're leaving," I told her. "This was the worst fucking day."

Her head snapped in my direction. I'd never seen her eyes so sharp before.

"Why do you always have to do this?"

The edge in her voice made my breath catch.

"What?"

"This is the perfect day. We're at a carnival. Why is it so hard for you to just be happy?" Every sentence was a punch to the gut. She shook her head like she was figuring things out. It gave me a second to regroup.

"Carnivals—" I said.

She cut me off with the wave of a hand. "No, you know what it is? You're a ruiner. You ruin things. That's all you're good for."

She stalked off toward our van before I could say anything back. Laid across the backseat and pretended to be asleep so she didn't have to look at me. I did the same thing on the middle seat so my parents wouldn't see me cry.

I got it now. It wasn't just McCloud. Or Anne. Or their stupid group of friends. *It was me.*

I am damaged.

I am toxic.

I take beautiful things and screw them up. I seep into

cracks and break things to pieces. My soul is made of dark and violent truths, and my brain is a fountain of hurt and pain turning me angrier, drearier, darker.

There is something permanently wrong with me.

And the worst part? I don't think it can ever be fixed.

Ellie

I PULL OUT MY PHONE WHILE I WAIT. IT'S 11:56. We're supposed to be meeting at midnight. The witching hour. But so far I'm the only witch here. If I end up waiting in this loft all alone—

Nope. Not even gonna let myself think about it. I pull out my phone. At least my be-more-authentic-on-Instagram campaign is still going strong. Except, suddenly it isn't. My mouth goes dry. They found me, the academy girls. I mean, it's not like my account is a secret. I want people to find me, and, you know, follow me. But none of the academy girls have ever commented on my posts before. And I know for sure Emily Rae wasn't following me two weeks ago.

When they say you're not supposed to read the comments, this is why.

Mace678: don't buy this girls' love and light bullshit for a second. some people are only caring about their own stuff. i play tennis with her IRL, so i know

EmRae03: She basically tried to break up our whole tennis academy with her drama queen attitude. Love how she's playing the victim on here.

AutumnJoy15: "Recovering" from food issues, my ass. Why don't you go throw up your cheeseburger, Ellie?

Just when you think it can't get any worse.

I set down my phone. If I read any more right now, I'll start crying, and the girls will be here any minute. I hope.

I hear the sound of footsteps downstairs, and I'm embarrassed by how much my heart leaps. There's the creak of the ladder. And then Amelia Grace's head.

"Hey," I say. It's a word and a sigh of relief at the same time.

"Hey," she says. "Sorry we're late."

We.

Because Scarlett climbs up after her, and then I'm looking for Sky next.

Only, she's not there.

"Hey." Scarlett winces as she meets my eyes. "Skyler's not coming."

"Oh."

"She said she was gonna hang out at the big house and watch *Great British Bake Off* with Mama."

Right. She doesn't have to give me another chance just because I want her to. I guess I can still apologize to the other girls, though. I've hurt them too.

"I'm really sorry about the notebook," I say. "And I'm sorry I lied. Especially when we're supposed to be 'no-holding-back, salt-in-the-wound honest.' Being more authentic on social media wasn't my impossible thing. I mean, I have actually been trying to do that, but my real goal was something else." I take a deep breath. This is beyond mortifying. "I wrote on my paper that I wanted to get you guys to be my best friends by the end of the summer."

There. It's out there. And I'm still a real girl and not a human puddle of embarrassment. Mostly.

Amelia Grace cocks her head to the side and looks at me with sad, puzzled eyes. "Why would you think that's impossible?"

"Yeah," says Scarlett. "I just don't understand why you felt like you had to do that to get friends."

I should tell them all the gory details. A simple apology *isn't* enough. But there's another way. A horrifically awful, embarrassing way. I can't even say it without cringing. I have to force each word out of my mouth.

"If you really want to know, come to my tennis tournament this weekend."

Next, I go find Sky. Not because I think she'll want to listen to anything I have to say, but because I still owe her an apology.

She's tucked up on the couch with her mom, watching people make hazelnut dacquoise.

"Hey, Sky?" She narrows her eyes. I backpedal. "Skyler. Can we talk for a second? I think you have the wrong idea about me."

Aunt Adeline announces she needs a cup of tea and scurries off to the kitchen. I sit on the couch beside Skyler, and she doesn't move, so I take this as a sign to plow ahead.

I clear my throat. Skyler doesn't—won't—look at me.

I think about telling her all of it. How I'm the biggest loser and everyone hates me. Showing her the comments on Discord and Insta. My throat starts to close up at the thought. Maybe not the whole truth.

"I'm really sorry I hurt you. When I wrote what I wrote, all I meant was that I thought it would be the hardest to get Scarlett to like me and that if the rest of you guys liked me, she might give me a chance. I wrote your name down first because I thought you were really kind to me, Skyler. Not because I saw you as a stepping-stone to someone else."

She meets my eyes, and I try to send her 80 billion telepathic messages. I haven't told her everything—the worst things—but I've told her enough that I feel completely naked right now.

"It wasn't just that," she says. "Scarlett always gets so much attention from my family, so it hurt for you to pick her too, especially when I thought you really saw me. And there was that list you wrote about me. Chanterelles, softball, blue nail polish. Do you even like any of that stuff? Because you can just be friends with Scarlett. You don't have to pretend to like a bunch of dorky stuff for me. It's fine."

"What? No! I wish you didn't see that. Ugh, everything I say or do comes out so wrong. Do you think you could come to my tennis tournament this weekend? I feel like it might help you understand."

She hugs a throw pillow to her chest. "I'll think about it."

"Okay, well, great. Um, I'll leave you alone now."

She doesn't ask me to stay, but I guess that's the best I can hope for.

Amelia Grace

SCARLETT GRABS MY HAND AND PULLS ME THROUGH the crowd of people on the dock. I know it's just so we won't get separated, but it still sends shock waves through me.

"Where are we going?"

"I want to jump off the top of the dock!" she yells. We squeeze past some guys mixing drinks on a table, and she snags a shot and throws it back without breaking her stride. She's been like this all night.

We make our way up the stairs to the second story of the dock behind Cooper's house, where there's a waterslide and a platform for jumping.

"We don't have our bathing suits," I say.

"So? We'll jump in with our clothes on." Her eyes are wild. She starts taking off her shoes.

"Is everything okay?"

Her face crumples. "I broke up with Reese yesterday."

"Oh." It's the only thing that comes out. Those are life-changing words. They could shift the tectonic plates of who we are to each other. "I'm so sorry to hear that." Of course, it doesn't mean that she likes *me*. "Do you want to talk about it?"

"No. I don't even want to think about him. He's the worst. I just want to feel free, like I can put this whole thing behind me." She steps up onto the jumping platform and grabs my hand again. This time she laces her fingers through mine. "Please? I really want to do this with you."

Her hazel eyes are searing into mine, and I'm trying not to hope, but this feels like it means something big.

I kick off my flip-flops.

"One. Two. Three!" she yells.

We take a flying leap together and crash through the water. She doesn't let go of my hand.

Our feet just touch the bottom of the lake, and we rocket ourselves back to the surface.

Scarlett throws handfuls of water up in the air like glitter. "That. Was. Amazing!"

It is then that I realize how much she's slurring her words.

"Let's get you back to dry land," I say. This time I grab her hand and help her along. Thankfully, she lets me.

We collapse on the sand and stare up at the stars. Tonight is so wonderful, I don't think anything could make it more perfect. Scarlett pushes herself up on her elbows. Leans over me.

"I'm, like, so lucky to have you. The luckiest." Her hair falls forward when she says it and hits me in the shoulder. "Ooops." She tucks it behind her ear. "But, seriously. I'm just like, there's people who are lucky, and there's people who are *lucky*."

Her arm is getting tired of supporting her weight, and her

face keeps getting closer to mine. "We're gonna be in each other's lives forever, okay?"

She definitely says forever with extra *r*'s, but I don't care. This is happening.

Scarlett leans closer. Smiles like she knows something I don't.

Then she sighs. "Ugh. I really have to pee. Don't move, okay?"

I wouldn't dream of it.

She runs off toward the house. I gaze out at the lake in stunned delight. I think she was going to kiss me. I touch my lips like they'll be able to tell me.

I look up at the house even though I know she wouldn't be coming back that fast. I decide to run up to the dock while she's gone so I can get our shoes and phones and stuff. There's a text from Zoe.

Hey, I'm back from camp! Can I see you tomorrow?

I sit down on the sand where Scarlett left me. I don't know what to say back. This feels like the start of something with Scarlett. I don't think I'm imagining it. But if she kisses me, should I kiss her back? She's had an awful lot to drink. Maybe I just kiss her back long enough so she knows I'm not rejecting her? I don't want to ruin things.

I put my phone down. I hate the idea of hurting Zoe's feelings, but this thing with Scarlett, it's huge.

I look over my shoulder again for Scarlett. It's been a few minutes now. I thought she would—

She's there, on the other side of the party. Dancing on a picnic table in her bare feet. She pulls a boy with shaggy blond hair up so he's dancing with her. I've never even seen him before. And then she wraps her arms around his neck and kisses him.

I look away, fast. Of course she wasn't interested. I'm a hopeless dreamer for manufacturing things.

I text Zoe back: Can't wait.

CHAPTER 42

Ellie

....

I HAVE NEVER FELT SO NERVOUS BEFORE A TOURNA-
ment. Momma and I came early for warm-ups, and I told the
girls to come later, but the minutes have ticked by so quickly,
and later is now, and I can't help but look at the stands. Every.
Freaking. Second. Skyler isn't here yet. I didn't exactly *expect*
her—I only mentioned the tournament to her a couple days
ago—but the tournament's in Augusta, and it's only about an
hour away. So, I hoped.

And then I see Scarlett coming down the sidewalk in a
short black skirt, a Mother of Dragons tee knotted at the waist,
and heart sunglasses. My entire body relaxes. Until she shakes
her head.

"She's not coming?"

"No." She gives me a sad smile. "And Amelia Grace couldn't
make it either, though that has nothing to do with you." A
storm cloud crosses her face for a second.

"Well, thank you for coming," I say. "It means a lot."

Scarlett shrugs uncomfortably because feelings. "Sure."

She goes to sit with Momma in the stands, and I get back to
stretching. Then my phone buzzes. It's from Skyler!

Sorry I couldn't make it today.

Well, at least she cared enough to tell me.

Also, I don't think I want to be in the club anymore.

I feel like I've been stabbed. I knew this was bad, but I thought I could apologize and make it better. Now the reality of what I've done is hitting me. Skyler and I are never going to be friends again. Because I don't deserve a friend like her. That's probably why I've never been able to have girlfriends all along. I'm not built for it. And it's not like I only ruined today or this week or this summer. That thing that our moms have? A life-changing friendship that binds them together for the rest of their lives? We were going to have that too until I killed it.

The tournament is uneventful. I do pretty well, but I don't win first place. Emily Rae cheats like a mofo, but at least I didn't have to play her this time. Everyone pretends I don't exist. I'm starting to wonder if Scarlett's going to be confused about why I asked her here in the first place.

And then it happens. Emily Rae waves her hand over her head to get everyone's attention before they leave. "Can I talk to y'all for a minute?"

I walk over because I figure she's going to bring up the Discord thing, and I want to be able to defend myself.

Emily Rae comes toward me, smiling. What in the world? But, no, she's smiling at the girl next to me. She gives her a hug and conspicuously avoids so much as a glance in my direction.

"I'm so glad you're here! I really wanted you to hear this!"

She turns to face the group so that her back is blocking me out. (I do not think this is an accident.)

"So, I'm having a Fourth of July pool party at my house tomorrow when we get back to DC." She clasps her hands together like there's so much excitement, she can't possibly contain it all. "You're all welcome to come.

"We're going to have a cookout and fireworks. Mace, you're coming, right? I want to see your new swimsuit."

"Wouldn't miss it," replies Macy.

"Autumn, bring your giant unicorn float, 'kay?"

Emily Rae does this to all the girls. Well, not *all* of the girls. Certainly not me, and she leaves out a few others as well. She thinks of some special thing to say to each person to make them know they're included. And to make sure everyone knows who's not. Her eyes skim right over me like I'm not there.

Right. I turn around to leave. And there's Scarlett waiting for me.

"C'mon," says Scarlett.

"Where are we going?"

"You'll see."

"Are you kidnapping me?"

"Yep. You'll thank me later."

We get out of her mom's SUV at a place that looks like a warehouse. There's a sign that says DINNER BREAK, but I have no idea what that means.

"Ummm. I was kidding about the kidnapping part."

Scarlett just rolls her eyes and leads me inside. She hands a guy at a counter some cash in exchange for a stack of plates. And then she walks me over to stall number seven. There's a brick wall at the back and partitions to separate us from the other stalls (which are currently empty) and also a counter on which she sets the plates.

She looks at me like she's waiting for something.

"Still not sure what we're doing here."

"We," she says, "are letting off steam over those malevolent she-demons you play tennis with. Also my loser ex-boyfriend. I take it you've never been to a plate-smashing place before, so let me show you how it works."

She grabs a plate and flings it at the wall in front of us. It shatters brilliantly.

"Um."

"Try it. I swear it'll make you feel better."

I pick up a plate. Take a step to the right so I don't accidentally elbow her. "This feels a little ridiculous."

"Trust me," she says.

I take a deep breath in, let it out, and throw the plate like a Frisbee as hard as I can. It hits the wall with a terrific smashing noise. I feel like a little bit of the poison I've been holding inside evaporates. Also like I'm kind of a badass.

"That was amazing."

"Right?"

Scarlett throws another plate and so do I. We are Olympic discus throwers and over-served Real Housewives and ancient warrior queens defending our kingdoms.

We're both panting by the time we get to the end of our plates.

"So, I guess you've figured out I'm a loser," I say.

"What?"

"Those girls at tennis academy think I'm a huge home-schooled loser, and I was pretending to be cool because I thought it would make you guys like me."

"Um. Those girls at your tennis academy are snaggle-toothed harpies. Well, except for a couple of them who I think might actually be cool if you give them a closer look. Also: It's time for activity number two."

"There's another one?"

Scarlett nods. "Oh, yes." She whips out a notebook and a pen and sets it on the counter in front of us. "I'm going to show you how to make a friendship notebook. Amelia Grace taught me how to make one in eighth grade, and it's still the best thing ever. What you do is you use the awful things people do to you to help remind yourself of the type of friend you want to be.

"For example, you can take this page here, and you can write, 'I will never be the kind of hateful hag who invites every person except one to something. I will be the kind of classy-ass bitch who waits until the person is gone before politely extending an invitation to other people.'

"And on this next page, you can put something like: 'I will always check around if I'm in a group to make sure one person isn't walking by themselves. I'd certainly never be the kind of rude-ass, backstabbing, spiteful daughter of a sea witch who would make someone walk by themselves on purpose.'"

I laugh, but I take her notebook and write both things down, hateful hags included.

"I don't know about you," Scarlett says, "but I'm already feeling a great deal better."

I grin. "I am. I very much am. Are you really supposed to insult the other people when you write down your pledge?"

Scarlett winks at me. "That's an added bonus.

"Hey, Ellie?"

"Yeah?"

"I'm sorry for being such an asshole to you at first. I

was dealing with a lot of my own stuff, and I didn't give you a chance."

I kind of can't believe she admitted it. "Thanks," I say. "I'm really glad you eventually did."

"Me too."

I'm feeling good for the first time in days, and then I remember Skyler's texts.

"About Skyler—"

"Yeah, I was going to talk to you about that too. You should try talking to her again. Maybe in a couple days? Based on my years of experience, that's my best estimate."

"I think we're over," I say quietly.

"What? Why?"

I have to fight to get the words out. "Skyler doesn't want to be part of the SBDC anymore."

"And?"

"And that's it. We're over. I've screwed up so badly, I ruined everything and there's no returning from it."

"Are you kidding me? You, with the lists and the plans and the everything? If you give up after this, you're not who I thought you were." She puts her hands on both my shoulders like I'm a boxer about to go back into the ring. "You're going to talk to my sister. And you're going to apologize again. And this time, you're going to be brutally honest about all that tennis girl bullshit, because you're a weirdo, and Skyler's a weirdo, and you're meant to be together. You just have to get her to see that."

CHAPTER 43

Scarlett

....

MY SISTER STANDS WITH HER FACE PRESSED AGAINST the glass doors that lead onto the back deck of the carriage house. Whispering to herself. Because that's not weird.

"Kiss her! Ohmygosh, kiss her already!"

"Sky, what are you doing?"

She jumps. "Nothing!"

I wait.

"I mean, I was just watching Zoe and Amelia Grace take a walk, and they are so cute, I can't even stand it. I'm pretty sure Zoe is about to kiss her." She presses her face back against the window. "Oh, c'mon, kiss her already!"

Skyler

....

How can two human beings bear to stand so close together without actually touching each other? ARE THEY TRYING TO MAKE EACH OTHER SPONTANEOUSLY COMBUST?

"It's pretty creepy to watch people kiss," says Scarlett.

Which, okay. Yes. It is. But also:

"Why do you have to kill my joy?"

She narrows her eyes. Sharply.

Whatever. I'm still inconsolable over Ellie liking Scarlett more than me, and this is cheering me up, so.

I turn back to the window.

"Doesn't it just make you so happy to know that there's love in the world?"

Scarlett

Sometimes I want to slap her.

When we first found out she had arthritis, I thought something really terrible. I thought, maybe this will make things different, the scale will tip in the other direction, and she'll be like me now. But no, it only makes her even more perfect.

"I'm gonna go back to the main house," I say.

Skyler turns around all offended. "Seriously?"

I throw my hands up. "I'm sorry. Look, I'm not trying to be an asshole, but you're being exhaustingly happy right now."

"Our friends. Are kissing right now. Of course I'm flipping happy."

So, they did? I mean, they are? Something pulls me to the glass doors, I'm positive I didn't walk there on my own. And I'm standing beside Skyler and I'm staring, and she's wrong. They're not kissing. Yet. But anyone with a brain can see they're about to.

In three.

Two.

One.

Zoe's lips touch Amelia Grace's, and I can feel the champagne supernovas from here. I ball my hand into a fist at my side.

Skyler

"See? That wasn't so hard, was it? You were happy for a friend, and it didn't—" I catch sight of my sister's face. "Kill you."

She tries to rearrange her expression, quick. It doesn't exactly work.

"Oh, Scar, I'm so sorry." I go to touch her arm, but she flinches away.

"I'm fine."

"I never would have set them up if I'd known. You told me you weren't—"

"Ohmygosh, Sky, that's not even it. I'm just upset about something else. Maybe you don't know what that's like because nothing bothers you because you're so damn happy all the time. Or maybe you just don't feel anything."

I shouldn't clap back, but there's so much I've been pushing down inside me lately, and Ellie's notebook is in my head and how I'm always less important than my sister in a million other ways, and I can't help it, I just snap. "Or maybe I feel everything you do, but I keep it all on the inside because I'm not as selfish."

"Excuse me?" I hear my sister say, but it barely registers. I am prowling the carriage house in circles, and the feelings, they are bubbling over. "I've been trying so hard, and it's like no one even cares, and oh, sure, Skyler can do it, and Skyler can be the strong one, and I am so freaking tired of having to pretend to be happy when I'm hurting and I can't play softball. Do you know what that's like? Having your body turn against you and take away the thing you love most in the world? Do you even know what I'd give to switch bodies with you for a day? You are making lemons out of your lemonade!"

"That doesn't even make sense!"

"*Your mom* doesn't make sense!"

"We have the same mom!"

I do one of those screams where your hands are clenched at your sides and your mouth is closed and no sound comes out but you are still definitely screaming. And then I launch two middle fingers in the direction of her head because I am nothing if not composed and classy.

Scarlett

Sometimes when my sister gets really angry, she looks like a kitten who thinks it's a lion.

Skyler

"It's not funny! I am so shit-damn angry. I shouldn't have to do all this stuff just to take my gall-darned fucking medicine."

Scarlett

I know that my snickering is only making the situation worse, but also, I have zero control over it. Did you not just hear her say "shit-damn"?

"I'm sorry, I'm sorry," I say, keeping a (mostly) straight face. I take a deep breath so I can pull it together before I say the next bit. "But, Sky, you know you don't actually have to do that, right? Mama and Daddy would have taken you to the doctor if you'd just asked them. You have to stop hiding that you're hurt."

"It's not that simple."

"It *is*. You tell them what's wrong. They take you to the doctor. Bingo. Stop being such a freaking martyr."

"You don't understand!" she grows more exasperated with every breath, but I talk over her:

"You don't have to do everything yourself, you just think you have to."

She clenches her fists. "I DO have to."

"*Why?*"

Skyler

I want to blurt out the truth. That I saw her cutting that day after the fair, and I know it's my fault. But, angry as I am, I'm scared to let that out in the open. So, instead, I lash out.

"Because nothing can ever be about me because everything has to be about you. That's how our family works. That's how *everything* works."

Scarlett narrows her eyes. "Skyler—"

I put my hands up. "I don't have the energy to be around you right now."

I stalk out of the carriage house before she can say anything else.

Scarlett

I don't try to stop my sister. There's no reasoning with her when she's like this.

She's right about Amelia Grace. But it doesn't make any sense. It's not like I'm in love with Amelia Grace. I care about her, and she's my friend, and maybe I just have a gut feeling that Zoe isn't the one for her. A second gut feeling follows, taking the shape of a question. If Zoe isn't the one for her, who is?

But it's not a question I'm ready to think about right now, so I push it away. Because Amelia Grace is so damn good, and I'm the kind of person who requires energy to be around.

Amelia Grace

Zoe drives away in a little motorboat. At least, I think it's a motorboat. It's a boat and it has a motor? I've been here five weeks, and I still know nothing of rich people and their boats.

We kissed. She kissed me. But I don't know.

I waited. For the fireworks and the shooting stars and the birds singing just for us.

And I felt. Lips.

Just lips. Like they could've been anyone's lips. They were nice lips. They certainly weren't slobbery lips. But it didn't feel like the entire world was attached to them. Even with Carrie, and the kiss coming totally out of nowhere, I felt . . . something.

I'm scared.

Because I felt more yesterday when Scarlett announced she'd broken up with her boyfriend than I did just now when Zoe kissed me. And if I kissed Scarlett, I know it wouldn't feel like just lips or strawberries or friendship. It would feel like everything.

If she loved me back.

CHAPTER 44

Ellie

....

I DON'T THINK I HAVE EVER BEEN LESS EXCITED ABOUT a party.

Reasons I should be excited:

1) It is the Fourth of July, and I have gone full T. Swift with the red, white, and blue clothes. And accessories. And make up.

2) The moms have given us permission to go to this party because there's parental supervision, and Bennett is picking us up in his boat.

3) A lakeside bonfire on the beach.

Reasons I am not:

Skyler and I aren't okay yet.

It's not like she's being vile to me Emily Rae–style or icing me out or something. More like: I'll ask if she wants help picking an outfit that will drive Bennett completely bananas, and she'll be like, "Sure." Only, it feels like someone sucked all the excitement out of her voice, and we don't gush and squeal over him, and I don't bother bringing up my Instagram stuff, and we're not glued to each other in the boat on the way over.

It's not easy anymore.

When the boat docks, Skyler rushes off to light sparklers with Bennett, and I don't chase her. Just watch the friendship I've waited my whole life for run away.

Instead, I have a veggie dog and look for a guy to kiss, and dance around the bonfire like a pixie and look for a guy to kiss, and write my name in the sky with sparklers and look for a guy to kiss. (Spoiler alert: I don't find one.) It's not that I'm desperate, but I've accomplished everything else on my list for the summer: tennis and PSAT practice and recipes and parties and letters to Ilhan Omar and Halima Aden and Yumna Al-Arashi and Saba Chaudhry Barnard. I like the feeling of completeness. It may also have something to do with the fact that "Make friends" is utterly and completely in the gutter right now. I can't make Skyler be my friend, but finding some rando to make out with for a sec? That's within my power.

Scarlett comes and stands beside me, only not *right* beside me, because fire hazard.

"Hey," she says.

"Hey." I light her sparkler with mine.

"You look about as happy as I feel."

I watch Skyler squeeze onto a hay bale with Bennett.

"Skyler and I still aren't talking."

"Welcome to the club. Did you talk to her yet?"

"No."

Scarlett gives me her most scathing raised eyebrow.

My sparkler fizzles out, and I put it in the bucket of water nearby. "What's killing your night?"

"Oh. Nothing." Her eyes snap to the lake, but I follow

where she was looking before. Amelia Grace. And Zoe. "Just not feeling it tonight, I guess."

Scarlett traces circles around her head, looking entirely too unhappy for someone holding a sparkler. I want to hug her, but she would hate that, so instead I say, "I haven't seen them hold hands."

She almost drops her sparkler. "What?"

"Zoe. She's big on the PDA, like with holding Amelia Grace's hand or finding an excuse to touch her."

"Oh," says Scarlett, flustered. "I mean, I don't really—"

"Tonight"—I steamroll over her excuses—"she hasn't so much as picked fake lint off of Amelia Grace's shirt."

Scarlett's mouth is still opening and closing like a fish's, but I just squeeze her shoulder. "You watch. I'm gonna go eat a s'more."

There's a table near the bonfire with marshmallows and sticks and stuff. I try to only look at Skyler a few times as I make a plate with graham crackers and Nutella. (Side note: Whoever thought to put Nutella on s'mores is a genius.) I head over to the bonfire.

Bennett's friend Cooper (of the gratuitous flexing) winks at me through the flames. It would be so easy to go over and say hi. To grab his neck and kiss him while the party swirls around us. Except now I'm hesitant. Because Muslim girls aren't supposed to just go around kissing random boys, and despite all my daydreams, I'm frozen where I stand.

And then suddenly there's a girl in a bikini top handing him a beer. And he's pulling her against him and he is. The. Worst. Kisser. Ever.

One hundred percent, this is not me being petty. I may

have never been kissed, but even I know you're not supposed to use that much tongue. She has to wipe her face with the back of her hand when he pulls away. Not just her mouth. Her *face*.

Whelp. Dodged that bullet.

Sometimes not getting what you want is the very best thing. Sucks though. I don't know why, but I have this feeling like tonight was my last chance.

I spike a marshmallow onto a stick. I should be more excited about these s'mores. I add another marshmallow. Fireworks burst overhead anticlimactically. Scarlett moves past the bonfire in the direction of the s'mores table. A few seconds later, I get a tap on the shoulder.

"If this is about Zoe and Amelia Grace, I—"

My brain registers the face in front of me. Mile-long eyelashes. Bright red hair poking out from under a ball cap. Shy grin. (Not Scarlett.)

"OHMYGOSH, IT'S YOU," the face is saying.

I can't help but giggle. "What?"

He blushes, and I feel like I have taken a taser directly to the heart. "I'm friends with Bennett? You were talking to our boat on the dock that day, and then I saw you at the sandbar party but Bennett was having some . . . trouble, and then there was that party at Nate's but a weird thing happened with a bullhorn and was that your mom?"

It is my turn to blush. "Maybe." Change the subject, change the subject, change the subject. I notice his shirt, a white tee with a logo that says MARATÓN SAN BLAS. "Is that from a race?"

"Yeah, it's a half marathon in Puerto Rico. I ran it last year when I went to visit my dad. I'm a runner."

"Cool." I can't believe he's been looking for me. I have been looking for a guy to kiss the whole summer, and this gorgeous boy has been looking for me. It occurs to me that I should probably say something else. "I play tennis." Smooth, Ellie. Really smooth.

He only smiles harder and touches his hat nervously.

"But sometimes I run for cross-training."

FFS, he does not want to hear your workout plan. I shove my marshmallows into the fire. The flames dance around them, turning them a light brown color, but I don't let them catch fire.

"Maybe we could go running together sometime," he says.

"I'd love that!" I say it too eagerly and wish I could pull it back.

I can feel my face turning red, but he's blushing too, and I am made of exclamation points, and ohmygosh, is this really going to happen—

"Ellie!" yells a voice from the dock. Scarlett. "Ellie, we gotta go. We have to be back by two."

ARE YOU FREAKING KIDDING ME?

This is supposed to be my romantic summer fling, first kiss, oops-we-live-seven-hours-apart-and-have-to-write-love-letters relationship, and I am not letting it slip away, dammit.

"I'm Ellie," I say, all rushed and breathless.

"Andres."

"Cool. If I'm going to kiss someone, I at least want to know their first name."

His eyes goggle. "Kiss, oh. Andres. My name is definitely Andres."

"Andres," I say. My first kiss is going to be with a boy named Andres.

I lean forward. So does he.

He closes his eyes, and I wrap my hand around his neck—the hand that's not holding the marshmallows on a stick. And I press my lips against his, and, oh. There are fireworks, both the real and metaphorical kind. And everything is glitter and magic and heat and fire and smoke. Wait, what's that smell?

We jerk apart. His hat is on fire. Well, my marshmallows are on fire, and his hat is smoking. I yelp and drop my marshmallow stick. How. Embarrassing.

"Ellie!" Scarlett yells again. "We're gonna miss curfew!"

Everyone else is already on the boat, including Skyler, who doesn't appear to be worried at all about leaving me behind. Andres pours a cup of water on the still crackling marshmallows. (In addition to being gorgeous, he is also resourceful.)

"Um," I say.

"You have to go," he finishes.

"But—" I say. Passion and longing and extreme mortification all war inside my brain. I can't let this end. I grab my charred marshmallow stick and scratch my number in the sand because glass slippers are for quitters. "Call me!" I yell as I run to catch the boat.

He waves. "I most definitely will."

Scarlett

THEY WEREN'T TALKING. MUCH.

I try to pretend like this is a mere observation and not
the sole thought occupying my brain for the entire Fourth
of July party. What exactly Amelia Grace and Zoe were—and
weren't—doing.

They weren't kissing.

Fuck, and now I'm thinking about kissing again.

"You okay?" asks Amelia Grace, and I jump.

I didn't realize she had leaned against the boat railing next
to me. Skyler's crossfaded knight in shining armor is chauf-
feuring us home in his boat (and is currently sober, which is
the only reason I'm letting him).

"I'm fine," I say. "Just kind of partied out and ready to
get home."

I brush pretend dirt off my blue lace dress. (Ellie insisted
we glam it up because that's what Taylor Swift would do.)

She nods. "Me too."

She looks . . . jumpy.

"Are *you* okay? You and Zoe hardly talked the whole night."

"Oh." She blushes. I don't know why her blushing over Zoe bothers me so much. "Zoe and I broke up. Well, I guess we weren't officially together in the first place, and I think I was liking her for some of the wrong reasons, but now we're definitely just friends."

"Oh, wow, I'm so sorry." I mean it. I don't want her to feel bad or hurt or anything like that. There is definitely no part of me that feels like a flower curling toward the sun right now.

But things do feel different. Now that I know.

I can feel it in the way she follows me quickly off the boat while Ellie and Skyler are still saying their goodbyes, slipping up the stairs to our bedroom in the carriage house. In the way my breath catches at the thought of us being alone for one fleeting moment. I have to take off my dress, and we've been changing in front of each other all summer, but my heartbeat knows secrets my brain doesn't, and my hands can't seem to work the zipper, and I feel suddenly brave.

"Can you unzip me?" I ask.

When I was a kid, I remember Mama asking Daddy to unzip her dresses, and I always thought it was so weird, because you can totally do that yourself if you contort your arms enough. Now I get it.

Amelia Grace says sure and crosses the room. "Sure" is a word that says, "It's fine. It's no big deal." Her voice doesn't say it's no big deal. It's terrified.

I realize I'm holding my breath. Maybe I'm a little terrified too.

She pulls down the zipper. Is it weird I'm disappointed that it's over already? And then she strokes her fingers down my back where the dress is pulled open and there is so very much skin showing. She starts at my neck and goes all the way down my spine.

I let out the tiniest gasp without meaning to.

"Sorry," she says, jerking her hand away like one of us has burned the other.

"It's okay."

There's a pause that stretches clear across the room. I don't move away. Neither does she. Her voice is soft in my ear. "It's okay I did that just now or it's okay you want me to do it again?"

I am dizzy with how much I want things. "The second one."

She doesn't say anything in response, just runs her fingers down my back again, only this time it's slower and more. I think I might explode. Is that a thing that can happen to people? Because I'm pretty sure it's about to happen to me right now, and I have no idea what kind of person I might be after the explosion. Maybe the kind of person who is in love with Amelia Grace.

The door to the carriage house swings open, and Amelia Grace and I jump apart. Ellie comes bounding up the stairs.

"Was that the most amazing party or what?!" yells Ellie.

"Yes." My chest goes up and down as I say it. Can she see it, how difficult breathing is right now?

I accidentally catch Amelia Grace's eye from across the room and have to turn around. What in the ever-loving hell just happened? I have only ever dated boys. I've never even thought about dating a girl. But when Ames touched my back just now, I couldn't think of anything else. So, now I'm what? Bi? But I've never. I mean, I haven't ever.

Oh.

McCloud Harris. McCloud Harris and her boyfriend and her talking about her boyfriend and *the feelings*. Oh, the feelings. And it's not just McCloud. It's also Sloane, Britney, Layla, Kayleigh. And it's not like it's every girl I've ever been friends with. More like I can suddenly look back at the history of my life and tell you which girls were my friends and which girls were my *friends*. And there's one friend who stands out above all the others.

"Are you okay?" says Amelia Grace quietly.

I almost jump out of my skin. "Totally." I smile brightly for Ellie's benefit. "I just need to, like, brush my teeth. So, yeah. Gonna get right on that."

"Okay," says Amelia Grace.

I rush into the bathroom with my dress still halfway off. I hate that it's my fault she looks so sad, but I'm more scared of what will happen if I stay.

CHAPTER 46

Amelia Grace

SCARLETT AND I STILL HAVEN'T TALKED SINCE, YOU know, The Dress. I mean, we've exchanged conversation, but we haven't *talked*. I feel like there's a wall between us.

The day after the Fourth of July party is especially sunny. We're sitting on the dock with Ellie and Aunt Seema (because we're never alone anymore, Scarlett and me, she makes sure of it), when by some stroke of luck or kindness Ellie says she needs a snack and Aunt Seema gets up to follow her. Scarlett's so into her quilting, she doesn't notice until they're halfway to the house.

"Oh," she says, jumping up from her chair after she sees the look on my face. "I just remembered I need to—"

I jump up too. "Scarlett, wait." I'll beg if I have to. "I'm sorry I made you uncomfortable, and it's okay if you don't like me, but please, I need you to be my friend."

I stand there, all desperate-like. Wishing/hoping/waiting/needing.

Scarlett sets down her quilting.

"Okay."

"Okay?"

"Okay, I'm your friend. We're always going to be friends."

It would be nice if I could cling to the word "always" and let the word "friend" go sailing past.

"That's all I need," I force myself to say. Lies, lies, lies, lies, lies.

There's the hum of a boat in the distance. Scarlett wraps her arms around herself protectively.

"I don't know," she says. Doesn't know what? If she likes me? "I've never liked a girl before, and I just don't know."

So she does like me! I don't smile though. This doesn't feel like the kind of news where you smile. Something about the way her mouth turns down tells me not to hope.

"It's just—I can't—" She looks like she's holding back something terrible. "What if we kiss each other, and it's like, Nope, definitely don't like girls. I would feel like such an asshole."

That's it? She's worried about kissing. I don't mean it to sound dismissive. Identity stuff is a lot to figure out. No one knows that better than me. But I got the feeling there was something much bigger/darker/scarier hurricane-ing behind her eyes.

"Well, there is a pretty easy way to figure out the answer to the kissing part." I can't even say it without blushing.

She blushes back. Accidentally looks at my lips. Blushes harder.

Holy crap, Scarlett Kaplan-Gable is thinking about kissing me. This is more than I could have ever dared hope for in life. The girl I've loved since seventh grade is maybe/finally/hopefully falling in love with me. Or at least is interested in my kissing abilities.

I take a step closer. Is this really going to happen? Scarlett's hair gets swept across her face by the wind, and she tucks it behind her ears. I've imagined this moment approximately eighty billion times. I reach out my hand to touch hers. Run my thumb across the back of her wrist just to feel the sparks that swirl around us like lightning bugs. Heck, maybe we don't even need to kiss. Maybe we could just hold hands for the rest of our lives. But then I look at her lips.

They're perfect. She's perfect. And if we could just—

Scarlett steps away.

She lets go of my hand, and the lightning bugs fizzle out.

"I have a lot of things to figure out," she says. "I'm sorry."

She runs down the dock and up the hill to the house.

Only, this time it feels like she's taking pieces of me with her.

CHAPTER 47

Skyler

I SIT ON A BARSTOOL IN THE CARRIAGE HOUSE AND shoot orange juice the way other people shoot gin. The loft is empty. Again. It's been over a week since we lit candles and talked about important things. Two days since we were kind of forced to hang out together on Bennett's boat on the way to and from the Fourth of July party. I'm not going to a meeting. Not after what Ellie put in her journal. Not after my fight with Scarlett. She and Amelia Grace seem to be going through something too, not that I'm getting mixed up in that. But I do climb the ladder and stare forlornly at the candles and papers gathering dust. In a twisted way, it makes me feel better.

Maybe it's because I'm in self-destruct mode or maybe it's that I have nothing else to lose, but I decide I'm finally going to talk to Mama. I am allowed to want these new meds, I tell myself. Talking to my mom about them and about how I want to play softball again might very well destroy life as I know it, but I don't feel like there's anything else for me to lose. I search the main house for Mama. Find her in the kitchen holding her cell phone like it's a poison-ous snake.

"I just got off the phone with Dr. Levy," she says.

I don't say anything back. Can't. This is the worst possible outcome. Even in my most pessimistic daydreams, I couldn't have conjured a scenario like this.

"How could you do this to me, Skyler? Especially after that talk we had the night you took the boat." Mama makes her wounded face. She's very like Scarlett in that way.

"My pain has been getting so much worse."

She looks genuinely flummoxed. "What are you talking about? You've hardly complained about your pain since we've been here."

"Only because I couldn't." You can do this without crying. You *can*. "You've been so upset, and you should be—things are awful. But then Scarlett always seemed right on the edge too, and every time I tried to talk to you about it, you started crying, and I felt like I couldn't talk to Daddy, and it's been so hard. The worst it's ever been."

She puts her hand on my shoulder. "Baby, you should have told me that. I want you to tell me things like that."

She's taking it so much better than I imagined. I duck my head. "I couldn't. I swear I tried really hard."

Mama hugs me tight. For a while. Then she lets me go so she can look me in the eye. Calmly.

"Make me a promise. If you ever can't get through to me again, write me a letter, get Scarlett to help, anything it takes, but just, make me listen to you. Please don't ever let yourself be in that much pain again."

"Okay." Is that really it?

"You promise?"

"I promise. And, um, now that you mention it. There's more."

"Oh, damn, are you pregnant? Ellie said there's a boy you've been seeing."

"What? No!"

"Oh, good. Is he Jewish?"

"Mama!"

"Sorry! Okay, but is he?"

I roll my eyes. "Every bit as Jewish as Daddy. But, listen. I—I want to play softball again. *Try* playing softball again."

There. It's out there. I wait for the ground to start crumbling around me.

But it doesn't.

"Well, that's wonderful news," says Mama.

I wait for the other shoe to drop.

"Baby, why were you so afraid to tell me that?"

I don't know how to tell her this without making things worse.

"Sky?"

"That last game I played, I could barely move after."

"I know. I remember."

"It's why you guys got in that fight." I shrug fragilely. "I don't want to be the reason."

She freezes, and I can see the pieces moving in her brain, see the moment they click into place. She lets out a little gasp. And then she starts crying.

I hug her and pet her hair. "Mama, it's okay."

"No, it's not. It really isn't. I'm so sorry, baby. Your daddy and I are having problems, but they are our problems. It is not and never has been your fault. Do you understand?"

I feel like weights upon weights have been lifted off of me. I can tell people what I need. I don't have to keep everything hidden. It won't break the entire world after all.

"Yes," I say.

CHAPTER 48

Scarlett

IT IS RAINING.

Amelia Grace and I feel like a spontaneous combustion waiting to happen, and now the weather and the universe have conspired to keep us confined to an enclosed space with six other women. Well, five. Aunt Val hasn't been over today because Heidi's really exhausted and keeps having these Braxton Hicks contractions, which Aunt Neely said is totally normal at this stage, but rest and water never hurt anyone.

"It's looking really good," says Amelia Grace.

"What?" I say stupidly.

"Your quilt." She sits down beside me with a glass of sweet tea. "It's beautiful. It's like artwork or something."

"Oh, right." I am quilting right now. That is a thing I am doing. "Thank you."

I concentrate very hard on pushing the needle down and back up through the layers of fabric. It is not an easy task with her making the question face. But I don't have any of the answers. Not ones she'll like anyway. Because even if I do have these feelings for her, she's the best person I know. Why would I unleash a train wreck on her?

Thunder crashes overhead, and the needle jabs through the fabric and into my finger. I let out a hiss.

"You okay, sweetie?" Mama puts her hand on my shoulder and eyes the needle meaningfully.

"I'm fine. It was the stupid thunder. My hand slipped."

Mama hovers. "Are you sure you don't want to talk about anything?"

Her eyes slide to my finger again. Ugh. I never harmed with needles anyway. She knows that.

Amelia Grace pretends to be very interested in the sweet tea she's drinking.

"Are you sure I can't go back to the carriage house?" I say it more sharply than I mean to.

"Sweetie, I told you, there are too many big trees over there, and that carriage house is tiny. One good bolt of lightning, and you'd be flat as a pancake."

"Right." I go back to stabbing the fabric in front of me.

Amelia Grace winces beside me. It's not her I'm mad at, but there's no way for me to explain that without making this situation even more awkward.

"It's really coming down out there," says Ellie from the table, where she and Aunt Seema are playing Exploding Kittens.

"There's a flash flood warning till ten a.m. tomorrow," says Aunt Seema. "We're supposed to get at least five inches. Do you think we should move the cars?"

"The cars will be fine, Seema. We're on a hill. But I wouldn't recommend driving anywhere till we get the all-clear." Mama eyes Seema's jittery hands. "How many cups of chai have you had?"

Seema scoffs. "A number."

"I'm cutting you off."

I snort and go back to my quilting. A phone rings a few minutes later.

"Hello?" says Aunt Neely. "All right. Well, how far apart are they?"

My head shoots up.

"Okay, and how long have they been going on? No breaks? Can I talk to Heidi? Hey, honey, how are you feeling? Okay, yep. I'd say you're in labor. Why don't you call the midwife, and I'll head on over."

She hangs up. And realizes we are all staring at her like OMGWTFBBQ.

"It's going to be fine," she says. She heads to the door, and the rest of us follow. "First babies take a long time to get here."

Famous. Last. Words.

Amelia Grace runs downstairs with our first update after just a few minutes. "She's already at six centimeters!"

"What does that mean?" asks Ellie.

I whisper an explanation in her ear.

"Oh, *gosh*, why would you tell us that?"

"I know," says Amelia Grace. "I had to hide my face when she checked so I wouldn't throw up. Anyway, it means she's pretty far along. It's okay though. The midwife still has plenty of time to get here."

Amelia Grace says all of this with a serene confidence.

This is why she's the perfect person to sit by Heidi and whisper words of encouragement during her contractions, while Val drives down to check the road. I kind of wish I was up there too, but Heidi asked for Amelia Grace. She knows her best. Plus, can you imagine if it was me up there trying to calm someone? I shudder. Some people aren't built to handle crisis situations.

I boil some water, while Sky and Ellie read the same *Teen Vogue* without talking to each other and Mama and Aunt Seema set about cooking a metric ass-load of food.

The next time Amelia Grace comes down, her face is paler. "So, Aunt Neely says she's hit the transition stage."

I wince. "Already?"

Amelia Grace shrugs and runs back upstairs. And Aunt Val bursts in soaking wet.

"The creek's risen over the road. The midwife can't get here."

Amelia Grace staggers downstairs. This time she is shaking.

"I think she's having the baby now. I shouldn't have looked. Oh, gosh."

She sits down, fast, and puts her head on her knees. I'm by her side in a minute.

"I'm so sorry. I didn't know I was so squeamish," Amelia Grace says into her knees.

"It's okay. You're doing great," I tell her.

She shakes her head. "Mom's going to need help up there. Can you take my place?"

"Me?"

"You've been shadowing her—"

"As a lactation consultant. I've never seen a birth in person." The thought of trying to help sends my heart racing, but underneath that, there's a part of me that really wants to.

Amelia Grace takes my face in her hands. Looks me right in the eye. "You can do this. You're the bravest person I know."

With her hands on my cheeks, I feel brave.

And then Heidi lets out a yell that echoes through the house. Mama, Ellie, Aunt Seema, and I run upstairs to make sure everything is okay. Skyler stays with Amelia Grace because she freaks over blood and needles and stuff. The rest of us freeze in the doorway. Heidi is yelling, "No, no, no, no. I can't do this." She holds Val's hand.

Aunt Neely stands up. "You can do this. And you will. You're going to get to meet your baby soon." She turns to us. "I need someone to get me some more towels. And wash your hands really well first."

I wait for someone competent to move. Someone strong. Everyone stares like their faces and limbs are frozen. I run over and start scrubbing my hands even though literally anyone else would be a better choice.

There's a lot of blood and stuff. I get why Amelia Grace almost passed out. But I focus on Heidi and on doing everything Aunt Neely tells me step by step by step:

Bring up more water.

Apply pressure here.

Help me change this underpad.

"I can't," says Heidi.

"You're doing great," says Aunt Neely.

"You sure are!" I say. "You are such a super badass. A total

BAMF at pushing out babies." Probably not what you're supposed to say, but at least there's a flicker of a smile on Heidi's face. Neely tells her to push again.

I hear Ellie make a noise behind me, and Aunt Seema leads her away, and Mama goes to make sure the food doesn't burn, but I'm too busy to really notice.

"I see hair!" I squeal.

"There's hair?" says Heidi, smiling.

"Beautiful hair! So much hair! Gorgeous hair!"

Val and Heidi share a sweet smile with tired eyes.

The pushing continues. Mama comes back at some point to squeeze my arm and ask me if I'm okay, and Amelia Grace comes with her. But I can't leave now, so I tell her I'm fine, and Mama pats me on the back and heads downstairs.

"There's a head! This baby is freaking beautiful, and you are a rock star!" I tilt my head to the side. Are they supposed to be so blue?

Val joins me so she can see the baby's face. "Is that—" But Aunt Neely silences her with a shake of her head.

"One more big push," she tells Heidi.

Amelia Grace had been frozen in the doorway, but now she moves to hold Val's hand. The inside of my head is a beehive, but I force myself to remain calm. The rest of the baby comes out, body red and wriggling. It has a cord wrapped around its neck. Aunt Neely unwraps the umbilical cord in two quick movements.

"Everything is going to be fine," she says. "You have a beautiful baby girl, and we're just going to give her a couple minutes with mom before we cut the cord. Get some extra oxygen and nutrients in there." She sets the baby skin-to-skin against

Heidi's chest. Even as she's been talking, more of the color has returned to the baby's face.

"She's perfect," whispers Heidi.

I feel like I can breathe again.

"Oh, thank goodness, she's going to be okay." Val walks with shaky legs back to her chair and keels over sobbing into Heidi's shoulder.

"We can cut the cord now," Aunt Neely says gently. She squeezes Val's shoulder. "Did you still want to do it?"

"I don't think I can," says Val.

"Why don't you let Scarlett do it?" says Heidi.

"*Me?*" I'm 298 percent sure I don't deserve to be entrusted with something so important.

Aunt Neely wraps her arm around me. "You were wonderful, honey."

I blush. "Thank you."

She hands me the scissors and shows me where to cut. It's kind of like cutting through uncooked chicken, but I manage. Then Aunt Neely tends to the baby and all the stuff that goes on after the baby, which no one ever tells you about, probably because it's actually pretty gross. I help her even though a part of me wants to flee in extreme disgust.

"Let's give them a minute by themselves before we bring everyone else up," Aunt Neely finally says.

Heidi and Aunt Val give me so many hugs and thank-yous that I feel embarrassed. Almost as many as they give Aunt Neely. I give Baby Girl a tiny kiss on the forehead before I leave. It's hard to take my eyes off her.

I pause in the doorway, take one last, lingering look. Val and Heidi are both crying, wrapped up around this tiny girl like she's their whole world. I realize Amelia Grace is standing beside me, staring too. We walk downstairs together.

"I can't believe I did that."

But she looks at me like she's always known I could.

"You're amazing."

Amelia Grace

I DIDN'T KNOW MY MOM COULD LAUGH WITH abandon. When we got here, at least. But now we're sitting on the deck eating lunch at the picnic table, and there's sunlight streaming down, and I will never get tired of hearing her laugh that way.

"Oh, I meant to tell you," says Val. "Heidi shared her birth story on this mom board she's on, and now two more of her friends want you to be their doula."

Mom flushes under the praise. "That was so sweet of her. I'll have to see when they're due though. Summer's only got a few weeks left."

Every time someone mentions how much time we've got left, my stomach feels like it's full of rocks. Thinking about going back to Ranburne. Thinking about seeing my stepdad again. It makes me say something stupidly optimistic.

"What if we just stayed? You're starting to get so much work here, and you could get your midwife license in South Carolina, and—"

"That would be amazing!" gushes Scarlett. One more reason to stay.

Mom cocks her head to the side, puzzled. "Baby girl, we have a life at home. Friends. Church. I don't think your stepdad would agree to move."

Kinda counting on it.

"I know. I just. I guess I don't want this to end." And I don't want to stop seeing you this way.

Mom squeezes my hand. "I know how you feel. But a few doula jobs isn't enough to move over."

Her phone buzzes on the table. Speak of the devil. She rushes inside to take it like she always does. Heaven forbid she have friends. Or happiness.

We finish our sandwiches, and I take Mom's plate inside in case she's still hungry. Aunt Seema and Aunt Adeline cackle over something as they start the dishes. Mom takes the plate from me with a smile and steps out of the kitchen.

"It's just Adeline," I hear her say. "Well, it is her house. She's here every now and again. Well, yeah, that was the twins. They came with her. What? No, there aren't any men here. I'm not lying. I just hadn't gotten around to telling you that Adeline was here. I'm sorry, please, I should have told you. No, you don't need to come here. I'm not scared of what you'll find, but you don't need to— I'm sorry. Please don't say that. Jay, please, I love you. Okay, fine, but you really don't need to. I can drive Amelia Grace and I back at the end of the summer like we— I know. I know. I'm sorry. Yes, okay, I'm sorry. I'll be ready."

Mom hangs up the phone and her face is different. I try and then try harder, but I can't find any trace of that woman who was laughing at the picnic table.

"You need to pack your things," Mom says. "Your stepdad will be here tonight."

Scarlett

She stuffs the clothes into her bag like they've personally wronged her. Socks–pants–sports bra. Bam-bam-bam. Her arm muscles are taut, and her face is screwed up and red, but she isn't crying. Yet.

"Ames?"

"Hey." She freezes mid-stuff, like she's embarrassed to be caught revenge-packing her duffel bag.

"I heard you guys are going."

She crosses her arms and won't look at me. "Yeah. He's coming here tonight."

"Don't go." I say it before I can help myself. I thought we had a few more weeks to figure things out, and if she leaves— And then there's her stepdad. She can't go back with people who treat her like that. She just can't.

"I have to," she says quietly.

"But what if we try to convince your mom—"

"You heard her at the table. This is what my life is in the real world. My mom will never change her mind about my stepdad, and she'll never change her mind about me. I'm going home, and I'm going to email Pastor Chris and tell him I'll stay in the closet for the rest of the time I'm in high school."

Horrified. I am horrified right now. "You can't."

Her voice is wobbly when she answers. "What other option do I have?"

"You could—"

She cuts me off. "I forgot some stuff at the big house. I better go get it."

I watch her walk down the stairs, feeling like I have absolutely no power over my life. Everything is slipping away, and I can't do a damn thing about it. And then I look at the attic.

An idea takes shape inside my head. This could work. It's my only shot. It has to.

I run outside and down to the dock. Ellie practices her PSAT words on a beach towel.

"Amelia Grace's stepdad is coming, and he's making her and her mom leave with him."

Ellie drops her vocab book. "What?"

"I know. We're having a club meeting. Now."

"But Skyler and I—"

"Don't care. This is bigger than that, and you know it. Meet me in the loft in fifteen minutes."

She gets this steely look on her face and nods the way you do when you're about to go off to war. Hell. Yes.

I rush off to find my sister. She's on the couch in the big house watching yet more *Great British Bake Off*.

I step right between her and Mary Berry. She opens her mouth in protest, but I run right over her.

"I know you hate me right now, but Ames needs us. They're gonna take her back to Ranburne and make her be in the closet. Club meeting in fifteen minutes."

I don't wait for her to say yes before I walk away. I know my sister.

I talk to Mama really quick since she's in the kitchen, and I need to get her permission for a couple things. I can hear Amelia Grace upstairs in Aunt Neely's room. I hope I have enough time. I race back to the carriage house and swing myself up the ladder. Open the little window. Locate the lighter and light each of the candles. Then I sit down beside the bowl where we made our pacts, and I wait.

It isn't long before Amelia Grace arrives. She lets out a little gasp when she sees me in the loft with candles all around.

"Can you come up here for a second?"

She doesn't say anything. She seems stunned. But her arms and legs carry her up the ladder anyway. She sits down in front of me.

"What's going on?" she whispers.

"I can't let you go. They'll never let you be yourself there." She has to listen. The club can make her listen.

"But I already asked my mom."

"Well, you could try again. And." Oh, gosh, am I really going to say this? "And if that doesn't work, you could stay by yourself. Just you. With me."

Something flickers on her face, and I feel a soaring in my chest, but then she shakes her head. "She's my mom. I have to—"

I cut her off. With my lips. Holy crap, I am kissing Amelia Grace. For a second, she's in shock. And then she's kissing me back, and there's this feeling, like the world is as it should be. And I'm trying to convince her, only not with words: Stay, stay, stay. Please, stay.

It only takes a few seconds for her to come to her senses and pull away. "What was that?"

I honestly have no idea. I didn't even know what I was gonna do until it was already happening. All I know is she can't leave. Not when I'm so close to figuring this out. There's another way to maybe possibly convince her to stay. And honesty is even scarier than kissing. But here goes:

"I know I said I was worried about the liking a girl stuff, but that was only part of it. And, um, based on how I felt when we were kissing just now, a very small part." I don't want to tell her the rest. Because what if she confirms that it's true? I don't think I could take that. I wrap my arms around myself.

Amelia Grace scoots closer to me. "Scarlett, are you okay?"

"I couldn't make things work with Reese," I say. "Because I have all these problems. And if I'm too damaged for someone like him, how could I ever be good enough for you?"

"What are you talking about?" Amelia Grace looks at me like I'm speaking another language. How does she not see this?

"You're supposed to want someone who's kind and brave and makes you kinder and braver. And you are and you do. But what am I bringing you?" I shake my head. "You know what? I don't even care anymore, just please stay, whether I'm good enough for you or not."

"Stop it," she says, so firmly it startles me. "Stop saying you're not good enough. Who told you you're damaged?"

Silence.

"Him?"

I still can't answer. My eyes flick to the train track scars climbing my arms.

She notices. "He has no idea what he's talking about. Your scars don't make you damaged. Being in recovery makes you a badass."

"I know that. I *say* that. In the mirror. It's a really cool thing that I do."

"Well, he wants you to forget. If you could see yourself the way I see you . . . You're so wonderful, Scarlett."

When she says it like that, I can almost believe her. Except. "But you're, like, the best person in the whole world. And I can't be like you. I'll never be able to be that good. You should be with someone like Zoe."

"Zoe's really sweet," says Amelia Grace. "But she doesn't make me feel like I could take on the entire world."

Wait. "I do that?"

"Are you kidding? You take care of Skyler and your mom and everyone, and you find the strength to do it even when you're hurting too. And it's been months since you cut, which is so amazing, because taking care of yourself is the most badass thing you can do, because how can you be there for the people you love if you can't be there for yourself, and, oh, you DELIVERED A FREAKING BABY." We both kind of laugh even though we're almost crying. She brushes my hair out of my face. "You're amazing, Scarlett. I wish you could see it."

If I try really hard, I can see myself reflected in her eyes. Only, it's not like any kind of mirror I've ever seen. This one shows some better superhero queen version of me. Maybe I am strong. And whole. Good enough for this girl who is so amazing, it's hard to believe she's real.

She brushes my hair away from my face again. But it's not in my eyes this time. I think she was looking for an excuse to touch me. The realization makes me feel warm all over. My skin is singing, waiting to be touched again. I want to kiss her, but more than that, I want her to kiss me. I stare at her lips.

Smile. I don't try to pretend that I don't want things. She takes a deep breath like this is something she has to work up the courage for, and it only makes me fall harder.

She kisses me.

And I think: How is it possible? For it to feel like a kiss is taking you apart and putting you back together again?

And I think: She tastes like cinnamon gum.

And I think: Please let me spend the rest of my life kissing this girl.

I take her hands when we finally pull away. "Don't go. Please don't leave when I'm just starting to figure all this stuff out. I don't want you to go back to that place. Those people don't deserve you."

She sighs. "I don't know how I can stay."

I squeeze her hands like I'm trying to send her my courage. "We'll figure it out."

"And we'll help," says a voice.

Ellie and Skyler come climbing up the ladder. Amelia Grace looks, if possible, even more shocked. Her eyes go red and glassy.

Skyler and Ellie don't sit as close as they usually do, but the fact that they're putting aside their own stuff for Ames makes this that much more powerful. Ellie raps her knuckles against the wooden crate. "I call this meeting of the Southern Belle Drinking Club to order. Our first order of business: figuring out how to keep Amelia Grace at the lake house."

Amelia Grace looks around the circle, meeting each of our eyes. Stronger with every one of us.

She smiles. "You really think I can stay?"

"Of course I do," I tell her. "For a few weeks or forever or whatever you want. Mama already said it was okay. Will you at least think about it?"

Amelia Grace stares at the house for so long I worry she's trying to think of a way to let me down easy.

"Yes. But I'm not the only one who deserves better than that place."

CHAPTER 50

Amelia Grace

HOW MANY TIMES DOES IT TAKE FOR HER TO GET pushed under before she can't find her way to the surface again?

He honks the horn. Doesn't even bother to get out of the car.

Mom jumps and picks up her bag. Aunt Adeline opens her mouth to say something, but Aunt Seema puts a hand on her arm. Adeline clenches her fists by her sides, nails digging into palms. I know the feeling.

Mom takes the long walk to the front door. It ages her in decades and pain and the taking away of pieces. I barely recognize her by the time she reaches for the doorknob.

I watch them through the blinds. He rolls the window down and leans an elbow out.

"Looks like a lot of cars for just you and Adeline," he says with an almost-smile that is not and never will be a real smile.

He's not yelling or hitting things. It doesn't always have to be an explosion. Plenty of times, he ruins things just sitting still.

"You can go in and look around if you want," she says, throwing up her hands. "I'm not hiding anything."

He glares at the house, thinking. "Just get in the car."

"I drove?"

"Yeah, so get in *your* car."

"Can we talk about this?"

"There's nothing to talk about. My wife is a fucking liar. How would you feel?"

She swallows. "I need to go get Amelia Grace."

His eyes pierce the house again. "Tell her to hurry up."

I pull back from the window and lean against the wall. The front door opens. Mom's eyes take longer than they should to focus.

"Are you ready?" she asks. And then she really sees me. "Amelia Grace, where are your things?"

I think about Scarlett, kissing me. How can I leave and what does it mean and was it just to get me to stay? I think about Ellie and Skyler too, this club and these girls. People who love me—all of me—who don't ask me to get rid of any of my pieces. And I'm scared that maybe my mom isn't one of those people. But I have to do this. Our town, our church—they're more like my stepdad than I wanted to believe. Sometimes you have to decide to let go of things.

"I'm not going."

"Amelia Grace, I know we were planning to stay till the end of the summer, but we need to go now." She keeps her voice low, and her eyes flick toward the kitchen, where everyone is pretending not to listen. There's something more embarrassing about being treated badly in front of people.

I need to make her understand what I'm saying. "I'm not

going at the end of the summer, and I'm not going ever. I wish you wouldn't either. You're so different when he's not around, don't you see it? You deserve to be that wonderful all the time."

Mom's eyes well up. "Marriage is complicated. You'll understand when you're older."

"I hope I never understand."

"Where's your bag? I'll put it in the car for you."

"I said I'm not going."

The horn honks outside.

"You're seventeen years old. What are you going to do?"

My heart beats faster. "I don't know. Scarlett said I could live with her. I'll figure something out."

The horn blares again. Mom starts to look desperate.

"I need you to do this. Please, honey. You are tearing this family apart."

I feel like I've been cracked open. I can only just keep from crying. "I'm not. I just— Please, you could stay too."

"We can't make it without him."

"You haven't even tried."

"I *have*. Do you remember fourth grade?"

"Yes." The midwife practice where Mom worked closed, and she was cobbling together work. I remember eating a lot of ramen for dinner and Aunt Adeline sending us grocery money a couple times. "I don't mind not having a lot of money."

He lays on the horn again—it tears through doors and curtains and resolve. She wrings her hands, glances back and forth between me and the window.

"Mom, *please*."

"It's more than not having a lot of money. If I hadn't met

Jay— Amelia Grace, I was going to have to send you to live with your grandparents."

My tears spill over. I never knew that. Mom cries too—no, sobs—and pulls me close to her like she never wants to let me go. Maybe that means she won't. That she'll stay. "I love you so much," she whispers into my hair. "But he's my husband and the head of this household."

I go numb.

He's only been here for eight years. How can she possibly love him more than me? But a part of me knew this would happen. She always picks him. I don't know why I expected things to be any different today.

I hear them drive away, but it hurts too much to watch. I sink onto the floor, alone. I'm crying so hard I don't hear the girls coming. Just feel one set of hands and then another, and then all their arms around me, holding me together.

CHAPTER 51

Ellie

....

SKYLER SITS AT THE EDGE OF THE DOCK DIPPING HER feet in the water. It feels so strange to have had my first kiss and not told her. It's like the tree falling in the forest thing. If I kissed a beautiful boy in the most perfect, daydreamy moment of all time, but I haven't told my best friend, did it really happen?

She doesn't ignore me if I talk to her, but this is different. Telling her would be like exposing the soft part of my heart. I need to know she'll be excited for me. But I don't know if I can wait another second.

I sit down next to her and dip my feet in too.

"Hey," I say.

"Hey."

She only barely looks at me. Am I really going to do this?

But then I think about the kiss and scraping my number in the sand and almost setting him on fire. This is not the kind of story you can keep to yourself.

"I kissed Andres!" I blurt out.

"Who?"

I blush. Right. "He's this guy! Apparently, he's friends with Bennett, and he's been trying to meet me all summer, and he finally found me at the party!" I do a cocky little dance with my shoulders. "And I kissed him."

"Wait, seriously?!" Her face lights up. Thank goodness. "This is amazing! I want to hear everything!" And then the sadness creeps into her face again, and she hesitates. "Did you tell Scarlett?"

"Not yet."

She lets out a sigh of relief that makes me realize she was bracing herself.

"I mean, I'm sure I will," I say. "But I wanted to tell you. You're my best friend."

The words "best friend" hang between us with a weight that feels significant. I have uttered the friendship equivalent of "I love you." I'm fairly certain my lungs have stopped working. This is more nerve-wracking than when I kissed Andres.

"I've never had a best friend before," I finally say. "I've been homeschooled most of my life because of tennis, and I'm totally cool with that choice, really, because tennis is everything. But, yeah. I've never had close friends and I'd never even kissed a boy, and Momma's always told me all these stories about her and my aunts, and I wanted that so badly. Like, in my notebook, I didn't just write 'chanterelles, softball, blue nail polish.' I wrote: 'Chanterelles! Softball! Blue nail polish!' It was a list of reasons I was excited to be friends with you. It's kind of ridiculous how much I wanted it. But I'm a loser. And a weirdo. And I never thought it would happen for me."

Skyler smiles. Really smiles. Not the sad, deflated ones she's been forcing for the past week.

"I really missed being your best friend," she says.

"Oh, thank goodness! Me too!" I hug her, but I'm so happy right now I feel like a human glitter-bomb, so I almost knock both of us into the water. "I've been feeling like that scene in *The Golden Compass*."

"When Lyra tries to walk away from her daemon familiar?"

"YES. And, okay, what I wrote in my notebook was awful, but I really, truly didn't mean it the way it sounded. And I don't know why I feel this weird desire to make people like me when it seems like they don't. It's like, 'Challenge accepted.' Which is stupid, because you're the best friend I could have ever asked for. So, but . . . do you forgive me?"

"Yes. And I'm sorry too. I'm . . . kind of the worst about holding on to things when I'm upset." Sky puts her hand on mine and gives me a sly smile. "Now tell me about this kiss."

Skyler

....

It must have been hard for Ellie to come find me and talk to me like that. I know because I can imagine how hard it's going to be to talk to my sister. But I owe her the truth. Everything got better when I told Mama. I cling to that fact.

When I find Scarlett, she's in the living room at the main house, working on this really intricate quilt she started in art class last year. She stops when she sees me. I jump right into it.

"I'm sorry for what I said. About everything in our family having to be about you."

I wait, nervous, but between baby Isa being born and all

the stuff with Amelia Grace, I feel like there's a chance that we could be okay.

Scarlett's face softens. "I'm sorry too. I know this year has been ridiculously hard for you, and I'm sorry I said everything was easy for you. Honestly? I'm jealous of how well you handle things."

She nudges me with her elbow, and my heart is so full. It almost makes me not want to tell her the next thing.

"You okay?" she asks.

"Yes." I say it way too fast. She gives me the eyebrow.

"You sure you're okay?"

I shake my head. "I wanted to talk to you about why I feel like I have to do everything on my own. The real reason."

"Okay."

Something about the way she says it, so gently, makes my eyes well up with tears.

"Sky, are you sure you're okay?"

Say it. Just say it.

"It's my fault you started cutting!" I blurt.

I've done it. Oh, gosh, how I've done it. If me needing things tears my family to pieces, me telling my sister this? It is the atomic bomb that ends us.

I want to take it back.

I watch Scarlett's eyes—soft, worried, resolute. That is clearly not an option.

"Sky, why would you think that?"

"Remember when we went to the county fair? And I said all those terrible things to you?" My voice is just above a whisper. If I say these things quietly enough maybe they won't cause as much damage.

You're a ruiner. You ruin things.

"I saw you that night when I went downstairs to get some water. In the kitchen."

Why is it so hard for you to just be happy?

"You never would have taken out that knife if I hadn't been so awful to you that day. You started cutting, and it was all because of me."

Anything else I was going to say gets lost in the sobbing.

"Sweetie, no." Scarlett stands in front of me and puts her hands on my shoulders. "I'm going to tell you something, and I need you to hear it: You are not the reason I started cutting. The stuff with McCloud had a lot to do with triggering it, but it was me, and my brain and my anxiety conspiring against me. There was just a lot of stuff happening in my life then, and I couldn't handle it."

I feel like a person who has grasped at a life preserver and only just realized they're not going to drown.

"It really wasn't me. You promise?"

"Yes," she says. "That wasn't even the first time I did it."

"It wasn't me. Ohmygosh, it wasn't me." I repeat the words like that will help me believe them.

But if it wasn't me, then that means that it was okay to be angry that day. That I can say strong words without dismembering someone and I can want things, like to fall in love with a boy, or to get new medication for my arthritis, without driving cracks into our family's foundation. I'm allowed to need things and want things and feel things.

"Ohmygosh," I say again. And then my legs won't hold me up anymore, and I'm sitting on the floor by the coffee table, and Scarlett is sitting next to me with her arms wrapped around me, and we are both crying, but it doesn't feel like hurting. It feels like healing.

"I love you. I love you so much," I say.

Scarlett squeezes me tighter. "I love you too, you weirdo."

She has to say things like that so she doesn't let herself get too vulnerable, but I know. The covering up only shows the softness more.

"Oh, and Scarlett?" I say.

"Yeah?"

"You're stronger than you think."

She tears up all over again. "Thank you. And also, good grief, this conversation should have come with a waterproof mascara warning. Is there anything else you want to tell me, because my makeup is pretty much massacred at this point."

"Oh. Actually, yeah. I had sex with Jonah last year, but I didn't tell you because I was worried about how you'd handle it."

Her eyes bulge. "Holy hell, Sky."

"Pretty sure that's it though."

CHAPTER 52

Ellie

....

I'M GOING BACK INTO BATTLE. AND BY "BATTLE," I mean I have another tennis tournament, and no, I'm not talking about the actual matches. Did the gladiators of old get driven to the Colosseum in their mommas' minivans? I'm gonna go with no. Though my tennis skirt does have enough pleats that it looks kind of like one of those armor things with the leather strips. If they came in lavender.

I'm going to ignore them all. Keep my head high. I'm already steeling myself for it. And then I think about what Scarlett said. About the girls who didn't look so bad. I pull out my phone and do something I promised I wouldn't do (again). I open Discord and read everything from that night.

There's more of it now, even though the General channel moved on to other stuff weeks ago. After I closed Discord that night, the replies kept going. And going. A lot of them are the same. Hateful, terrible things from Macy/Autumn/Stephanie/Riley/Emily Rae. But I'm not interested in what Emily Rae has to say anymore. I focus on the two likes on my apology—from Sadia and Heather—and I search to see if they've posted. I scroll down down down. They definitely don't seem to be part of the dragging. Yet. And then there it is, Sadia's profile picture. I wince as I read.

Sadia: Hey guys, I'd like everyone to keep in mind that those were Ellie's private thoughts, and that she probably would have worded them differently in a group setting. I'd also like to remind everyone that Ellie is in a vulnerable position, calling out potential cheating by someone who has a lot of power on this team. Please think of the difference in privilege here. I don't think Ellie should be dragged for having her honest feelings revealed.

Ohmygosh, she stuck up for me. It gives me a warmth that spreads to my toes. There's only one like on the post, Heather's, but just the fact that I'm not alone means everything right now. I rush to hit the like button too. Crap, this reply was weeks ago. She probably thinks I don't even care.

I scroll further, knowing instantly that the next set of posts are the inevitable backlash, holding my breath as I read. It's everything bad you might imagine. And then a post from Heather.

Heather: I really have to agree with Sadia here. Ganging up on Ellie is not cool, for the reasons she mentions and others.

These girls are amazing—Sky would love them. They don't take any shit from anyone either. How am I not friends with them?

A reply from Emily Rae is next: Ohmygosh, I'm not dragging her. Just because I'm defending myself. I'm allowed to do that.

Right. That's how. I was so busy trying to get Emily Rae to like me that I missed out on making friends with some really great girls.

Sadia: Thanks for the support, Heather ♥

I wonder if I'm too late.

Momma pulls into the parking lot of the tennis academy that's hosting this weekend. A bunch of girls are already warming up. Two in particular are stretching by the bleachers.

There's only one way to find out.

"Hi," I say.

They stop stretching to look at me. Not the way Emily Rae and her crew do—like I have tentacles sprouting out of my face. More like they're surprised. I guess I can't blame them.

"I'm sorry I ran off after the last tourney." I fidget with my ponytail. "There was . . . kind of a lot going on. And I'm also sorry for not replying back on your replies on that Discord thread, the awful one? I stopped reading it after the first few hours, and I only just read everything today. It was really cool of you to stick up for me." I hesitate, trying to find the right words, the ones that will tell them I wish I was their friend and I'm sorry for probably seeming stuck-up and oh, man, how do I say this without seeming weird? "I'm sorry I didn't notice before. I should have noticed."

I try to pack all of my feelings into that last sentence so they'll know what I'm trying to say.

"Well, yeah. It's important for us to stick up for each other," says Sadia, and I can't help but wonder how many opportunities I've had to stick up for her but didn't.

"Yeah, Emily Rae had it coming. She's Prince Joffrey without any of the redeeming qualities." Heather grabs the bleachers with one hand and pulls her leg back in a quad stretch.

I laugh. "Um, well, cool." And then there's one of those awkward pauses. "So, uh, I guess I'm gonna go warm-up. I'll see you guys."

I give a little wave and walk away, but before I can get more than a couple of steps, Sadia calls out, "Hey, Ellie. You want to stretch with us?"

"Yeah." I grin. "Yeah, that would be awesome."

I glance across the court at Emily Rae, who happens to be glaring daggers at me. But you know what? It doesn't sting the way it used to.

CHAPTER 53

Skyler

BENNETT THROWS THE SOFTBALL TO ME, AND I catch it and toss it back. I'm capable of throwing it twice that fast, maybe three times that fast. But today, I don't throw it like a pitcher. Just like a kid having fun.

I'm learning to listen to my body instead of fight it. Playing when I can and resting when I can't. I go swimming with Ellie most days because it's low impact. I don't know if the meds are working yet—it's too early to tell. And I'm still not sure if I can be a varsity pitcher again, but right now, playing catch with Bennett by the lake feels pretty great.

The moms are sitting in lounge chairs on the dock. After the initial meeting and mortifying exclamations over how adorable he is, they mostly don't watch us.

I hear a car pull up out front, but I don't really think about it. Then I realize that my dad is walking toward me with the biggest grin on his face. I forgot he was coming today.

"Hey!" He runs over and gives me a hug. "Well, this is great! Why didn't you tell me?"

I shrug.

"Wow, I can't believe it. You're back. You wanna throw the ball with me? I can't wait to call your coach."

I clench the ball tight in my fist.

"Um." You can do this. "Look, this isn't going to be like how it was before. I need to be in charge of this myself, because otherwise, I get all worried about what you're going to think and I try to push myself too hard."

His goofy frat-boy face goes serious. Bennett pretends to be very interested in the horizon. "Hey, I'm just so excited you can play again. I don't mean to push."

"I appreciate that. I may try to play again this season. But you can't just walk in here and play softball with me like everything's fine. I need to be able to be honest with you about how I'm doing health-wise."

"Okay." He rubs my shoulder. "Hey, Skyler, I'm sorry. All I want is what's best for you."

I nod. "Good. And I need to be able to talk to you about how I feel about the affair."

His eyes go wide. "Whoa, hey, are you sure that's something we need to talk about?"

"Yes." I glance over at Bennett and blush. "I mean, not right now, obviously, but someday. If you want to be in my life, I have to be able to be honest with you."

"Well, okay. That's what we'll do."

He claps me on the shoulder awkwardly. The silence is so uncomfortable, he finds a reason to go into the house, stat. (Apparently, "sweet tea emergencies" are a thing.)

Mama watches him walk up the stairs to the porch. Then she comes over and squeezes my arm, eyes soft and intense at the same time. "Are you okay, sweetie?"

Which is weird, because that's usually a question she asks Scarlett.

I smile. "I'm good."

This time, it's the truth.

Scarlett

I actually hug my dad. Well, I let him hug me and I don't flip him the bird or anything. I still don't know if she's going to take him back (neither does she—it changes weekly, if not daily). But I've learned to accept that whatever is going on between him and Mama is their own mystery. I don't stick around while he finishes his sweet tea though. My newfound clarity only takes me so far.

Amelia Grace is in the carriage house getting her stuff together—sunglasses, towel, sunscreen—like she's about to go down to the dock, but she stops when she sees me.

"Hey."

"Hey."

We smile at each other in that awkward way where you try to contain your joy because it's too embarrassing to show it all on the surface. Just when I think the sheer force of our dorky smiles may explode through the windows, Amelia Grace asks, "Do you want to go ride Jet Skis?"

Thank. Goodness. "Yes!" I say.

I realize the carriage house is unusually quiet. "Is Ellie here?"

"No."

It is a heavy no, the kind that contains a message: We are alone. And like every other time we've found ourselves alone the past couple weeks, we end up winding toward each other. She stands in front of me. I grab her hand.

We both let out humongous sighs of relief.

Look, there are only so many covert glances you can exchange before you start to feel like a walking taser.

"How are you doing?" I ask. She knows I'm asking about her mom without me saying it.

"Okay." She looks at our clasped hands and smiles. "Better."

"Thank you for staying."

"You don't have to keep saying that."

"I know. And I know it wasn't just for me, it's about you too, but I'm so glad you're here, and I'm sorry I keep—"

She presses her lips against mine, and the words and the worry disappear, and there is only us and this moment and no matter what happens next, we'll be fine. Every time I try to apologize, she kisses me. It's probably my 376th favorite thing about her.

The door opens, and we jump apart. Skyler bounces up the stairs. Amelia Grace's cheeks are so red, you could melt a popsicle on them.

"Think I'm gonna go Jet Skiing," she announces loudly and with absolutely zero stealth. She looks back at me.

"I'll meet you down there," I say.

Skyler watches Amelia Grace walk away. She raises her eyebrows at me.

"Can we talk?" I ask in my gentlest voice. I gesture toward the couch.

My sister looks shocked. Probably because she was expecting a sarcastic remark and not an invitation to share our feelings.

"Yeah, totally." She sits down, and I sit next to her, stiffly, like I'm not sure how we do this.

"So, how are things with Daddy?" I ask.

"Oh. Um, they're good. It went okay." She frowns at me. "Is—is that what you wanted to talk about?"

"Not exactly."

I clench and unclench my hands on top of my legs. Skyler will be totally cool with this. She will be happy for me, I know it, and there's a 200 percent chance she will hug me. So why is this so hard?

"Do you remember when you asked me if I liked Amelia Grace?" I finally ask.

"Yes." Her grin is bordering on a smirk.

"Well, you don't have to look so cocky about it."

She laughs. "I'm sorry! I'm not! Yes, I remember asking you that."

She is no longer smirking (on the outside).

"I do like her." I say it to my cutoff shorts. "She and I are . . . together."

She doesn't reply, and I hazard a glance at her face, and her eyes are positively beaming out joy, but she's trying to keep it contained.

I smile, I can't help it. Apparently, that's the straw that breaks her because she emits a high-pitched squeal and practically jumps into my lap, hugging me.

"I am so excited for you! And her! And you! Aw, I'm so excited for both of y'all because you're both so wonderful and you deserve to have that wonderfulness back tenfold, and I'm sorry, am I making you uncomfortable?" She disentangles herself.

"It's fine," I say. It actually feels really good, but I'm not telling her that.

"Does anyone else know?" she asks.

I shake my head. "I'm going to tell Mama and Daddy. Eventually. And I'm also going to tell them that I'm bi."

Skyler gives me another big smile, but she keeps her hands clasped in her lap this time. I appreciate that she does that.

"Well, whenever you're ready to tell them, I'll come with you. I mean, if you want."

I think about how support doesn't have to feel like some embarrassing thing you need because you aren't equipped to do things by yourself. Because I could. Tell my parents myself, I mean. I'm strong enough to handle it. But I want my sister with me.

"I'd like that."

CHAPTER 54

Amelia Grace

. . . .

"HI. HI THERE," I SAY.

Baby Isa looks up at me so serious. I can feel the warmth of her tiny body against my chest. I'm snuggled up with her on a couch at the big house so Val and Heidi can have a second to eat lunch. Heidi sits at the kitchen table, and Val brings her a plate, and it's such a small thing, but there is. So. Much. Love.

"You have the best family in the world," I whisper to baby Isa. "I hope you know that. Your moms and your aunts and me and Scarlett and Ellie and Skyler."

I sniff the top of her little head. She smells like magic.

The moment only lasts a few more minutes before she starts making a grumpy face and tries to eat my shirt.

"Um. Heidi?"

Heidi turns. "Yep. Bring her here. It's time for her to nurse. I'll just try to eat the rest of this sandwich without dropping any tomatoes on her head."

I get up, but I am clearly not moving fast enough because baby Isa goes into full-on rage crying. I pass her to Heidi.

"Hey," says Heidi, pulling down her shirt on one side

and popping Isa on with precision. "It's okay. You're okay. So hungry today. I know."

Isa stops crying.

"I feel the same way when I'm hungry," says Heidi.

Ellie comes in and plops down beside me on the couch. "Mom says I have to start packing soon."

I wrinkle my nose, and she makes a sad puppy face. It's hard to believe there won't be many more days like this. In a week, I'll be starting senior year at a new school. But I'll be starting it with Scarlett.

"Thanks again for all your help with the new school paperwork."

She smiles. "Anytime."

There's a knock at the front door, and Aunt Adeline goes to get it.

"Hey!" she says, and I can't hear what the other person says back, but I do hear footsteps, and then there is Aunt Adeline in front of me, and she is not alone.

"Mom?"

It's really her. Standing in the living room in khaki shorts and a ponytail and looking like there are a million things she wants to tell me. Everyone else is as speechless as I am, even the aunts, and I wait, and for a couple seconds, we just look at each other. And then she finally finds the words.

"I thought we could look for an apartment tomorrow. It'd have to be something small, but—"

Her voice breaks off mid-sentence, and everyone is watching me, and her eyes, they're scared. She's afraid I won't forgive her.

I almost cry. Almost say "I love you." Almost everything.

We've been through something so terrible that I didn't think we'd ever make it through to the other side, and now we just might. But she chose him over me, so many times and for so many years, and I don't know where to begin or if it's possible to find enough forgiveness for someone who hurt you so much.

But somewhere in the shapes of her face, I can find the woman who used to read Nancy Drew books to me when I was sick and who works magic with newborn babies and who could do so many great and unimaginable things now that she's out from under his shadow.

I smile. "I'll go pack my stuff."

AUGUST

CHAPTER 55

Amelia Grace

....

WE PLAY POKER UNTIL THE STARS COME OUT AND
the frogs and owls and crickets sound like they're right outside
our little window. Ellie makes us take a photo of all four of us
lying against the floor of the loft, chins in hands, legs kicked up
behind us. She already enlarged the one of our moms, framed
it, and hung it in the carriage house. She's going to add ours
right next to it. Then Skyler has us all sign a letter she wrote to
whichever girls come after us, and Scarlett declares it's time to
give our final updates because Ellie is leaving tomorrow. Scarlett holds a candle in front of her and speaks in a solemn voice.

"I need to know. Did you accomplish the impossible before
the end of the summer?"

I start to answer, but she cuts me off.

"First. Rule number two."

We glance around at each other. What is she talking about?

She wiggles a small glass bottle out of her purse and plunks
it on the crate in front of us. Southern Comfort. Ohhhh.

She pours some of the amber liquid into the mason jars
from the first night and adds Diet Coke. Except for the last

glass. She only puts Diet Coke in that one and passes it to Ellie. Ellie smiles and passes pearls to each of us.

"I'll go first!" says Skyler. "My impossible thing was to play softball by the end of the summer." She can't even stop grinning, she's so excited about it. "And I definitely played catch with Bennett this week in the backyard AND I feel like I actually know when to take it easy now AND I told Daddy to stay the heck out of my softball business, so." She brushes imaginary dirt off her shoulders.

We clink our glasses together over the crate, and Ellie yells, "Woo-hoo!"

"I still have no idea about varsity, but I feel like finding my voice was so much more important. And"—Skyler hesitates—"I realized it's okay to need help and to not always be okay, and that was mostly because of you guys, so thank you," she finishes quietly.

Ellie squeezes her hand, and Scarlett messes up her hair.

"I'll go next," Scarlett says. "This summer, I was supposed to figure out how to be in a healthy, grown-up relationship with my loser ex-boyfriend. And you know what? You can cross that off the list, because he's not worth it. And you know what else? I don't really give a damn." Day-um.

Skyler snickers.

Scarlett pretend-glares at her.

"What? You say it just like Mama."

Scarlett rolls her eyes. "Anyway. I may have had to kick his ass to the curb, but I did learn a lot about the kind of person I am when I'm not doubting myself. And about the kind of person I want to be with."

With that, she slides her hand across the floor to mine

and laces our fingers together. I grin at her, but only for a second, because Skyler's the only person we've told so far, which means—

"WAIT. WAIT. WAIT." Ellie throws her hands in front of her. "You guys are TOGETHER?! How long has this been going on? Why has nobody told me? Do you know I totally called this weeks ago? Tell them, Sky!"

"She did."

"See!" she squeals gleefully. "OMG, I'm so happy for you guys!"

She practically tackles us into a group hug.

"Do your moms know yet?"

"No," says Scarlett. "So you have to keep it a secret until we're ready, okay?"

"Absolutely!" She looks positively ecstatic about the idea of keeping a secret.

"Um, so I can go next," Ellie says. "You guys know what my real goal was now: I wanted to be friends with all of you before the end of the summer." She glances at Skyler. "And I almost screwed everything up, but. You guys are the best friends I've ever had." She stops for a second and blinks furiously. Skyler holds her hand. "And I feel like I learned a lot this summer about who I want to be friends with."

We clink our glasses again. There's something so victorious about that sound. Scarlett raises her eyebrows at me, and I realize I'm the only one who hasn't gone.

"Right." I smile sheepishly. "So, my thing was that I was supposed to get myself reinstated as a junior youth minister at Ranburne Baptist Church. And it turns out maybe that is impossible. At least, right now. Which is funny, because I guess that means I failed, but." I stare at my hand clasped in Scarlett's and shake my head. "I've gotten everything. I had all these dreams of things I thought I wanted, but real life ended up being so much bigger."

We stay up all night talking and playing cards and eating world peace cookies from the Tupperware Scarlett snagged from the main house. None of us want this night to end. In the morning, we walk down to the dock to watch the sun come up. We stand, hand in hand in hand in hand, and we look out at the water and the sun shines on my face in a way that feels packed with meaning.

I stare out at a future I never could have imagined. We are going to move into the new apartment we found yesterday, and I am holding hands with the girl I love, and I found a church that loves me, the real me.

Well, Skyler found the church. And Scarlett and I found each other. Ellie gave me that last critical nudge to take a chance and open myself up to new people, even though I was terrified. And if it weren't for my aunts, I know my mom would still be back in Ranburne right now instead of drinking her morning coffee on the deck of a lake house.

Sometimes people are more than friends. They become your family. They help you understand that life doesn't have to be the thing that you thought. They pull back the curtain on a world you didn't know existed. They make you reach for the impossible.

Maybe that's all of our mission in life. To find the people who can show you there's another way of living.

Acknowledgments

I couldn't have written this book without the help of a whole lot of people:

My phenomenal, thoughtful, brilliant beta readers: Kate Boorman, Jaye Robin Brown, Maryann Dabkowski, Lauren Karcz, Alina Klein, Dana Lee, Dana Alison Levy, Terra Elan McVoy, Sahara I. Mehdi, Aisha Saeed, Laura Silverman, and Jenn Woodruff. This book is so much better because of you. Thank you for your ideas, your feedback, your support, and your friendship.

To my Atlanta critique group: I'm so grateful I get to learn to be a better writer and better person from you. You are imperial goddesses, and I will make you inappropriate rainbow meringues anytime.

To my online critique group: I simply could not write books without you. Or mom without you. Or really anything without you. I love you all. (MoB forever!!!)

To Gilly Segal and Kate Goodwin: Thank you for being my friends, for your constant encouragement, and holing up in the mountains with me while I cranked out the first 10,000 words of this book.

To the five other writer girls from the French retreat: You know who you are, and you know how much cheese we can put away with our powers combined. I will dream about writing in that farmhouse forevermore. Slow down, Leenda.

To Catie and Emi: Thank you so much for helping me understand Discord so I look like I know what I'm talking about. ☺

To Cara M., thank you for answering a billion questions about competitive tennis. Tennis help thank-yous also go to Lindsey Roth Culli and Jeanne McKeon.

To Erica Landis, thank you for awesome talks about representation and for your encouragement.

To Alpha Gamma Delta: I write sisterhood books and books about women changing the world because of the friendships I made as an Alpha Gam at Georgia Tech. Loyally. ♥

To this amazing writing community that I get to be a part of, especially these little pockets: OneFour KidLit, the incomparable LBs, the Not-So-YA Book Club, Kidlit Alliance, Yay YA!, and my Atlanta writer crew. To Little Shop of Stories, which is like my very own Hogwarts, and to all the librarians, bloggers, teachers, and book people who make Kidlit awesome. Special thanks to Becky and Aisha for making me feel like I could do this over strawberries and cream.

To my agent, Susan Hawk. I can't believe this is book four (FOUR!) together. You are always in my corner, always making my dreams come true. Also? You're really freaking fun to work with. Thank you.

To my editor, Erica Finkel, thank you for helping me take this book to the next level, for caring about words as much as I do, and for helping me decide if lines are too much cheese or exactly the right amount of cheese. Thank you for being the kind of person to champion a book that makes relationships between women the most important thing. To Nicole Schaefer, Trish McNamara, Mary Wowk, Elisa Gonzalez, Andrew Smith, Michael Jacobs, Jenn Jimenez, Hana Anouk Nakamura, Emily Daluga, Jody Mosley, Melanie Chang, Jenny Choy, Mark Harrington, Pam Notarantonio, Amy

Vreeland, Tessa Meischeid, and anyone else at Abrams who worked on this book in any way, I'm so very grateful to have you as my publishing home.

To my family, who are the very best at supporting me and making me feel like I can do this, especially Mom, Mica, Bekah, (little) Zack, Hannah, Aunt Amy, Nana, Dennis, and Maxie. I love you guys.

And to Zack, Ansley, and Xander Allen. I love you all to the moon and back. Thank you for being my heart.

About the Author

Rachael Allen is a scientist by day and YA writer by night, who does her best writing holed up in a lake (or mountain or farm) house with friends as close as sisters. She is the winner of the 2019 Georgia YA Author of the Year Award whose books include *17 First Kisses*, *The Revenge Playbook*, and *A Taxonomy of Love*, which was a Junior Library Guild selection and a 2018 Book All Young Georgians Should Read. She lives in Atlanta, Georgia, with her husband, two children, and two sled dogs. Visit Rachael at rachaelallenwrites.blogspot.com.